A Stranger in the Village

Sara Alexi is the author of the Greek Village Series.
She divides her time between England and a small
village in Greece.

http://www.saraalexi.com
http://facebook.com/authorsaraalexi

Sara Alexi

A STRANGER
IN THE VILLAGE

oneiro

Published by Oneiro Press 2016

ISBN-13: 978-1535149648

ISBN-10: 1535149647

Chapter 1

The corner shop in the Greek village

Those present –

Marina, the village shop owner

Stella, who runs the hotel and local eatery

Juliet, an English woman who moved to the village

Frona, an older woman of the village who has lived in both Australia and America

Vasso, who runs the kiosk in the village square

Marina holds court in her corner shop. Stella, Frona and Juliet have all found somewhere to sit.

'It's like buying a pig in a sack. We don't know what we get till we open the sack.' Marina laughs.

'I got lucky with my "pig",' Frona says, her shapeless black cardigan quivering as she giggles.

'Thank God I got lucky second time around!' Stella says, crossing herself three times and kissing her thumbnail as she shifts her slight frame, tucking one leg under her on the wooden chair. She is hemmed in by barrels of rice, lentils, pasta and dried beans, and by the *komboloi* hanging from a nail on the edge of a shelf, by her head.

'Ah, but he wasn't in a sack then, was he, your second pig?' Marina's face is red with laughing. 'He

3

was out in the daylight. You could see all of what you were getting!' She dabs at the corners of her eyes with a tissue from up her sleeve.

'My piglet was running around for all to see, so cute then, but I didn't know he was going to grow to be a boar,' Juliet says, but the joke does not translate well – it would have sounded so much better in her mother tongue.

But Marina, Stella and Frona howl with laughter anyway, the sound muffled only by the plethoric jumble of goods and produce that lines the walls of Marina's shop. Fly swats, shepherds' crooks, balls in plastic string bags and a variety of other items hang from the ceiling. The shelves on the three back walls sag with the weight of jars of honey, tins of *dolmades*, packets of tights, bottles of chlorine, and countless other things. The counter extends from under the window at the front of the shop, at right angles to anyone coming in through the door, its top overflowing with sweets, cigarette lighters, *kolourakia*, packets of nuts in colourful wrappers and a shiny set of scales at one end. The door, which is permanently open, leads out to the village square. On the pavement outside there is just enough space for a couple of drinks cabinets and a wire rack of locally grown produce.

At this time of year the sun does not have the intensity it will later in the year, but it is warm enough to lure Juliet out daily. She will step out for something as simple as a bottle of milk and then linger for hours simply because the sun makes everything delightful and the world has transformed from the grey of winter into a wonderful place promising the excitement of summer.

This morning she loitered to admire the yellow flowers blooming along the roadside, and the almond and cherry blossom creating splashes of white and pink in the gardens, announcing the arrival of spring. The whitewashed walls and houses reflected the bright blossoms that are appearing in their gardens. The sudden warmth makes everything happen more slowly: the household chores, the shopping for the evening meal, even the conversations. There is no rushing to get out of the cold, there are no clipped exchanges to limit the minutes spent with frozen fingers away from the fire. Instead she has the luxury of being able to take her time. She has been in the corner shop half an hour already and she only came in for one item. Her chair is beside a barrel of rice. Stella is behind her, near the back shelf, which is loaded with cleaning products.

'And what are you girls gossiping about?' Vasso stoops slightly, protective of her lacquered hair, as she steps in through the door, eager to join her friends. The shop is almost in darkness for a moment as she fills the door frame.

'Pigs in sacks.' Frona giggles, her eyes bright in the gloom. Her soft old skin pleats all the way up her cheeks as she smiles.

Vasso frowns slightly and looks at Frona. She is sitting under the television, which is permanently on with the sound turned down, and she is separated from Juliet and Stella by a set of low shelves piled high with bars of chocolate and packets of biscuits and crisps, set centrally down the length of the shop.

Marina pulls out empty wrappers from the box of sweets she keeps on the counter for children sent to buy things for their parents.

'Husbands,' she clarifies, not even looking up.

'Ah.' Vasso leans against the door frame, a content look on her face.

'We were the lucky ones.' Frona twists her worn wedding ring around her finger.

'We were,' Vasso replies. Her husband died young. Frona's reached a good age but now she too is alone.

'Very lucky.' Stella looks down at her own shiny wedding ring and then gazes past Marina, through the window, to see if she can catch a glimpse of Mitsos over at the *kafenio*. She never talks of her first husband. It is as if he never existed.

'But lucky or not I sometimes think that it might have been fun to have had the chance to shop around a bit. You know, try before you buy, to see what the variations were.' The light in Frona's eyes turns to a mischievous twinkle; Marina starts to snigger.

'Did you not sample the goods at all then?' Marina stifles her laugh, putting the collection of sweet papers into the bin under the counter and dabbing her eyes again.

'Well, there was this one time, but I was so young I'm not sure if I knew what I was doing. Up

6

under the pines over there.' Frona nods to the open door, across the square, past Vasso's kiosk and up past Stella and Mitsos's house, where the trees on the hill are silhouetted against the deep blue sky. 'We just had a kiss and a cuddle.' Her face takes on a dreamy look. 'He'll be an old man now, wrinkly and grey.'

'I wouldn't have dared.' Stella looks at Frona as if she will find something new in her features, something she has not seen in her friend before. 'But then I'm not sure I ever had the opportunity …'

She trails off. Her childhood was not easy, since she is of gypsy stock, and her friends are aware of the struggle she endured. Schooldays were full of bullying, isolation and loneliness, and it was a source of much gossip in the village when she was married to a Greek!

'Well, I am almost ashamed to say that I tried pretty much the whole shop!' Juliet interjects and Marina stops laughing for a second to stare at her, then laughs even harder, Vasso joining in.

'There was this one guy whose surname was Fiddler.' She translates the words so the point is not missed. 'Mark Fiddler. We, or rather I, tried to pretend we weren't a couple but he had this really embarrassing and irritating habit – when he said hello – this was at school, you know, in a corridor, between classes – he would pat me on the shoulder, then his hand would slide down my back and ping! With a pinch and a quick twist of his finger my bra would be undone!'

Frona laughs the hardest, but they all suck back their mirth when a tall, broad-shouldered stranger comes in. There is a tense silence as he asks for a packet of chewing gum in a low, smooth voice, looking just a little nervously around the shop. Stella stares at her shoes and tries to stop herself giggling. Juliet stares at the man.

'Thank you,' Marina says as he places the coins in her hand. The man thanks her in return and smiles, and the smile remains as he glances at each of them before he leaves, ducking through the doorway. As soon as he is gone their laughter bursts out uncontained.

'Well, he was no pig,' Marina chuckles, looking after the man, the grey at his temples silver in the sun.

'Ah, but we all know you did a little trying before the buying, Marina,' Stella says.

'When the evidence is nearly two metres tall, I cannot hide it, can I?' Marina stops gazing after the stranger and turns to look at the framed picture of her son on the wall behind her. It was taken when his son Angelos was just born, and he is cuddling the child. Next to him is Irini, who looks tired in the picture. That was over a year ago, just after the young couple were married. How the time flies!

'You didn't ever meet up with his father again, did you?' Juliet asks.

'No, he went into the army and his baba moved back to Athens.' Marina is no longer laughing. 'You know, I don't even know his name. I called him Meli, because he was so sweet, and he called me his Melissa, his little honeybee. I knew him for just one night. What can I say?'

The four women become still.

'I had a love.'

They all turn to look at Vasso.

'You know, before I married.'

Marina and Stella gasp. Frona smiles.

Thinking back on this time, even after all these years, makes Vasso feel strange - the confusion of trying to understand the unspoken urgency that her girlfriends seemed to develop once they had left school, the odd way the boys she had always regarded as friends suddenly becoming tongue-tied or, worse, cocky and arrogant around that time. Of course she understands what it was all about now, but when she was younger it had been a bit of a mystery until that day she went to the post office. Then she had a very clear insight but it was one that had frightened her and no sooner had she met him than she was pushing him from her memory. It is only since her husband died that she has allowed herself to think of him at all.

'He was from Saros town too, not from this village.' Vasso hesitates, not sure whether to smile or not. 'We had such a passion. He met me in the post office, and we went swimming together and held hands under the water.' She sighs. 'The army took him as well. I would have been married around the time he got out.'

'I never knew that!' Stella sounds almost hurt that such a secret has been kept from her.

'Well, it is not something you brag about. My husband may be dead but I still respect him, and there is Thanos. He doesn't want to know that his mama could have behaved in such a way.' They all giggle again.

'But, oh my, he was sweet, and tender. But, unlike with Marina's man, it never got passionate enough to produce a child. I think we were too scared.' She turns to Frona. 'It's funny to think of them as old men now, isn't it?'

'Does he still live in Saros?'

'I've never seen him, so I expect he moved away–'

'Vasso!' Marina interrupts her and points through the window. There are three people waiting at the kiosk in the square.

Vasso leaps up and trots out of the door, the silver threads in her black cardigan bright in the sunlight.

'Who would have thought?' Frona says when she is gone. 'Never would I have thought Vasso would have a secret like that! I wonder where he is now? She could do with some company.'

Stella watches Vasso going into the kiosk to serve, looking for signs that tell of her friend's secret lover, but Vasso is the same as always. Stella's view is interrupted by another friend coming into the shop, in an acid-green T-shirt dress.

'*Yeia sou*, Ellie,' Stella greets the girl. 'Are you on your way?' Ellie works on reception at Stella's hotel down on the beach.

'Yes, I go. What's happening?' Ellies's Greek is heavily accented and not grammatically correct.

'Pigs in sacks,' Juliet says in English. Ellie's eyebrows draw together and unwrinkle again.

'Husbands,' Marina explains. Her English is as accented as Ellie's Greek. Ellie glances at her own engagement ring, the stone of which has slipped around her finger. She turns it to face up.

Chapter 2

Cigarette smoke curls up into the high corners of the *kafenio*. The walls, which were whitewashed many years ago, are yellowed with nicotine. The front corner of this masculine domain looks out over the village square and across the road to Marina's corner shop, through tall, floor-to-ceiling windows that let the light flood in, making this the perfect vantage point from which to observe the comings and goings in the village. During the day, the circular metal tables nearest the windows are preferred, but in the evenings those at the back, around the pot-bellied stove, are favoured. As summer comes, that will change and customers will take tables and chairs over to the square in the cool of the evening. At night, Theo will chain them all to the telegraph pole on the square's edge. He used to leave them out but one night some gypsies took the lot. But for now they are inside, the painted wooden chairs neatly tucked under the tables, four to a table, ten tables arranged in rows.

Theo stands with his hands on the counter, his eyes seemingly fixed on the village square. But he doesn't see the view. From the inside, when the sun is at this angle, it picks up all the smears and handprints on the windows. He picks up a cloth with the intention of giving them a wipe, but then that would mean getting out the stepladder, which is out at the back, and the whole job starts to look too big for the moment and so he puts the cloth down again. The men, his customers, who are also his friends and who were once his school chums, are taking up four of the tables. At the one in the front corner by the two windows, with the best view, are Mitsos, Thanasis and Nicolaos.

'This damned toothache!' Nicolaos feels his jaw with one hand. His morning coffee sits untouched.

'You want an ouzo for that,' says Thanasis.

'Too early,' Nicolaos grumbles.

'Not to drink, to rub on your gums,' says Mitsos.

'I am not a teething baby!' Nicolaos lifts his head and looks at his coffee, but he does not pick it up.

'Well, if it works for them why would it not work for you?' Thanasis takes a sip of his own coffee, noisily sucking the bubbles off the top.

'Just go to the dentist, it's not so bad,' Mitsos says, but his focus is on a bird that has landed on the roof of the kiosk over in the square. He cannot tell what type it is, and as he watches it flaps lazily off and over the terracotta roofs of the houses, climbing higher and higher, until finally it stretches out its wings and begins spiralling down very slowly, gliding on the currents.

13

'What are you watching?' Theo asks, peering up at the sky, following Mitsos's gaze.

'I need an ouzo,' Nicolaos says.

'Just a bird,' Mitsos says.

'One ouzo then.' The *kafenio* owner straightens up, using both hands to smooth his hair down the back of his neck. He needs a haircut. It bounces with its own wiriness when he walks, and when the bounces tickle his neck he knows he needs a haircut. He pours the ouzo, fills a bowl with ice and looks around to see if anyone else needs anything.

'Another coffee,' Petta says. His chair looks comically small under him. He has broad shoulders, thick wrists and long, muscular legs that dwarf his surroundings. One of his feet jiggles continuously.

'I'd better go and deliver the letters,' Cosmo says, but he makes no attempt to move. He picks at the cuff of his shirt where his mama has darned it. The stitching is coarse and untidy. Her eyes are failing. A man should have a wife. His mama is not getting any younger, and it is not good for a man to be on his own. He wonders, as he tries to snap off a loose thread, if he has left it too late. It is not a new thought but one that pesters him daily, like a splinter that won't work its way out.

'I'll have another coffee too,' Thanos says. He can see his mama, Vasso, inside the kiosk in the centre of the square, just a moving shadow behind the glass. She is up at dawn most days, tiptoeing around the kitchen so as not to wake him as she boils the water for her coffee on the little gas stove, and by

14

the time she returns at *mesimeri* he will be in Saros, preparing the taverna for the evening. Most nights he is home long after she has gone to bed, especially in the summer months.

He has come into the *kafenio* out of frustration. He was sitting at home trying to think up twists on some of the récipes, ways to give his menu something just a little different from last year, in case tourists return and to keep the locals interested. The taverna is on the main strip along the waterfront in Saros; it's a busy location but he is in competition with a number of other tavernas, most of which are well established. But he is fast gaining a reputation for good service and quality food. Still, it's important not to get complacent. He was getting frustrated at home, wasn't able to concentrate, and reasoned that a change of scenery would encourage new thinking; however, since he arrived all thoughts have left his head.

Theo balances the *briki* on the portable gas stove and lights a match. The smell of sulphur momentarily burns his nostril. He pulls his hand back hastily from the blue flame, blows on the match and puts it on top of a little pile of other used matches. He adds two teaspoons of sugar to the tiny copper pot of water and waits for it to dissolve and the mixture to boil.

'Water, sugar, patience,' he mutters to himself. That is the trick to making good Greek coffee: let the sugar really dissolve before adding the dry coffee powder, and that way when it boils the bubbles will glisten, hold the sweetness, soften the coffee granules so there is no grit.

Petta's and Thanos's coffee is served in tiny cups, each with a tall glass of water. Two men have come in whilst he has been making it and have seated themselves at the next table.

'Yes, but you can't. I need it then.' Vangelis is arguing with his companion.

'To do what?' Grigoris retorts.

'To plough round the olive trees.'

'How can you say you want it to plough around the olive trees when I just said I was going to use it to plough around my trees?'

'Vangeli, Grigori,' Theo greets them; they immediately stop arguing but breathe heavily for a while. 'The usual?' Theo asks.

Chapter 3

'Can I help you?' The girl behind the reception desk at Stella's hotel is wearing an acid-green T-shirt, her eyes wide, her expression open. She speaks to him in English. The wall-to-wall carpeting of the foyer muffles any echo the empty space might otherwise have offered back.

The man takes his time to look at her; there is no hurry. Life is not a race, and why not enjoy the bloom of her youthful face? He smiles.

'Do you have a room, for a night, maybe two?' he asks. The mechanic in the village garage said the part should be here tomorrow. A simple fix, he said. 'Yes, two days should be fine,' he confirms.

'For one?' the girl asks. She has delicate eyebrows and they arch to emphasise her question, but as she picks up her pen it is her hand that draws his attention: slim fingers, manicured nails.

'That's a beautiful ring.' He leans over the counter slightly for a better look. It is a small stone set on a thin band, probably not very expensive. It has slipped and is slightly too big for her. Maybe she has lost weight recently, or perhaps it was the only ring to be found locally within budget. As he

17

straightens up he notices that her cheeks have taken on colour.

'I am to be married the day after tomorrow,' she confesses.

'I wish you joy.' He says it with feeling. Lucky girl, lucky man. He wishes them nothing but happiness and he smiles again to let her know the sincerity of his words.

'Yes, for one.' His smile remains. 'The room, I mean. For one.'

'Name?' she asks.

Miltos gives the girl his name and, with the key in his hand, he thanks her, assures her he can find the room by himself and pushes through the double doors to make his way along a carpeted corridor. Number ten. There it is.

Once he's inside, the door clicks shut behind him and he is alone. He pulls the voile curtains aside so he can see across the hotel's lawns to the sea; the sun floods in, the room instantly becoming hotter. He looks around for the air-conditioning switch. Unable to find it, he sits on the bed; his emotions overcome him and his tears fall.

As usual the saline trails come without noise or juddering, just coursing slowly down his cheeks, the sorrow that accompanies them deadening the weight of his arms. His shoulders drop, his chin too, and his bottom lip trembles. He allows the full wave of his emotions to flow over him, suppressing nothing. He wants to vent it all, let every last bit out until he is spent. But it never happens like that. His tears dry before he feels the true depth of his emotion has even been accessed and it is most unfulfilling – like the promise of a sneeze that never comes, but deeper and more important. He swills his face in the sink in the bathroom and presses a white fluffy towel against his skin. It smells of lemons and fresh air.

Outside, a hiss indicates that the lawn sprinklers have come on. Through the window he watches the grass soak, turning from a pale green to a deep emerald hue. Beyond the lawn the sandy beach is a pale yellow, almost white, and then there is the sea, the wavelets flashing silver and blue as the sun catches them, sparkling as if it is alive. Moments like this make it so much worse. When the world is so beautiful it is at odds with his feelings. He wants either to rid himself of the weight or to stop being capable of appreciating the magnificence of the world. But it is a futile wish.

His hand seeks his jacket pocket. It's a safe haven, worn smooth with years of fondling. He takes out the curling white shell, his fingers finding the jagged part where a piece broke off. At one point he drilled a little hole in it and wore it on a chain around his neck, but it got caught on something, he forgets what, and the shell broke free of the chain. For an awful moment he thought it would smash. It landed and rolled, and then the fear came that he could lose it, but with a quick movement he stopped it rolling under … What was it that it nearly rolled under? He forgets. There is so much he forgets these days.

There is a knock on the door. With a quick movement of his hand across his eyes he wipes away the new tears that are flowing and forces the smile back onto his face.

'Sorry to disturb you …' It's the girl. 'I forgot to say that the dining room is open until eleven and that breakfast is from six till ten, unless you request otherwise. Oh, and the air-conditioning gadget is in the drawer of the bedside table. It seems I forgot to tell you everything!' The girl smiles brightly, but shyly. *Ellie*, her name tag says.

'Thank you, Ellie.' He smiles in return and looks into her eyes, looking for her happiness, for the love she holds there for her fiancé. It is all visible. She will not spend her free time alone crying. She probably doesn't spend any time alone.

Ellie leaves and he closes the door.

His vision blurs again. 'I am not ungrateful for my life. My God, no!' he mutters to himself. It has been the most amazing and adventurous life – the things he has done, the places he has been, the experiences he has had! But then, has it been so exciting because of his relentless drive, pushing him ever onwards to try to rid himself of his darker feelings, in his perpetual and insistent search for … for what? The question is unanswerable. It is why he never stays anywhere for any length of time, no matter how much he likes it. Why he never sticks at a job, even if it is fun. Well, he may not have found whatever it is that he is looking for but he cannot deny that he has nevertheless been rewarded with experiences that he would not have missed. He refuses to be ungrateful. He sniffs and lifts his chin.

He spends a while gazing out of the window at the sea, trying to make out where the water ends and the sky begins. There seems to be a cocktail bar on the beach, a simple hut with a palm tree roof and stools sunk in the sand. He will go down for a drink, chat to the barman, chase away this feeling or numb it with alcohol. He'll while away the hours until he feels sleepy enough to go to bed.

Chapter 4

The young man behind the bar is drying glasses, staring out to sea, and he looks round as Miltos approaches. The young man nods and half smiles, and puts down his cloth, ready to serve. He leans, hands spread wide on the bar; his expression is open.

'And where were you going as you stared across the sea, my friend?' says Miltos. 'I'll have a beer, a Mythos.' He sits on one of the high stools.

'Actually I was going nowhere. I was contemplating my work!' The young man pours the beer into a glass and fills a small bowl with cashew nuts.

'Is there much to contemplate about running a bar …? I am Miltos, by the way.'

'Loukas,' the barman says, and they touch finger ends and then he straightens himself. 'There is much to everything if you look for it,' the barman replies lightly, his careless tone inviting banter.

'And nothing to all of it,' Miltos retorts, accepting the invitation.

Loukas settles onto his own stool, leaning on his forearms on the counter, hands clasped, his eyes narrowed against the sun. 'Ah, you could say there is nothing to any of it, but it all depends on the circumstances.'

'Ah, circumstances.' He takes a napkin from the pile on the bar and wipes the back of his neck. The day will cool off in an hour, once the sun has set.

'Here's the thing.' Loukas pours himself a glass of water and they both settle. Miltos turns a little, and they both look out to sea. 'I am getting married the day after tomorrow.'

'Ah! To Ellie on reception?' Miltos exclaims.

Loukas confirms this with a movement of his chin, a sideways nod.

'Yes, to Ellie, and it has made me wonder if I am doing everything right.' He looks around his domain. To Miltos it is a small world. A fridge, some glasses, rows of bottles. He'll need to remember how to make the cocktails. But maybe that no longer requires learning; Loukas will be able look it up on his phone, no doubt. There is bound to be an app. The whole world seems to be running on apps these days.

'I mean, I'm not sure what more I could be doing. I stock the bar and I serve drinks and I love my life, and my work, but there is a niggle in my head, like the wiggle of a tequila worm, and it says, "Have I missed something? Am I doing enough?"' He puts on a little voice when he says this and then laughs. His neck goes red and he briefly glances at Miltos but without making eye contact.

'What more could you do?' Miltos asks, still gazing out to sea to allow the boy to recover from his embarrassment unobserved.

'Well, that's the question – how do you know? And how do I know I am doing everything I should be doing right?' Loukas asks.

Miltos can remember a time when he took life so seriously, and one of the tales of his life, one that he has told so many times, to so many acquaintances, comes to mind.

'Ah, you know, this brings something to mind for me. Have you ever been to Cairo?' Loukas shakes his head, looking puzzled. 'Well it is a big city and a noisy one,' says Miltos. 'I was there once. I couldn't have been much older than you. How old are you? Twenty-four, twenty-three?'

'Twenty-five,' Loukas replies.

Miltos nods and examines the young man's face before looking out over the beach. The sunbeds are empty. There is only an old man left and he is gathering up his towel and bottle of sunscreen. With a bent back he heads towards the hotel on skinny, sun-reddened legs, his round stomach forcing the waistband of his trunks over. The sand is taking on pink hues as the sun begins to sink into the sea. The water is almost purple, darkening to black, and the tips of the wavelets glow orange.

'What were you doing in Cairo?' Loukas settles again.

'Do you know, I'm not sure.' Miltos chuckles, a slow burbling sound. 'I was in Rhodes, visiting someone I met when I was doing my national service, and I have a feeling that when I was leaving I got on the wrong boat. It's possible – not that I can really recall now.'

That is the way he has always told it, but a little nugget of truth inside him knows that, really, he had no place to go, nowhere to be. Cairo was as good as anywhere and if he was to be alone then he also wanted to be lost. At the time it felt like there was some romance in that, which seemed to matter.

'Anyway, the boat landed at Haifa, in Israel, and I stayed in a kibbutz for a while, but I got bored of that and I left and hitched all around, saw the place a bit, and at one point I went across the desert to Cairo. I can remember that I arrived late in the day and I needed somewhere to stay.' He can still remember the noise of the streets now. He takes a handful of the cashews and crunches them as he continues. 'With very little money, I began to wonder if I had done a very rash thing to go there. Cairo itself was such a mix of old and new. High-rise blocks, twenty storeys high, so much traffic and everyone using their horns, and then suddenly there would be a donkey pulling a rickety cart half full of fruit, the animal running along at full speed and the driver almost in rags.'

He lifts his bottle, but it is empty so he pushes it across the countertop towards Loukas, who drops it with a rattle into a crate and then points to the fridge, where there are more.

'Sure, why not?' Miltos says. No glass is offered this time. After a slug of the cold nectar and a moment to watch the sun, which is now half submerged in the rapidly darkening sea, he continues his story.

'So, the man I hitched a lift with stops driving and points to an alley where he says there are many cheap hotels. I ask the first person I come to which is the cheapest hotel of them all, and as he points the call to prayer begins. There are speakers attached to the buildings and the sound is coming from everywhere.' He takes another swig from the bottle. 'Well, blow me, but the street begins to fill with men and each man has his own prayer rug and they lay them down, carpeting the street. It was the most amazing sight – the street a rainbow mix of colours.'

Loukas has been watching Miltos's face as he talks. Just now, Loukas breaks off to top up the bowl with nuts and then becomes still again, waiting for the tale to continue.

'But I digress. I was looking for a hotel and I found the cheapest of the cheap. It was on the third floor of this grand old building that had seen better times. It was hot, so I took the ancient lift that creaked and groaned its way up. I could have walked faster … But then it stopped and I hesitantly pushed back the metal doors to stand in the corridor. It was called the Nefertiti Hotel, and there was a statue of the ancient queen there in the hall, badly made and with one eye missing. If I remember rightly it was painted gold, and the paint was peeling off, and the whole thing was lit by a series of lights, half of which didn't work, and around it was a moat of stagnant water that gave the impression that at one time it flowed and gurgled … Ha, ha, there I go again, off course. But I just wanted you to get a feel of the hotel. At the other end of the corridor was an enormous pile of sheets, and in front of me a reception desk that was cluttered with papers, old cups and overflowing ashtrays.

'I waited for a while, but no one came, and then I called out, and there was a noise from the half-shut door behind the reception desk. I called again but no one came. I was tired, and so, with a little desperation, I stepped behind the desk and knocked on the door, which swung open. Inside was a large bed with two men about my age lounging on it, with a dog, and the air was rich with the smell of the marijuana that had leached the life out of these two individuals.'

Loukas gives a knowing snort.

'They invited me in and the herbal cigarette was passed to me. I was alone in a country whose language I do not speak, with very little money, no prospect of food and nowhere to stay. Anyway, I took the cigarette, took one puff and looked around to find somewhere to sit down. The herb was strong and my legs instantly needed to be relieved of my weight.'

He pauses his narration to watch as the last sliver of sun sinks into the water and the sea turns inky black. The sky now lightens to a softer blue where the orb was. Loukas flicks a switch and lights come on along the raised paths to the hotel; there is also one on each of the tables, one between each pair of sunbeds, and a stripe of soft lights above the bar.

'Well, my noble hoteliers eventually got around to showing me to a room. Most of the rooms were full of boxes and discarded furniture, and one was full of dirty sheets. Apparently the washerwoman had given up on the place. One room was so dark I could see nothing, and then they turned the key to a bright room that was so big it had a double bed and two singles in it as well as a shower in the corner. The windows went down to the floor, and they opened onto a long, carved stone balcony that looked down on one of the major streets. It was noisy.'

Miltos clears his throat.

'There were no sheets or pillowcases. Not even any blankets, and the mattress was swarming with bedbugs, so I laid out my sleeping bag on the floor.' He pauses to clear his throat again and takes another swig of beer and a handful of nuts. Loukas takes another bottle of beer from the fridge and they drink in silence for a while as the darkness gathers. The sound of goats bleating and the dull clonk of their bells drifts on the soft air from behind the hotel.

'Did you leave the next day?' Loukas asks.

'No, not exactly the next day. You see, I had enough to stay one night and I had enough to eat for one day but then I would have been broke. So I made the suggestion to the two men who ran this hotel that, perhaps, for a room and a plate of food, I could help them out. They were very happy at the idea of lolling around all day, never to be disturbed by a lost tourist or a tired Egyptian, and they were happy for me to man the reception desk. And of course, to celebrate this new arrangement they rolled a herbal cigarette, and I took on the running of the hotel!'

Chapter 5

'I started my work at that hotel with enthusiasm, cleared the corridor of the sheets, stuffing them into the room that was already full of dirty linen, and tried to find out how many rooms were available. There was only one other room that was suitable for guests, apart from mine, so in one way I felt I had fallen on my feet. Managing one room was not too much to deal with, but on the other hand, if it was so little work why would these two characters be hiring me?'

Loukas becomes a little more alert, perhaps sensing that the story has some relevance to him.

'So I decided I would make myself indispensable. I cleaned the corridor, I got bug powder for the beds, I tried to fix the lift, I replaced the stagnant water around the statue – and I tried to get the pump working to circulate it but to no avail. Oh, and I managed to locate some toilet paper for the one toilet.'

He shifts his weight on the bar stool, turns slightly to Loukas and drops the pitch of his voice. 'Someone had plumbed in a very thin copper pipe from under the rim of the toilet to the centre of the bowl where it bent upwards. The result was that when the toilet was flushed, water shot out of the end – you know, so you could clean yourself. I believe that is the way in Eygpt, but can you imagine an American or a British woman being faced with that?'

He leans back again and assumes his normal voice.

'So I got the toilet roll and waited for someone to arrive. But of course, who would find us, tucked away down that narrow street, with no sign? So I went out onto the streets and touted for business. I looked out for tourists, and the first day I talked a pair of backpackers into staying. Italians, a lovely couple. They left the next day but I was on the streets again and I found a really nice couple from Holland, and the day after that, a fun group of Americans. The characters who owned the hotel seemed very pleased with the sudden flow of money and each time I handed over the takings they celebrated with a herbal cigarette, encouraging me to share.'

Miltos chuckles. 'Ah, I can remember, even now, standing on the balcony to my room after that first week, before bed, with the feeling that I could survive anywhere. The cars below making so much noise, the red tail lights and the white beams, people driving badly, stopping to let passengers out, car horns sounding and the smell of something rich with spices being fried somewhere. The buildings in that area were made of stone, some intricately carved, others with mosaics around the doorways. Men in long white robes, women in burkhas. It was all so exciting.'

He sighs.

Something swoops over the bar.

'Bats,' says Loukas, and he points across the lawn to the swimming pool, which is lit up, shining blue, under the water. The bats are swooping over the surface, drinking, clicking their way, missing each other by a hair's breadth. Loukas takes a napkin from the bar and rubs his hands, dries between his fingers. Miltos too feels sticky from the day's heat now the air is cooling, and he takes a napkin and rubs the back of his neck again. The change in temperature is such a relief.

'So you did well at the hotel then?' Loukas encourages.

'Well, here is my point. In the beginning I had energy and I was on the streets, fresh-faced, looking for business, and things were fine. But the celebratory herbal cigarette became an evening ritual, and getting out of bed to find tourists became more difficult as a result. So the evening ritual became an afternoon ritual and the tourists stopped coming after a while. If I got down to the streets at all, the only people I could tempt were lone Egyptian men in Cairo on business. This upset me, but instead of taking a shower, stopping smoking the herbs and sorting out the sheets to be washed to get rid of the lingering smell, I spent more time with the hotel owners and began to enjoy their way of life, lazing around all day. And then to mark the evenings they would open a bottle of illegal alcohol and the nights would become a blur.'

Loukas sucks his teeth and nods gravely.

'When you are on an unknown path, the trouble is you don't know where the end of it is. Just when I thought I could sink no lower, a girl of the night came and asked if she could take a room for the evening. You know what I mean, yes? Well, money is money and with no other customers I took her piastres and let her use the room as she liked. She was in fact a very sweet girl, and at that point I didn't understand why she did what she did for a living. It didn't suit her. Nevertheless she used the room often, and paid every time, and so with this regular customer the hotel owners and I could lounge around on their oversized bed, unable to say more than a few words to each other as we watched Arabic television. We spoke English as the common language, but none of us could speak it very well. But really, no one cared as long as a herbal cigarette was being passed back and forth.'

'Argh.' Miltos groans as if the wounds of this time are fresh. He stands and downs the last of his beer. 'Anyway, to cut a long story short, the girl began to bring her boyfriend, and I realised her lifestyle was not a choice. This man was dark. You know, spiritually, really dark.'

Loukas nods as if he understands, but a brief frown crosses his forehead and Miltos is reminded how young he is. He lightens his tone.

'But if life thwarts you in one way, it seems to me it also offers opportunities in another. You see, when we ran out of food it was my job to grab a few pounds from the dish where Ahmed kept the money and go out to the market and bring back food. Near the end of my time there it was the only thing that reminded me of normal life, that there was indeed a world outside the hotel walls. But when the girl began to bring her dark friend to the hotel I would return from the market to find him also smoking on the bed with the hotel owners, and the mood was different. The herbal laughter was gone, the air felt heavy, and the girl, who I didn't even notice the first time this happened, would be curled up with her knees to her chest, and her arms around her legs, eyes wide and staring. She was in a very bad state.'

'I didn't understand it at first but then I saw syringes by the bed and it all became clear. Ahmed's eyes were rolling in his head and I felt a flash of fear and clarity. I had followed these men down their path so far. Was I going to accompany them even further? … Do you know what stopped me?'

'No.' Loukas answers, eyes wide.

'I once had a girl, just for the briefest of time, and I loved her. It was her memory that stopped me. I knew I would never do such a thing if we were together and I knew she would never want it for me even though we were apart. So I asked Ahmed if I could take some money, just like that, straight out. He gave me it all with a wave of his hand and I took it. I took it, my bag and myself and I left that very moment, never to go back.'

'That sounds like a really grim adventure,' says Loukas, collecting the bottles and the glass.

'Ah, but nothing is grim if you learn from it,' Miltos says. 'You see, you said you feel a little niggle, wondering if you are doing all you can, wondering if everything you are doing is right. But all the time, I suspect, you are looking in the wrong direction to see clearly.'

Loukas stops drying the glass.

'What told me that things were not right was not what was going on within my head. Not the niggle, as you put it – nor was it the mess, the dirty sheets, the drop in quality of guests, or the company I was keeping. No, what told me was putting my feelings for the girl I had loved into the equation. If the situation fitted with the love then everything was fine, but if it jarred with the purity of the love I had felt for her then it was not. It was that simple. And it's an equation I have used time and time again, and it works. The only problem is there have been some occasions when I asked the question too late. But for you it is hardly too late. So, if you look at your situation and all you are doing here to run your bar, the question I would ask – or should ask – is "Does Ellie approve?"'

Miltos hitches up his jeans so they sit better and puts his hand in his pocket to check he has his room key. His fingers trace the rim of his broken shell.

Loukas replies with a smile, his hairline shifting backwards as if a weight has been removed.

'Then you do not need to do more. If you wanted advice,' Miltos says, 'which I'm aware you haven't asked for, but I will give it anyway – she is your happiness, son. She will give you all the signs you need to know if you are doing right and doing enough. Just keep your focus on her, and whatever you do don't let her slip through your fingers.' The last sentence has a weight to it.

'Are you around for a couple of days?' Loukas starts to vigorously wipe the bar.

'Not sure, any reason?'

'Just thought, if you are around the day after tomorrow it would be nice to see you at my wedding.'

'Ha! If I'm here, it would be my honour.'

And with this Miltos turns towards the hotel, jangling his keys. He keeps the smile plastered to his face but his own advice has disquieted him. He might have told that tale in a few different ways in the course of his life but, now he thinks of it, he has not told it recently. It seems a long time since he thought of Cairo and even longer since he thought of the girl he met in Saros all those years ago, and her influence on him.

Chapter 6

The bed is very comfortable and Miltos has slept longer than he expected. Actually, that is not accurate: he has been awake since the first ray of sun crept into his room, but he lingered in a state of semi-sleep, drifting in and out of dreams in which he was travelling from one beautiful location to another, and in each of which he would meet a different exotic girl and think he was in love. But then his first love would appear, her face veiled, and the other girl would fade in comparison and then disappear so he was alone with his first love, and he would reach for her hand. But just as their fingers touched, she would turn to mist. It is a recurring dream that he has had for years, as long as he can remember, and although it is heartbreaking he also relishes the closeness to her, just for those minutes. It brings a sweet melancholy which will stay with him all day, a familiar feeling. It is like an old friend.

'Come on then,' he tells himself. 'Let's go see if the car is fixed.'

He has missed breakfast but he is rarely hungry this early in the day. He runs his tongue over his teeth and chews a piece of the gum he bought yesterday after dropping off the car.

'Good morning,' says Ellie the receptionist with a smile. 'Did you sleep well?' She looks scrubbed, as if she has just come out of a shower.

'Thank you. I'll go to the garage today and see how long I will be staying. I won't know for sure until I know more about the problem with the car.' He offers her his room key.

'Well, we are not so busy so you won't have to change rooms if you decide to stay on. Do you want to settle up now so you can just go if you want to?' She looks at the computer screen, and her hands click on the keyboard. 'Room ten – here we are.'

A part of him wants to tell her that he met Loukas last night, but he is not awake enough to chat. He pays for last night and without another word steps into the heat of the sun.

The day is as glorious as yesterday: warm, but not too hot. He often thinks that Greece is wasted on the Greeks – not in an unkind way, just matter of fact. If they have always lived here what do they have to compare it to, so as to realise what a wonderful place it is? Having lived in so many places he knows the cold grey damp of northern Europe, the moist heat of the tropics, the parched heat of the deserts. Lush greenery comes with heavy rain, and temperate climates tend to be accompanied by a cloud covering and make him long for the changing of the seasons. No, the Greek climate is special. Not even Italy has it, although it comes close. The seasons in Greece are strong. Spring erupts with a boldness that takes his breath away, the flowers exploding into colour in the hedgerows and on forestry land. The summer has a heat that pulls all his happiness to the surface and chases all his fears away, and then, just as he begins to take it for granted, those ten or so days in August hit like an illness, so hot he cannot function. But then, just as he gives up hope of ever being able to do anything again, the air cools to a perfect temperature and a dramatic autumn sweeps over the land, with bronzes, tans, golds and burnt umbers, and the oranges hanging in huge bunches like jewels in evergreen trees. Such beauty.

But even so, he never seems to be able to stay in Greece long. It is not so much that other places call him; it is more that the intensity of the beauty in Greece needs to be shared. Experiencing it by himself makes him feel lonely, and the best cure he has ever found for loneliness is to travel, to keep himself alone. The desire is burning deep now, to get away, to stifle his emotions. As soon as the car is fixed he will return to Athens, quit this job, give up his rented room and go to Morocco, or maybe Israel again.

The walk from the hotel to the garage in the village takes him past the church, where a group of boys are playing football, laughing and calling to one another. Miltos watches the game as he approaches, and as he draws closer a wild kick sends the ball in his direction, and he finds he is on his toes, dribbling between the youngsters looking for a goal. The boys instantly move more quickly, legs extended, feet reaching for the ball. The new player adds excitement to the game and they all seem to want to prove themselves his equal. After a rough intertwining of feet the ball is taken from him and he walks on, hands back in his pockets, a bounce to his step.

A smell of oregano and caramelised onions is leaking from one of the houses. There is geranium and just a touch of jasmine too, but then, with a shift in the slight breeze, these delicate aromas are replaced with the scent of fresh washing. Miltos is level with the corner shop now, on the edge of the village square.

The garage is off to his right but he is thirsty, and the drinks cabinet outside the kiosk calls to him. A cat curled up asleep prevents him from opening the door of the fridge, and he wakes it with a stroke and a nudge. The animal yawns, rolls onto its back for a stomach rub, then slinks off across the road, and settles itself on a wooden chair in the shade of a tree that appears to be decorated with fairy lights, outside an eatery.

'Just this, please,' Miltos says to the woman inside the wooden hut. There is barely space enough to balance the bottle of water on the shelf that goes all the way around the kiosk as he fishes in his pocket for change. He glances at the front pages of the newspapers stacked on the floor. The headlines seem to be mostly concerned with the economic crisis, and one bemoans the number of Greeks moving abroad. Perhaps he will join them – perhaps it is a good time for him to move on too.

'Have a sweet,' the woman in the kiosk says, pushing a box of assorted single wrapped sweets towards him.

It is an unexpected offer and it makes him smile and look her full in the face. He hasn't really noticed her until now, and it is a nice face. It has none of the bloom of youth that Ellie's has, but there is a kindness, and humour in the eyes. She has perhaps overdone the lacquer in her hair, but she is a handsome woman. His first instinct, as always, is to flirt, but this is swiftly followed by a reminder that he has made an agreement with himself not to do that any more. How many relationships has he ended up in that he never intended to? They could all be thought of as just 'fun', but then it is never his heart that is broken. Instead, it is he who walks away and the woman's heart that is bleeding. But what if she is the one? Can he just pass by without finding out? His early morning dream comes to him again. He knows its meaning. Every woman he has ever met, and every relationship he has ever had, has been judged against that one brief passion all those years ago. His first love set the bar, and unfortunately for him no one else can ever match up.

'Thank you.' He accepts the sweet, gives her the money, takes a good long look into her eyes, smiles and forces himself to leave without another word.

'You are welcome.' The reply is mixed with a giggle. He likes that and feels tempted to return.

Looking around him distracts his attention from the encounter. Alongside the kiosk in the square are a small fountain and a palm tree surrounded by a low wall. Chairs and tables are arranged under the palm tree, presumably for customers of the *kafenio* over the road. It looks like a pleasant place to sit, and perhaps he will have a coffee later, but first he needs to go to the garage and find out when the car will be ready.

Overall, the village is pretty, and he can imagine sitting in a chair on a porch here, letting the days drift by.

He drinks deeply from the bottle and then he rubs the condensation on its surface against his forehead as he weaves between the *kafenio* tables in the square. There is no one sitting here – the sun is too high in the sky for that now, but this evening, if he is still here, these chairs will be full. If there is space he will allow himself to sit for a coffee, or a beer, and talk nonsense to people he will never meet again as he watches the world go by.

Down the side of the *kafenio* is a lane with a few houses, and rows of orange trees further up. But there on the left is the garage. The front yard is full of cars, tractors and piles of tyres. In amongst the engines and bowls of oil a line has been strung on which white washing is drying.

'*Yeia sou, file.*' He addresses the man as his friend, and eyes the worn and faded sign propped up on the porch that announces *Aleko's Garage*.

'Ah, yes,' says Aleko, rubbing his hands on an oily rag. 'It is not a big problem, should take an hour or two to fix.'

Miltos shifts his weight slowly from one foot to the other. So the car will be fixed and he can leave! This time next week he will be on the African continent. To up and leave Greece is a sensible choice based on how he is feeling, and it is one he has made many times before. But this time it just doesn't sit as well. It disturbs him. He digs his hand deeper into his pocket.

'Great,' he says to Aleko. 'I'll wait at the *kafenio*.'

Chapter 7

'Well, you could wait in the *kafenio*,' Aleko says, 'But as I said the part I need has to come down from Athens. So a day, maybe two?' He looks back at the engine he is working on. 'Will that be a problem with your boss?'

Miltos rubs his chin thoughtfully.

'Well, it is as it is.' Dropping off and picking up hire cars is not the worst job he has ever had, but it often involves a lot of waiting around, which he never suspected when he took the job.

'If you don't have the part you don't have the part.' He shrugs. It seems as if his plans to travel will be put on hold for a little. But that's all right – he can find work at any time in Marrakesh, or maybe, even, at this time of year, Essaouira. Maybe Ghita is still unmarried. Beautiful, loving Ghita. Ah, now that was a summer. The image in his mind of the wind blowing her long hair straight out behind her, as she stood on the wall by the sea, is still crystal clear. Such a gentle nature. She knew how to soothe a man's soul. Yes, he should see if she is still unmarried, and hope her baba is not around. It feels like a good decision, positive, and the melancholy he so often

44

feels settles down in such a way that it is less acute, convincing him that Ghita is the answer.

'Well, I should have this one and that one' – Aleko points at one car after another –'finished today, and then I have to get to those three tomorrow. They are booked. I will get your part put on the bus from Athens, and with some luck it could be here tomorrow. If so, I can work late.'

Aleko eyes Miltos's water bottle. He steps towards the house, takes a grubby-looking mug from a windowsill, fills it from a tap in the wall and drinks deeply.

'That's a lot of cars that need fixing for a small village,' Miltos observes. They both step into the shade of the tree, the trunk of which grows up at the boundary; the wall has been built around it, and the roots crack the impacted mud of the yard here and there. The place would look barren without it.

'Yup. I have created a little hire car business on the back of Stella's hotel. You staying there?' Miltos nods that he is. 'The business is going all right,' Aleko states, 'but I don't understand them.'

'Who?' Miltos asks. The orange trees in the grove adjacent to the yard rustle suddenly, the leaves lifting in a light breeze. The same wind cools the back of his neck.

'Tourists,' says Aleko. 'On the one hand, they complain that something will go wrong before it has happened. This means I always expect a big argument when they return the cars. But then, when they do return the cars, there is never any complaint,

45

only smiles and thank yous. I am finding it very stressful.'

'Different cultures, different thinking,' Miltos says.

'Have you been abroad? Do you know foreigners?' Aleko's face is stippled with the sunlight coming through the leaves and it reminds Miltos of petite Florentine, her face dappled in the sunlight of Fontainebleau forest in France, Gus and Henry standing next to her.

He was there for climbing, the boulders in the woods perfect for practising.

'That's a good one to start on,' Florentine said, dipping her hands into her chalk bag so they wouldn't slip on the rock. 'You start off there and then go straight up the face.'

She patted her fingers together to get the surplus off and a small cloud of dust drifted away on the breeze. The sun was brilliant through the pale-green deciduous leaves. The floor of the forest was so flat it didn't look natural, and there were climbers all over the other boulders like ants, using them for practice and to perfect particular climbing moves.

'It's got a long reach at the top,' Florentine added. 'Actually, I'll try something with less of a stretch on the other side. You coming, Henry?'

And the two of them went off, heads together, sharing lovers' secrets, holding each other's chalk-dusted hands.

'Personally I don't like it. It's a thuggy route, all brawn and no brain. They've never done it.' Gus was still looking at the route, but he nodded in the direction that the lovers left in. 'Needs too much height for Florentine and too much bottle for Henry.'

He always spoke directly like that – straight. It never felt offensive, because of his smooth French accent. Then he walked away, around the huge boulder, and Miltos was alone. The birds filled the branches above his head and children's shrieks of delight could be heard all over the forest. He looked up the rock face, saw where to place his hands and his feet and decided he could do it.

His chalk bag hung behind him from a cord around his waist. Usually it hung from his harness but as he was not going up any roped routes today he had left all that kit back at the campsite.

When he arrived the night before he had pitched his tent in the black of night, and the campsite had been silent. But when he had awoken this morning he had been greeted warmly by strangers in the other tents. That was the way it was in the climbing community: everyone accepted, everyone treated like family. It was one of the reasons he did it.

The moment he poked his head out of his tent in the morning Gus introduced himself and asked, 'You been here before?'

'No.' Miltos admitted. They spoke English, their mutual language.

'Well, my friend, be prepared to learn how to climb all over again.' Gus's chuckle was a little smug. 'Try to understand what the problem requires and just enjoy solving the puzzle, eh?' But he was friendly enough.

A small, lithe girl walked, catlike, towards them from another tent.

'This is Florentine, my cousin,' Gus said, and then another head popped out of the girl's tent. There was an edge in the way Gus introduced Henry.

'It is all slopers and mantles,' Florentine informed Miltos as she sat down on the dusty, bare earth beside them.

'And there's a lot of pressing and squeezing,' Henry sniggered, tripping on the guy ropes as he tried to get out of his tent and running forward to gain his balance.

'The routes are generally beefy and gymnastic, not for girls.' Gus's eyes flicked to Henry rather than to Florentine. Henry put a possessive arm around Florentine's shoulders.

'Strong legs are helpful, as well as strong adductors. There're a few heel hooks on some of the routes. Also, on some of the slabs you just basically want to do a one-leg squat and you may also want to glue your fingernails to your fingers too.' Florentine grinned at her own joke and examined her nails, which were short and ragged.

'But you are in the right place,' Gus reassured him, and then he set about making breakfast for them all.

Now, standing in front of the route that Florentine and Henry had never attempted and that Gus had described as thuggy, he felt strangely isolated. He wondered if he was the only person who felt like that before a climb. But it was what made him a bold climber because it gave him the sensation that he had nothing to lose. At that moment, death would have been just a part of – the final curtain to – the adventure of youth. So he faced the route, looked up its height and made the first move, stepping on a low, broad rock on the ground to gain the first hold. It was easier than he expected until halfway up, at which point he knew that if he went further he would be committed. There could be no climbing down after that point. He pressed on.

The greatest demand was now on his upper body and, as he continued, the build-up of lactic acid in his forearms became unbearable. There was no hold on which he could stop to rest, and each manoeuvre demanded more of him than he felt he had left to give. His fingers would no longer curl because of the acid in his muscles and the only way out of the situation was to make an effort to reach the top as speedily as possible. He was two handholds away from the summit, the end so close, but his legs, by this time, were trembling, and the next hold was a long reach. It would need a dynamic manoeuvre and he did not have the strength left. His calves began to give. He looked at the ground and knew that if he hit it there would be no avoiding the rock at the bottom.

If he jumped he would be looking at two broken legs, and if he fell he could crack open his skull. There seemed to be no choice left, and he summoned all his strength to bear the impact as his grip gave way.

Chapter 8

The fingers that locked around his wrist were so unexpected he could do nothing but stare up into the face of Gus, whose grip on Miltos's arm was strong and sure. Without hesitation, Gus, shorter than Miltos by a head but presumably fuelled by panic, summoned the strength to lift Miltos vertically from the rockface. Then Henry appeared and grabbed Miltos's free hand, and between them they hauled him up, his belly scraping against the top edge. For a few minutes the three of them lay sprawled on the flat top of the rock, then Henry began to laugh. Gus grunted, and Miltos felt another gaze on him. He looked around to find Florentine there too, staring at him, a look of ashen horror on her face.

'Never climb up what you cannot climb down,' Gus spat and took an easy route back down off the boulder.

'Wow, man, that was epic!' Henry exploded. Florentine's colour came back slowly, but her staring increased with everything he did after that. For the rest of the day he chose easy routes, Henry joining him, and Florentine occasionally making suggestions, and the dappled shade under the light-coloured leaves of Fontainebleau seemed to be the most perfect spot on earth.

Two days later, however, he did fall. Not off a rock, but on the wet bathroom floor following a drunken evening with the others. It was a clean break that made him shriek more in surprise than pain. Florentine was first by his side, kneeling beside him and resting his head on her knee. Henry flapped about without a clue what to do and Gus ran to get help.

The hospital was new and well equipped, but soulless; however, things looked up when a pretty young nurse was assigned to him. She confirmed that the X-rays showed a break, and she spent some time strapping him up. A night's stay would be enough to check for concussion.

The nurse was very attentive. Several times she looked him in the eyes for no real reason. It was only when he was shown to a bathroom, where there was a full-length mirror, that he saw what the nurse saw and realised she must have been flirting. There in the reflection, instead of the tall skinny youth he had always been, was a man whose muscles had all filled out, presumably from the climbing, and his olive skin had tanned from spending so much time outdoors, and his dark hair had flecks of gold put there by the sun. So, on returning to his bed he did what was the most natural thing in the world. He flirted back. That was when things became weird.

'How are we feeling today?' the nurse asked as she came in the next morning to plump up his pillows. She had more make-up on than the day before.

'Hey.' Henry came in. 'No climbing yet, there was dew in the night and the rocks are wet, so I'm here to kill time until the sun dries them out.' He grinned and offered Miltos a paper packet with a croissant inside. He politely accepted, but as he had eaten bacon and eggs half an hour before he put it to one side. The nurse was changing his water and made eye contact with him as if they were already in the middle of a steamy relationship.

'I brought you some flowers.' Florentine came in behind Henry. They were wild flowers and they had wilted somewhat, but Miltos was touched by the thought. Something was different about her, and Miltos had to look twice before he realised that her face, usually scrubbed, was also made up. 'Henry, go get us coffees,' she whispered quietly and, like the docile hound he was, with a cheerful smile Henry was gone. The nurse's eyes flashed at Florentine and Florentine looked daggers back at the nurse. In the same awkward second they were both smoothing the bed, one on each side, and Miltos suddenly felt like a pawn in a game he had not agreed to play. The nurse tried to outdo Florentine by moving from the sheets to the pillow, arranging it behind his head. Florentine might have been petite but she was feisty on the rocks and just as fiery, it seemed, in the rest of life. Without hesitation, she took his comb from the

53

bedside table and started combing his hair, blatantly staking possession. Miltos could only think of poor Henry, who would walk through the door with the coffees at any moment.

The nurse countered by picking up his wrist and looking at her watch. 'Pulse steady, that's a good sign. Nothing here to make it race,' the nurse said.

At this, Florentine looked the nurse straight in the face and then bent over and kissed him full on the mouth.

The nurse huffed her indignation and left the room. When Florentine pulled away, Henry was already standing in the door with three coffees balanced between his extended fingers. The look on his face told Miltos that although he was hurt by what he had just seen, this was not the first time.

Henry and Florentine left the hospital that morning together, but Florentine looked back at Miltos.

'No, I don't understand them either,' Miltos tells Aleko who, having finished his water, is picking at the oil and dirt on his watch strap.

Miltos was discharged later in the afternoon, and when he returned to the campsite Gus and Henry were still there but Florentine was gone. Neither of them mentioned her and Miltos presumed the topic was not for discussion. But it left him feeling very awkward so he left in the night, the same way he arrived, with no one seeing him.

For a while after that, he felt very alone; it was almost a physical feeling as if something was tearing at him from the insides. He wandered aimlessly until he found himself in Paris. But his days were purposeless and he wandered aimlessly there too. It was just chance that took him into that museum, but it was as if another world had opened up to him. He discovered French painting, or, to be specific, impressionist painting, and that was the first time he felt that other people like him existed in the world, saw life as he did.

'No, I do not understand them at all,' Miltos repeats to Aleko, and he finds that now his decision to go to Morocco to find Ghita is no longer the right one. The exotic is not what he wants any more. He wants something more personal, more real. Someone closer to his soul. A good old-fashioned Greek girl, perhaps?

Chapter 9

Miltos wanders back towards the village square with this thought in his head. It teases him. A Greek woman of his age will be married, with children, and grandchildren, no doubt. If she does not have a man at home then the chances are she will be in black, the shawl of mourning over her shoulders, weighing her down so she cannot lift her head to contemplate the possibility of new love. Such attitudes are cultural, of course, but for him these are also a problem with no solution. Unless he can find himself a feisty woman, one who flouts the rules, runs to the beat of her own drum – that woman would be his equal, someone who is capable of standing up to traditions and making her own decisions. But before he can dwell on it any longer he is distracted by the thwack of wood upon wood. An animated game of *tavli* is being played in the *kafenio*.

Miltos trots up the three steps into the masculine domain. Above the men's heads, just below the ceiling, hangs a billowing cloud of tobacco smoke. It hovers thinly, and will no doubt thicken as the day goes on, but for now its acrid aroma does not reach his nostrils. Rather, it is the smell of Greek coffee that dominates. A man with a fuzzy mop of hair is standing behind a long counter by the back wall, watching a *briki* balanced on a gas stove. This man looks up as Miltos enters and smiles in welcome.

But he is still thinking about the women in his life and wondering why he has never stayed with any of them for very long. He has had his chance with Greek women as well as with foreign girls, but the Greek women, back in the days when he was courting them, always seemed to have a mama not too far behind them, a combination that generally seemed rather formidable and put paid to any romance that might have bloomed.

He sits at the counter in the depths of the *kafenio*, half turned so he can see some of the room and through the window to the side where the corner shop is visible.

'What can I get you?' The man with the mop of hair has a gentle, easy way of talking, the sort of lilt that is only gained by conversing with people all day every day. Milton's own drawl is similar but slower. He has removed all the rush from his life.

'Theo, I'll have a refill when you have a moment,' another man calls.

'Make mine a coffee, *metrio*.' On the rare occasions when he does drink coffee, Miltos likes it strong, black and medium sweet.

Theo gathers the used cups that are piled on the counter and puts them in the sink, then starts on Miltos's coffee. With a well-practised movement he stirs a spoonful of sugar into the water and puts it to boil. The granules dissolve slowly and the water takes on a sheen. From a shelf behind him he takes a new packet of coffee, snips off the top and holds it out for Miltos to smell.

'Good, isn't it?' But it is not really a question. Theo gently drops a spoonful of the fine granules on the water where they float, and Miltos watches as the grounds absorb the water, sinking with a satisfying plop.

'I wish everything just took time and patience,' Theo says.

'Such as?' Miltos is looking forward to this drink. Theo has lifted the *briki* from the heat twice already when the froth has threatened to boil over. There will be no traces of grit left.

'Women,' Theo says. He pours the coffee into a waiting cup and then fills a glass with water from a bottle in the fridge before presenting them both to his customer.

'Thank you. Miltos, by the way.'

'You're welcome. Theo,' Theo replies, introducing himself in turn.

'Women can be controlled but not all women can be controlled the same way.' Miltos shares his knowledge.

'Well, I cannot control my woman in any way,' Theo huffs.

'How long have you been married?' Miltos is not sure he wants this conversation; so far, it is only serving to remind him of what he came in to forget.

'Oh no, we are not married, and that is just another example of the problem.' Theo starts another coffee and looks up to scan the room. 'No. I want to marry her, and I have asked her, many times over the years. She does not deny her love for me and yet she will not say yes. Then, as if to rub the situation in my face, there is Loukas and Ellie. He's a young man who works at the hotel. You might have met him, he runs the beach bar.'

Miltos grunts, his lips on the cup. He cannot wait to taste the deep-brown nectar.

'Well, he is not even thirty yet and he is marrying in two days' time. And there is another problem.' He lifts the *briki* off the heat as it begins to boil over.

'What's that then?' The coffee could not be more perfect and Miltos is only half listening, responding automatically to Theo's chatter.

'After the church they have arranged to celebrate here in the square. You know, put all the chairs and tables out.' He turns off the gas with one hand and lifts the *briki* with the other. 'And we will use the chairs and tables from the eatery too.'

He looks up in the general direction of the *ouzeri,* cup in his hand. 'Together we will do the food and the drink – only, and I don't even know if Stella is aware of this, we have already agreed to do Petta and Irini's baptism party, and it turns out that that is on the same day.'

Miltos doesn't ask Theo to clarify who Petta is but he is becoming curious about this Stella.

'But surely the priest knows he has booked these two ceremonies on the same day?' Miltos says, readying himself for a second sip. If he had a choice he would rather sit in silence to drink the coffee, but Theo seems like a very gentle man, and besides, Miltos doesn't mind indulging someone who turns coffee-making into an art.

'Hrumph.' The sound comes from the back of Theo's throat. He pours a glass of water and takes it and the latest coffee to the waiting customer, before coming back to the counter and wiping everything clean. Hanging the cloth on a hook and mirroring Miltos's pose, he leans on the counter.

'The priest is all rush, rush, rush, as if he still lives in Athens. It would make not one bit of difference to him if he had booked them both on the same day. He would be happy to run the church like a conveyer belt.'

'That's not right. Rushing is rarely, if ever, a good idea. Life is too precious to hurry. Better to savour every moment, even the low ones.' Miltos slowly taps his short nails against the cup.

Theo shrugs and reaches into his pocket, takes out a packet of cigarettes. Miltos declines and Theo stands slowly puffing away.

'There must be a way to control a feisty woman.' Theo speaks quietly, after a long pause. 'After every wedding we attend she even promises that we will be the next.' He looks out of the window and down the street, but his eyes are glazed.

60

'I dated a feisty woman once. Scottish. Temper like the devil himself. Red hair, skin so white – she was such a beauty. Not beautiful in the traditional way – she had a high forehead, puffy cheeks, her lower lip bigger than her upper lip – but there was just something about her.' Miltos allows himself to dwell on her for a moment, sinking into her essence, remembering her fully.

'What happened? Did you find out how to control her?' Theo looks hopeful.

Chapter 10

The sun is slanting through the large windows, lighting up half the floor and half the tables and chairs, forcing the men into the shady side of the room. A butterfly hurls itself repeatedly against the large front window, stopping periodically for a rest before beginning again. It is too high to be reached with cupped hands.

'I was in Hebron,' Miltos tells Theo. 'In Israel,' he expands, in response to his new friend's blank look. I was staying on a kibbutz and I thought that whilst I was there I should visit Jerusalem.'

Theo nods his head as if this is the most natural thing in the world.

'Well, from where we were to Jerusalem, the most direct route was through the West Bank and a town called Hebron.'

He hasn't thought about this since the day it happened. Why was he walking in Hebron, and not on a bus? He would not have the courage now to do half the things he did back then, but then he probably just thinks a little bit more before he does things these days, is more aware of the consequences. He goes on.

'Isla was with me, this fiery Scottish girl. We met on the kibbutz and I was taken by her colouring, her temper, her accent, but she showed no interest in me. She told me the worst of all things that she could have told me. She said she thought of me as a brother!' He pauses, sighs and takes a sip of coffee. Theo chuckles his understanding. 'So we were walking through Hebron, with me wishing I was not in a brotherly role. At the time there was peace in Israel, but it was tentative peace. The people were not happy and Hebron did not feel like anywhere else in Israel. There was a tension, you know, like it was an unsafe place to be, and there were only men out on the street, no women at all. But I was walking with Isla down the main street. We could hear the roar of a crowd as we drew near to some gates, and beyond we could see the concrete terracing of a small football stadium. But the sound was not a cheer for a goal, or a foul, it was people arguing, a lot of people, and we realised a meeting must be going on.

'Isla had on a long skirt and a long-sleeved top but her hair was blazing in the sunshine and she looked so Western she was attracting attention just being there. Like I said, there were no women on the street, only men, everywhere you looked. So I suggested that we turn around, or find a hotel, anything to get us off the streets.'

'"I dunna care," she hissed. "No man's gonna intimidate me." And she strode on in front of me.'

Theo stubs out his cigarette and begins the process of making a coffee, but no one has asked for one and so Miltos presumes he is making it for himself.

'Well, just as we drew level with the gates of the football stadium they must have finished their meeting, because a sea of men swarmed out onto the other side of the street. Isla's red hair was catching everyone's attention and I felt suddenly under threat.

'I leaned forward and hissed "Cover your hair" in her ear. She turned to defy me but she saw the men and quickly brought the scarf up from around her shoulders and over her head, and pulled it forward so her hair and most of her face was covered. But the men flooding out of the gates continued to stare as we walked, with Isla a pace ahead of me, and that's when I realised what was wrong. She should have been behind me.'

The quickening of his heartbeat felt so strong. The crowd had begun to filter across the wide street, and he feared for himself but, more than that, he felt terrified at the possibility of what could happen to Isla. His mouth was so dry, his tongue sticking to the roof of his mouth. His fists were balled and his legs twitched as he walked, ready to run, but he knew he would not run, not unless Isla was running too. Without moving his head he swivelled his eyes, taking in who was where, how big they were, the way they were looking at him and, knowing he was outnumbered, he thought quickly.

'Rather than draw attention to her being a step ahead of me, I took control of her,' he tells Theo, who is pouring his own coffee, slowly and carefully. 'I put my hand on the back of her neck as if I owned her. At first she shrugged to loosen my hand but I tightened my grip and I pushed her in front of me. It felt strange, aggressive, but it immediately had a pacifying effect on both Isla and the men. Within a few minutes we had moved quite a way down the street and lost the attention of the men. It was as if I had performed a magic trick. But all I had done was imply my ownership. I thought that the moment the streets were clear and we were alone again Isla would slap my hand away and say something. But she didn't. My hand stayed there and I slowly changed it from a dominant gesture to a loving one, and by the time we arrived, I forget where now, I was fondling her earlobes and she was a kitten, cosying up to me and showing me such affection.'

'Hummmm,' Theo says thoughtfully, his elbows on the counter, balancing his little coffee cup on the ends of his fingers in front of his nose. 'Hummmm,' he repeats, his eyes losing focus, lost in his own world as he stares across the china rim.

Miltos didn't like it then and he doesn't like the memory now – that feeling of dominance does not suit him. Isla gave him all the signals later on that day that she was open to having a relationship with him, but it didn't take much imagination to see how that might unfold. Her quick temper firing up at the least provocation, him putting up with it until he could tolerate it no more, and then only being able to settle her down again by letting his irritation come out as dominance. It would be a never-ending cycle.

No, he wasn't ready to lead such a life, so he left the kibbutz life and Isla behind him.

It is strange how one minute he can feel so sure of what he wants. Like just before he came into the *kafenio*, when he felt sure the answer to his dreams lay in a Greek woman who would flout the rules, run to the beat of her own drum. He had even used the word 'feisty' in his head. But now he is not so sure. He wants a peaceful, slow life, no more drama.

'So you think if I was to dominate Anastasia she might succumb?' Theo asks.

'Who knows? It was just something I remembered. Only you know your relationship.' He is tempted to get a second coffee, it is so good, but he would be better off lining his stomach with some food first.

'I have never dared. To be honest she frightens me just a little.'

'I understand. That's how it was with Isla. But when the fear was gone, so was the excitement.' His eyebrows lift at his own words. 'I never thought of that before. But yes, that was her attraction. Once I knew how to be in control there was not much left for me and her.'

Theo looks a little saddened by his words, and he still has a contemplative expression on his face.

Miltos is intrigued by his own revelation. He doesn't want someone bossy, then, or domineering, or feisty. Maybe all this time he has been drawing in the wrong type of woman. Does that mean he wants someone sweet, with no edge? Maybe that's just how it is as age creeps up on you. He shudders at the thought, mentally defying his advancing years. There is still time for adventures. Maybe he should go back to Thailand, Cambodia, Vietnam, maybe even Burma, and spend some more time there, become lost once again in their unspoilt beauty.

'Theo, can I get some service here?' a grey-haired man at one of the tables calls out. Theo puts down his own cup and, with a spring to his step, his hair bouncing, is quick to attend the customer.

Miltos fishes in his pocket for a euro and leaves it by his cup. He will find some breakfast now and spend a little time thinking. If he is to go to the Far East, what are his plans exactly? When will he go, and does he intend to come back? The Thai girls are as sweet as they come, but, from his experience, they cannot be pushed around. The ones he has known have had very stubborn cores. But maybe that is exactly what he needs.

Chapter 11

Miltos leaves the *kafenio* and as he passes the kiosk he turns to look between the fridges and into the shade of the awning for a glimpse of the woman who serves there. If he could think of something to buy he could talk to her again. It is a pleasant surprise to see that the woman from the corner shop is also there. She seems to be just passing the time. The two women speak quietly, the woman inside leaning out, the one outside leaning in, their heads meeting over the boxes of sweets on the counter. They chat as if they are sharing secrets. The lady from the corner shop's blue dress suits her, hugs the curves of her waist, which, thank goodness, is not unnecessarily thin. Both she and the lady inside the kiosk are handsome women; the kiosk lady is taller and more vivacious, but the one in blue has a twinkle in her eye that promises fun.

There's nothing he needs to buy, though, and the women do not make eye contact as he passes them.

Past the kiosk a fluster of voices can be heard within the eatery. Opposite this is a tiny sandwich shop, with a selection of sandwiches and cakes in the window. The girl in the doorway looks up blankly. She is dressed in jeans and a light-blue sweatshirt the colour of the sky, her dark hair up in a ponytail held by a matching ribbon. She is nice-looking but too young for him, perhaps in her twenties. He strolls towards her.

'Can you believe it?' She addresses him before he is much closer. 'Nothing happens forever in this village and then everything on the same day. Look!' She waves her hand in the direction of the eatery. The double doors across the road are open and the grill top is visible behind the counter. The acrid fumes of the charcoal mix with the smell of the sandwiches, which in turn mingles with the aroma of fresh bread that is leaking from the bakery next door. A childlike woman in a floral dress is standing, hands on hips, in front of the grill opposite and it is her voice that is projecting for all to hear. A tall, broad young man who cannot stand still is speaking in harsh but very hushed tones as if he does not wish to be heard by everyone.

'But how many times do you think we will baptise him?' he hisses, the tension audible in his voice. 'So far Irini does not know, but when she finds out everything is double-booked what do you think she will say, Stella?'

'Petta, I do not know what you expect me to do. My role may be the godmother but I am not a fairy godmother.' She makes an attempt to laugh but she sounds exasperated. 'I cannot undo what is done. When I suggested doing the catering and having the celebration on the square it never occurred to me that it was the same day as Loukas and Ellie's wedding day.'

'Why can't they have it at the hotel?' Petta asks, his voice cracking like a child's about to cry.

'Because they work there, Petta. They wanted a break from where they work on their wedding day, to be with the village. And besides, Theo is doing all the drinks as he's Loukas's *gambros*, so it is natural that it should be on the square outside Theo's *kafenio*, isn't it?'

'But with you and Mitsos as the godparents it is natural that we should have our baptism celebrations on the square near the eatery.' Petta exclaims. 'Besides, I think after the years it has taken my mama to build up that corner shop, surely she deserves to have her first grandchild baptised in the village church and have the celebration on her doorstep.'

'What I don't understand is why the priest double-booked you, or is he packing you in one after the other?' Stella asks.

'It sounds as if they have a problem,' Miltos says to the girl on the stool. 'But I have to say, as problems go, it's not so bad.'

Her eyebrows lift and she looks at him, waiting for an explanation.

'The whole village thing,' he says – but, judging by her eyebrows, which are still held high, she has not understood him. 'I have no family,' he explains, 'and no village. I have nowhere I belong, so there is no one and nothing with which I could double-book anything. Hearing two people arguing about weddings and godparents and baptisms, and everybody integrated with everybody, the whole village life bit, it all seems, so – well, so … lovely,' he ends lamely.

The girl slides from the stool.

'Well, it's not lovely for them, they have a problem,' she says matter-of-factly, and her tone makes him realise that she has no idea what it might mean to be without a village or family or friends. 'Can I get you anything?' she asks.

'Oh, yes, right. Do you have any *bougatsa* left?' He wonders if perhaps he has annoyed her a little, but he cannot put it right, and nor does he want to waste his energy actually trying. She will forget him the minute he leaves.

'Sugar or cinnamon?' She packets the custard pastry and her hand hovers by two canisters, each with holes in the top, one dusted with white and the other brown.

'Cinnamon, please.'

She picks up the brown-topped shaker and shakes cinnamon liberally into the packet.

The pastry tastes good, and Miltos had not realised how hungry he was. For a moment there is nothing else in existence. He closes his eyes against the sun and lets his taste buds have his full focus. His tongue swirls around the flavours in his mouth; his teeth grind against the flaky pastry. The sweetness warms against his tongue before it slithers down his throat. It seems like seconds before the sugar gives energy to his limbs and he opens his eyes again and becomes aware of the strength of the sun. He would be better off out of its direct glare. He remembers that beyond the kiosk, not visible from where he is standing now, is a bench in the shade of the wall that runs along the back of the square. It is the foundation wall, if he remembers rightly, of the first of a line of houses that are built one behind the other up the steep hill behind the kiosk. He will sit there.

With long, easy strides, his eyes half-closed against the light, he walks beyond the now-unmanned kiosk and prepares himself to sit before the next bite. But he is brought up short. The man who was in the eatery just now, the man who was addressed by the woman in the floral dress as Petta, is sitting there, an elbow on each knee, his head in his hands. He must have walked there whilst Miltos was paying for his pastry.

Miltos moves more slowly, softening his footfall, and sits carefully so as not to disturb the man.

Chapter 12

Miltos nibbles at his *bougatsa*, but the young man's obvious distress, just at the other end of the bench, tempers his enjoyment somewhat. Maybe he can cheer the poor fellow up? He tries to weigh him up with a sideways glance. With wide-set eyes and a generous mouth, he is a good-looking young man, and built like a horse. His nails are short and his hands look like they have seen some work, but he is wearing deck shoes with no socks, which seems odd in this rural farming village. Maybe he is a fisherman.

'You sail?' It is a shot in the dark but the young man's despair is almost tangible and it seems worth a try. There is no reply, but then he looks up, not sure if it is he who is being addressed.

'Sailing? Do you like it?' Miltos asks again.

The man answers with a forced laugh that nevertheless seems to release a little tension. 'Best feeling in the world,' he says. 'Sailing, motoring, anything on the water. I used to run a taxi boat service' – his thumb points over his shoulder – 'on Orino Island, over the hills there.' As he speaks, the energy in his voice increases and he becomes decidedly animated.

'I have been on the water a fair amount myself too,' says Miltos. It's good to see the young man smile, and it's a nice smile: open, warm.

'Miltos.' He offers his hand.

'Petta.' The young man's shake is firm and strong and he sits upright, his worries temporarily forgotten. 'Where have you sailed?' he asks.

'Well, I skippered a flotilla of sailing yachts here in Greece one year, and I won't ever forget that,' Miltos says, and they laugh together. 'Then I got into delivering yachts from France. You know, bringing over the new boats. Bavarias, Beneteaus, Jenneaus. The straits of Messina, now those are strange waters. It was like the ocean was billowing up from the bottom and creating huge cushions of water on the surface. Almost like the whole sea was boiling, but in slow motion.' He can still envisage that in his mind, images that can be recalled so clearly. 'They say the legend of Scylla and Charybdis comes from there, and I can believe it! We saw whales, and lots of dolphins. But the best bit of sailing I ever did, can you guess where that was?'

The expression on Petta's face shows that he has forgotten all about his troubles, and Miltos slows himself down; there's no need to hurry now. He takes a bite of his *bougatsa* and waves his free hand about to indicate that he will talk after he has swallowed. He takes his time, lets Petta anticipate. Anticipation is one of the most enjoyable feelings.

There is something about the excitement, the waiting for the pleasure, that can often be even more enjoyable than the experience itself. The *bougatsa* filling is delightfully creamy and sweet, the contrast with the crisp pastry exquisite. His lips hover over it before taking another bite. How often has he wallowed in anticipation? The anticipation when he meets a woman, the chase, that unsure feeling of not quite having established a relationship, is so exciting. But then, also, how often, as soon as the anticipation is over, and the relationship is sealed with a kiss, has he thrown the whole connection off balance again so that neither of them is on firm ground, just so he can have the whole experience over again?

Petta has moved a little closer, put an arm, bent at the elbow, on the back of the bench so he can shield his eyes from the sun to see Miltos clearly. Miltos swallows. The cinnamon was a good idea but he will try the icing sugar tomorrow, for variety.

'Egypt,' he says, licking his lips, in response to his own question. 'That's where I had my best sailing.'

'You mean in the Mediterranean, off the coast of Alexandria?' Petta has started shuffling his feet; his legs twitch, and his hands gesticulate, suddenly needing to expend some energy.

'Ah, the coast of Alexandria! Where did he not conquer, eh, that Alexander the Great? But no, my favourite place was not even on the sea. It was on the Nile, down at Luxor – you know, across from the

Valley of the Kings where all the pharaohs are buried.'

Petta nods vigorously.

'Well,' Miltos continues, warming to his story, 'I had taken the bus from Cairo to Luxor with the intention of seeing the tombs. What a place! I've never been so hot in my life.' He lets his head drop back, looking up at the blue sky, which is dotted with birds floating on unseen thermals. The great ragged leaves of the palm tree in the square move ever so slightly in the lightest of breezes. The sun has moved and the bench they are sitting on is out of its shade now. 'I had very little money, so I looked for the cheapest place to stay I could find in Luxor, and it was cheap! Just a few cents it cost me a night. But once in my room, by midday, I realised why. I could not move. The building was a block of concrete and it absorbed the heat and, with no air conditioning, I lay on my bed and watched the ceiling fan turning around. In my mind I pretended it was actually cooling the air, but in reality it just blew the heat about a bit, possibly making it worse. I was so hot I just could not move. So the next day, I set out to see the tombs before the sun was fully up and the day was fresh. I could not afford the bus so I had to walk, and so the earlier the better. Well, Luxor is on one side of the river and the trail to the Valley of the Kings is on the other side, and there was no avoiding spending a few piastres to get across. So I wandered down to the water and there I saw the most graceful of sailing craft. They call them feluccas, and they have huge triangular sails to catch the light winds on the river. Beautiful things. Well, the owner was asleep but his little brother – Mohammed was his name – took me across to the other side. He was a good lad, wise and so full of life, like a forty-year-old in an eight-year-old's body. Anyway, I went up to the tombs and when I came back Mohammed was there again, as if he had not moved in all the time I was away. His elder brother was still asleep at the back of the boat.'

Miltos folds the paper packet that his bougatsa came in and puts it in his pocket.

'The tombs were interesting, don't get me wrong, but it was the felucca that really caught my attention. Mohammed was full of questions about Greece, asked if I had been to Germany, England, America. For such a small boy his English was perfect, and strange, coming from a youngster the colour of a burnt chestnut. In his long cotton robe he looked as if he was straight out of the Bible.' Miltos stops to smile at the memory.

'But I digress! I was talking about the boat. It was an old wooden open boat, and she was a thing of beauty. Pretty soon Mohammed started the patter. "Hey mister, you take a tour with me down the river?" That kind of thing. His hair was so bleached by the sun that it was a kind of dark red, and the whites of his eyes were so white, as were his teeth. He was a good-looking little chap. I could see his future ahead of him, doing so well with the tourists with his grin and his wit, but eventually finding he was a big fish in a small pond and wanting more. I felt for him.'

He has had that feeling himself once or twice, when he has been somewhere too long. His solution, back then, was to move on, usually to another country. These days he always feels like a big fish because he has seen so much of the world, experienced so many things. Not that this makes him better than anyone else: it's just that he always sees the bigger picture and the small stuff loses its intensity. On the positive side it seems to have slowed down his haste, but the price of that is that there is nothing to ground him. He returns his thoughts to his storytelling.

'So I said I couldn't afford his tour. We were about halfway across the Nile then, on the way back, and he let go of the rudder. He had been steering with his foot, his toes curled over the tiller. But he just moved away and lay down. The boat began to drift – we had been side on to the current, but the bow began to shift round and once in the current we began to pick up speed.'

Petta is smiling as he listens; all the signs of the adult life he must have lived are wiped away and he looks like a small boy. It pleases Miltos, and he continues.

'I cannot afford your tour even if you force me,' I told Mohammed as I took the rudder and steered us back to the bank. It didn't make any difference to him, he just shrugged and let me steer the boat, and let me tell you, she handled beautifully. Well, it

78

seems the young lad had been thinking as I sailed us across, because he asked me to go in with him. "You come with me," he said, or something like that. "We make tours together. I do the chat-chat with the women and you do the steering." Just like that! "He's no good," he said, meaning his brother, who was still half-asleep. And that's how it happened, and I spent the summer taking tours up and down the Nile. I tanned a dark brown with being out in the intense sun all day long, and Mohammed gave me a *jelabiya* to wear, and for all the world I looked like I had been born there.'

He sighs. Mohammed became like a younger brother and a son all in one, and because of it, for the months that he spent on the Nile, he felt very grounded. But by the end of the summer his care for little Mohammed began to worry him. He thought that if he grew too fond of the little man he might become stuck. At least, that was what he told himself at the time. The truth was that the feeling he had for the boy, the love he began to feel, as if Mohammed was his own offspring, began to ignite a spark that made him think about having children of his own. That frightened him, and although he was only half aware of it at the time, it was why he left.

'What an adventure!' Petta says. 'This is the sort of adventure I want to have with my son when he is grown. I can see us sailing from island to island, with Irini – that's my wife – making the food, and watching the dolphins. This is my dream.'

'Oh, you have a boat then?' Miltos asks.

'Ah, no, that is my first dream. I have had this dream since before my son. The dream to build a boat with my own hands.' Petta spreads his hands out before him. He has a big span.

'That is a fine dream, and one I have had myself. But it looks like I will never fulfil it.'

'But why wouldn't you?' Petta curls his fingers into his palms and drops his hands to his lap.

'Well, for one I have never stayed anywhere long enough to make it happen.' The corners of Miltos's mouth twitch downwards.

'So stay somewhere. Stay here. Maybe we can build such a boat.' Petta's eyes sparkle, a broad grin on his face. His legs have started jiggling about again, his toes tapping. 'If you stay long enough my son can help too.' He is laughing now.

Miltos scrunches up the paper packet his *bougatsa* came in and smiles at Petta.

'Ah, to have a son, how lucky are you. It is him you should build your boat with. Now, that is a luxury I can never have.' He stands. 'I think I will take a short walk. Where does the little lane on the other side of the kiosk go?'

Petta is also on his feet now. Miltos notes that he has to fractionally look up at him, which is rare. He doesn't often find men taller than he is.

'Up to the pines on the hilltop. There's a beautiful view from there,' Petta tells him.

'Sounds perfect. See you.' He says the words but he does not really want to leave this man's company. He would love to stay and start to build

80

boats with him, maybe even stay long enough to watch Petta's son's small hands grow and learn to use woodworking tools. But this desire makes him feel vulnerable, and his legs jiggle involuntarily, ready to run.

'By the way, my son's baptism is the day after tomorrow – if all goes well,' Petta adds, and his brow wrinkles. 'But if it does, it would be a pleasure to see you there.' He does not wait for a reply. He turns his broad shoulders and strides across to the corner shop. 'Come and we can talk some more about the boats we will build,' he calls back over his shoulder.'Ah yes, I think I heard something about that,' Miltos replies, and he watches Petta stride across the square towards the corner shop, but before the young man reaches it he is waylaid by a dog and stops to rub its head.

'Ah, so the lady in the blue dress that runs the corner shop is the mama,' Miltos says to himself as he makes the connection, also noting a resemblance.

Chapter 13

'The priest has only gone and double-booked us,' Stella announces as she enters the corner shop.

Frona is perched on a chair close to the counter, chatting with Marina, who is busying herself with a carton of mini ouzo bottles, arranging them on a high shelf on the back wall. Juliet is standing by the shelves of cleaning products, picking through a box of rubber gloves, dishcloths, rubber sink plugs and pan scourers.

'Double-booked who?' Frona asks casually.

'Do you have any of those metal things with holes in that sit over the sink plughole to catch peelings and teabags and so on?' Juliet asks.

'Yes, they are in the button and zip box.' Marina points to where it is on the shelf Juliet is looking at.

'Of course they are! Where else would they be? Oh, it says that it is only one hundred drachmas!' Juliet pulls out her find and holds it up to show the price tag.

'I've been busy,' Marina says.

'Since 2002?' Frona wags a finger at Marina and laughs.

'Did you hear me?' Stella says.

'Who has double-booked who, Stella?' Frona asks.

'Petta and Irini's baptism and Loukas and Ellie's wedding.'

'Surely not?' Juliet says.

'Please tell me this is a bad joke?' Marina abruptly stops organising the bottles and sits heavily.

'No joke. I have just been talking to Petta.' Stella looks behind her, out of the door. He is there on the bench by the kiosk talking to the stranger with the broad shoulders.

Marina looks through the window and asks, 'What's he doing with that man?'

'What man?' Juliet peers out of the window, as does Frona.

'Oh, it's the tall man who was in here yesterday.' Frona says. Marina starts to smile, as the memory of their discussion about pigs in sacks comes back to her, along with the look the stranger gave her. A thrill runs down her spine, making her wriggle.

'It looks like they are chatting, but he is not the point. The fact is we are double-booked.' Stella turns back to Marina.

'Well, that's the priest's fault, surely?' Frona says.

'Yes, but our problem,' Stella says.

'Well, if it is the priest's fault, get the priest to sort it. I'm sure he hasn't double-booked anyone, and someone has heard the date wrong.' Frona sniffs.

'Well, I didn't.' Marina is adamant.

'I really don't think Ellie is going to get her dates wrong – this is her wedding,' Stella retorts.

'So you are suggesting I don't know what I was told?' Marina is back on her feet facing Stella.

Stella's hands are on her hips and she is about to reply when Frona says quickly, 'Ask the priest.'

'You are right. Come on, Marina.' Stella relaxes her stance and the two of them bustle out of the shop. Frona, who is still sitting, struggles for a moment to stand and then hurries to catch them up. She pauses in the doorway for a moment to beckon Juliet.

'I'll keep an eye on the shop,' Juliet says, and she watches the three women hurry away, up towards the church, before her gaze returns to the stranger on the bench opposite.

Behind the church there is a large grand house with a balcony that overlooks the paved area around the church, and seated on this balcony, sipping coffee in the sun, is the new priest, in his black robes. He is the second new priest in fairly quick succession and the villagers do not really know him yet.

'Papa?' Stella calls up. He starts over his coffee and then draws a hand over his long beard before wiping the same hand down his cassock.

'Papa, can we talk?' Stella takes a step closer.

'Of course,' he says amiably, but he does not offer to come down, nor does he invite them up.

'The last priest might have been a bit vacant but he was not rude,' Frona says quietly. Then, loud enough for him to hear, she adds, 'You have double-booked a wedding and a baptism the day after tomorrow.'

A noise behind them makes them all turn. The old widow who lives opposite the church has come out of her house with a broom, and she begins to sweep her spotless porch.

'No, no, no, no, no.' The priest chuckles to himself. 'I have booked the wedding for eleven, but the baptism is at ten.' He stands with his coffee and comes to the edge of the balcony.

'Exactly!' Stella says. 'And I am supposed to do the catering for both, and both celebrations are meant to be held in the village square.'

'Oh.' The priest pales.

'Yes – oh.' Stella folds her arms and looks up at him.

'Well, I'm afraid after today I have a lot of diocese business to take care of this week and I will not be here except that morning. Maybe the wedding or the baptism can be moved to next week?'

'People are coming from long distances. I think there are cousins from Crete and Corfu, maybe even from abroad. We cannot reschedule.' Stella is firm.

'Is it not possible to use the hotel for one of the celebrations?' the priest asks lightly. He doesn't seem concerned.

'For our own reasons we want both to be in the square,' Marina says.

'Well, ladies …' The priest takes a sip of his coffee, and appears almost to enjoy looking down on them and receiving all this attention. 'I am not sure what you are asking of me now?' He smiles, his face muscles growing soft, the skin around his jowls sagging.

Stella opens her mouth and then closes it again.

'What are we asking him?' Marina hisses quietly through her teeth, keeping her face still.

No one says anything. The priest shifts his weight, the corners of his mouth drop and he scratches at his belly under his cup and saucer as he waits.

Stella suddenly shrugs and walks away, leaving Marina and Frona hurrying after her. They all come to a halt outside the shop.

'So, it is as it is,' Stella states. 'Someone will have to give way. Marina?'

'It makes more sense that Loukas and Ellie have their reception at the hotel,' says Marina. 'After all, all of Ellie's family will be staying there.'

'Yes, that's true.' Frona nods.

'But they work at the hotel. Don't you think they need a break from the place?' Stella says.

They are now back at the shop, where Juliet is standing in the doorway, ankles crossed, arms folded.

'That's true too.' Frona nods.

'We need to tell Ellie and Irini and see what they have to say. Let them decide,' Stella suggests.

'Ah, but we were trying not to stress them,' Marina says.

'Can't be helped,' says Frona, then adds, 'He's still there.'

'Who is?' Stella turns to see where she is looking.

'That man with Petta,' Juliet says, not averting her gaze.

'You know, Marina, if I was your age I would speak to him.' Frona giggles.

'What do you mean, "my age"? You make me sound like a spring chicken. I am fifty-three and have been a widow for twenty-five years.'

'Exactly! Twenty-five years alone.' Frona's eyes shine and she is looking from Marina to the man on the bench next to Petta.

Vasso, across the road, is looking back at them, watching them from within her kiosk. Finally she releases herself from her confines and hurries over.

'What's going on?' she asks, arms folded, ready to gossip.

'Frona is matchmaking Marina with Mr Shoulders over there,' Juliet says.

'What are they talking about, do we know? I could hear them, from inside my kiosk, but not the words, just the tone. He has this lovely slow way of speaking,' Vasso says.

'Then you have him, Vasso. You are more of a spring chicken than I am,' Marina says, but she is still looking at the stranger.

'We are the same age,' Vasso replies, but now she is staring at the man too.

'Perhaps he is married,' Juliet adds.

'No ring,' Frona responds without hesitation, as if this is the most natural observation in the world to have made. 'But actually, Juliet, perhaps he is the man for you?'

'Me?' Juliet exclaims, as if the thought is unthinkable, but then she looks more carefully at the stranger.

Chapter 14

The air-conditioning unit sends a blast of cool air into the shop. Mounted over the doorway, it chills the air that enters the shop, and Frona, Marina, Vasso and Juliet continue to stand in the entrance where the air is coolest, watching the stranger talk to Petta. Petta stands and begins a slow walk towards them, stopping halfway to pat a stray dog.

The stranger now stands and with long, easy strides walks around the kiosk and up the lane that leads to the pine forest on the hill. As he turns a corner and is lost from view, the women shuffle a little. Marina folds her arms, Vasso pats at her hair.

'Right, well, I'm going too,' Frona says. 'I have my bees to tend to.'

Marina follows her out into the heat, and looks up and down the lane for potential customers. On her way back into the shop she takes three bottles of water from the drinks fridge by the door, hands one to Juliet and one to Vasso, and opens the third herself.

'He would be that age,' Vasso says.

'Who would be what age?' Marina asks.

'The lad I cuddled with before I married – he would be about the age of that man.' She points in the direction of the hill.

'Ah, yes, and so would Meli,' Marina says.

'Meli – that's an unusual name,' says Juliet. 'Do you mean *meli*, as in the sweet stuff the bees produce?'

Marina blushes, but her eyes twinkle.

'He was sweet, you see, and to him I was his Melissa.'

'His little bee,' Juliet says, looking up at the sun, which is at its hottest, just past the zenith. The occasional bang of a shutter can be heard around the village, signalling that people are preparing for their *mesimeriano*. Even the dogs are quiet in the heat and there are few people on the streets.

'What was your boy's name?' Juliet turns to Vasso, who is drinking deeply.

There is a moment's of silence as she wipes her lips on the back of her hand. 'You know, when we met it was instant! He was standing in the post office and my knees went weak. I saw from the look in his eyes he felt the same. Mama was with me so I could not do or say anything, but later that day, when she stopped to sit in the square for a coffee, I said I would take a walk along the seafront. I didn't have a plan or know where he was or anything. I just wanted to be alone to think about him.'

She pauses, her face taking on the glow of youth, the years dropping away.

'Well, I went to the harbour end and when I turned to go back, who was there, straddling his moped, staring? I stopped walking and we just looked at each other. Then, ever so slowly, he let his bike creep towards me. My cheeks began to heat up and I was struggling to think what I would say when he got near enough to speak.'

Juliet rolls the cold water bottle across her neck, her eyes on Vasso.

'He spoke first. Oh my goodness, he sent chills down my spine. This low, husky voice. "I have three days," he said. "Then I go to do my national service." Well, I was about to be sent off to Orino Island to work in the taverna, and so I told him that. It seemed like fate, and we just stared at each other, not speaking, until finally he said something like, "Realistically this is not going to work, my love." Can you believe it? He called me his love the first time we spoke. So I said that two days were better than none, my love, or something like that. I can still remember the thrill of saying those words to him, and how I blushed afterwards!'

Vasso hugs herself, her water bottle spilling a little as she does so, making a dark patch on the floor that is quickly sucked into the hot concrete.

'So did you get two days with him?' Marina asks.

'Not full days. We arranged to meet later that day on the beach. I told Mama I was meeting school friends. The next day I said I was going to a friend's house. He picked me up just outside the village and

91

we went to Saros and spent the whole day doing nothing really – holding hands, learning to kiss in quiet corners. But you know what? I still did not know his name. I called him "my love" and he called me "my love" and I sort of didn't want to know his name or tell him mine in case he stopped calling me his love.'

Vasso's chest lifts with a deep breath, her ample breasts rising and then, as she releases the air again, falling just as dramatically.

'I never found out my Meli's name either. How extraordinary is that?' Marina says.

'Maybe, or maybe we just don't put as much importance on real names at that age,' Juliet suggests. 'I know I had a boyfriend whom everyone called Click, of all things, but I thought it was a cool name so I never did find out what his real name was. Not until I returned home to visit years later, after my boys were born. Anyway, I bumped into him and it turned out his real name was Walter.'

Juliet looks at Marina and Vasso, anticipating their laughter, but the name makes no impression on them. 'Walter is a very old-fashioned name in England,' she explains. 'Conservative, even, and rather a soft name for someone who was pretending to be streetwise.'

It's clear the other two do not really understand.

'Ahh' Marina says non-committally.

'Mmm.' Vasso agrees.

'So, how long were you with Meli?' Juliet changes the conversation, putting the focus onto Marina.

'One night,' she replies.

'One night!' Vasso breaks into a whoop of laughter and nudges Marina with her elbow. 'I guess that's all it takes.' She nods her head in the direction of Petta, who is now talking to Theo, who stands with his arms across his chest on the *kafenio* steps.

'It was beautiful, gentle, warm,' Marina says in her defence. 'You know, I don't think I even knew what was happening exactly, it just felt right and close and loving.' Her voice becomes quieter as she remembers. 'And let's face it, with that Manolis as a husband, Meli is the only warm loving memory I have.' There is a hard edge to her voice at the mention of her dead husband.

'I was lucky,' Vasso says. 'My Spiros was a good man from the beginning to the end and I did love him, I really did.'

'Being with someone again, sharing the same rooms with them, being accountable – for ages I could not bear the thought,' Juliet joins in. 'But it's amazing how we forget how painful relationships can be, just like we forget the trauma of childbirth.' She gives a short dry laugh and finishes her water. 'Right, I'd better go and do some work.'

'Are you teaching at the hotel?' Vasso asks, taking a step out of the cool of the shop, towards her kiosk.

'No, I have some translation to do, a short story for a novelist.' Juliet follows Vasso out into the sun, her hand automatically rising to shield her eyes.

'Right, I might get around to pricing up all that stuff you found with the sink plug this morning,' Marina says.

'Oh no, don't – it's nice to find things still in drachmas,' Juliet says, and she gives a little wave.

Chapter 15

The walls either side of the lane are built of stone but the layers of whitewash have smoothed over the edges and corners, as though a white blanket has been draped over them. How many hands have whitewashed these walls, how many children have watched? How many Easter celebrations have been anticipated, as this ritual of whitening the walls has been repeated? Miltos reaches out and lets his fingers skim along the undulating surface as he makes his way up the hill. The route is steep and demands a measured pace, but it does not steal the air from his lungs. Tractor tyres have carved deep ruts up the track; a line of grass grows in the centre, but already it has browned and withered in the early summer heat. He passes the last of the houses, listening to the muffled voices in their courtyards. A woman, hanging out her washing, is talking to a dog, or maybe a cat. She is hidden behind a high wall, chastising the animal, but without malice. Soon the woman's voice fades and the sounds of birds dominate. Here the walls lower and he can see into the orange orchards either side. The first of the summer cicadas have begun their harsh mating call. Up ahead, the oranges give way to olive trees and the wall is reduced to a jumbled pile of stones, mostly hidden by long dry grasses, as though whoever built it was distracted long ago and abandoned the task. He will walk up past the olives, cut across to the right just where the wall ends and make his way up to the pines.

A bird swoops across the lane and, further up, what looked like a twig on the rough tarmac zigzags away: a small snake – an adder, perhaps, that was basking in the sun.

On the right a little further up is a gate, with a strange home-made letter box wired to it. The top of the box has a brass handle attached to it as if it was once the front of a drawer, and on the handle a lizard basks in the sunshine, its tongue darting out and back, tasting the air.

The noise of a motorbike coming up the lane startles the lizard, and it lifts its head and slides out of sight behind the wooden box.

Miltos watches as the bike approaches and then splutters to a stop by the gate. It is the postman, who calls out a cheery *kalimera* over the nose of his moped.

'*Kalimera,*' Miltos responds. 'And a beautiful one it is too.'

'Yes, I suppose it is.' The postman is chubby and slightly balding, and he looks about him as if he has only just noticed where he is.

'Many letters to deliver?' Miltos tilts his head in the direction of the village, which is laid out before them.

'Always.' The postman twists on his seat to look in his sack. 'When I first took the job, nearly thirty years ago now, I was given to believe it would be easy. Even my mama joined in. "Cosmo," she said, "take the job, it has a good pension. And how many letters can a village have?" Well, no one made allowances for things changing.'

'I would have thought there weren't so many letters now, as everyone has a computer and sends emails.' Miltos puts his hands in his front pockets, his fingers fiddling with the broken edge of the shell. He relaxes his spine so he is sitting back on his hips, his stomach sinking in.

'Yes, exactly – that's what everyone thinks. But do you know how much stuff people order from the Internet? No. Exactly. I can tell by your expression it has never crossed your mind. Well, up to a certain weight and size I will deliver. Like these seeds for Mitsos, for example. I have no problem delivering them.' Still straddling his bike, he pops the packet in the home-made box. 'If they are too big I cannot, but I still have to deliver a card to tell people to collect the thing. No one thinks of that, do they? No! The number of cards I deliver seems to grow every month! And then they lose them and come to pick up their packages without a reference and who do they blame for that?'

97

'Ah, but in the late spring days, what a job, wandering about the lanes, nothing but blue skies and birds above you. The satisfaction of a good day's work done, and home to the wife for a well-earned meal.' Miltos tries to sound positive.

'I wish.' The postman – Cosmo, as he called himself – swings his bag behind him and looks at the cuff of his shirt. Miltos can see big clumsy stitches holding frayed edges together. 'Look at that.' He holds his arm out so Miltos can inspect it. 'You think a wife would do that?'

Miltos shrugs.

'She means well. My mama has always meant well, but – well, her sight is going, and, the simple fact is that one day she will be gone and I will be alone. But I am not sure she thought about that when she was vetting my girlfriends.'

'You have had many, then?' Miltos asks.

'Well, no, not really. One or two when I was younger, but after my first girlfriend – more of a friend, really – I knew Mama would find fault every time, so after a while I just stopped looking. But now, of course, now I am past my prime, I am thinking what a fool I was – how I should have ignored her harsh judgements and found myself a girl.' Cosmo turns his hand over to inspect his cuff again.

'Life is tricky, but there are women around,' Miltos says non-committally. Cosmo is not the only one to suffer; he himself has found a hole in his front pocket. He knows it would be best if he were to leave it alone, catch it with a stitch at the first opportunity, but he cannot resist fiddling, and, unseen by the world, he pokes his finger through, traces little circles in the hairs on his thigh.

'You make it sound so easy,' Cosmo responds. 'At one point in my life maybe it would have been a bit easier, but now, at this age? … Are you married?' Cosmo stops looking at his cuff to stare Miltos in the face.

'No. But I was.' He can see he has Cosmo's attention. He takes a breath and looks at the horizon.

'I was married for three years. It's amazing how three years can pass so quickly. And also so slowly.'

'Sorry?' Cuff forgotten, Cosmo rubs his forehead with his fingers, the beads of sweat soaking back into his skin.

'Oh, don't get me wrong,' Miltos adds quickly, 'I am not complaining, I have been lucky. I've had a rather adventurous life, been here and there, done this and that. I've also had the pleasure of a number of girlfriends. But' – he sighs, a wisp of a breath that is only just noticeable – 'you are right. Until a certain point in your life it feels like you have a duty to the world. My baba died when I was a young man, and my mama when I was only a child. But my uncle, whenever I saw him – would he acknowledge any of the things I had achieved? No! Instead he would pressure me to join him in his business, as if I owed this to him and my baba!'

'Oh? What business was that then?' Cosmo takes the heavy bag off over his head and puts it on the floor, settling more comfortably on the seat of his moped.

'Ball bearings. Oh, the joys of ball bearings. Do you know how ball bearings are made?' Miltos asks, a half-smile teasing his lips.

'No.'

'It is so exciting.' His voice is flat and one of his eyebrows is raised. 'You take a piece of wire which you cut into tiny pieces and then you cold-head the pieces and heat them up and cool them down and temper them ... I could bore you for hours with the intricacies of ball bearings. But let me just tell you, the process of making ball bearings is one of the dullest things in the world.

'Ball bearings are so dull that I thought nothing in the world would tempt me to work with my uncle manufacturing them. But you know what, there came a time when, although my life was exciting, I thought that there was something missing. You know that feeling, when you don't feel complete?' he does not wait for a response. 'Well, I had that feeling and my uncle, with his arm around my aunt, suggested that it was because I was living my life too freely. He suggested that if I committed to one woman and settled down to have a productive life I would find the satisfaction I was seeking.'

'Please tell me you did not acquiesce just to please him?' Cosmo sounds genuinely concerned.

'I'm afraid I did. I took his job offer and a year and a half later I married the woman he suggested and that began three of the most uneventful, unsatisfying years of my life.'

'Did you have children?'

Chapter 16

'No, she claimed she couldn't have children.' Miltos can hear the cold calm in his voice.

'Was she?' Cosmo's eyebrows are raised.

'In year three she left me for the accounts manager because she was pregnant by him.'

'Ouch.' Cosmo squirms.

'Actually, not so much ouch, more sort of phew! You see, although our courtship was much like any other and the wedding was every woman's dream – you know, the fancy dress, flowers everywhere, big celebrations – she came with a heavy burden – her mama – and her mama came to live with us! In fact, when we returned from our honeymoon she had dinner on the table and was already running the house. Within a month I could not tell the difference between them when they spoke to me. It was as if Aphrodite had turned into her own mother overnight. I had married one woman, and got another into the bargain, and one was a good thirty years my senior and didn't seem to like me very much. Also, she wanted everything to be a routine because that was the way her mama before her had always done it. Breakfast at eight, lunch at three, dinner at nine, that sort of thing. We went out for coffee on Saturdays and to church on Sundays. There was no spontaneity.'

He pauses and turns to his companion, who seems quite happy sitting in the sun, halfway up a hill, listening to a stranger's tale.

'But do you know what the scariest thing is?'

'Tell me.' Cosmo smiles encouragingly.

'You try to fit your round self into this square hole, and at the beginning it hurts, so do you know what you do? You try even harder, thinking that if you succeed the struggle will be over. But you never fit, and then the scariest thing is that one day you stop trying. You are neither out nor in, but you stop hurting and you're just stuck there in this numb impasse and you no longer have the energy either to get through to the other side or to wriggle back to where you came from, and you don't even complain. You just watch as the minutes, the days and the years of your life tick past.'

His mouth has gone dry at the memory so he licks his lips and turns so the sun is on the back of his head, putting his face in the shade. Cosmo stares at him, waiting for more, so Miltos tries to round his story off. A dragonfly hovers between them and then darts away.

'Whilst I was in this position the cuffs of my shirts were always darned very neatly, my friend, but take some advice – be careful what you wish for.'

Cosmo heaves the bag of mail back over his head. He has not spoken but he is nodding, his eyes on the ground as if he is deep in thought. He revs the engine of his little bike and with a deeply worried look wishes Miltos a good day; he turns to freewheel back down the track, kicking up stones, his bag of mail hanging heavily off his shoulder.

Miltos remains standing, watching him go. Telling Cosmo the story of his marriage was like listening to someone else, as though it was another man's tale and nothing to do with him; this is a familiar feeling, one that was present during the years of his marriage. It is remarkable that the feeling is so fresh after all this time.

Aphrodite often said that he was not a team player. She complained that he was detached from the world and the events in it. In the beginning, he just dismissed what she said. But then her mama began to say it too, and over time the two of them wore him away. He began to wonder if there was any truth in what they said. He certainly didn't feel as content as the other people he worked with appeared to be, and so he began to seek out books and journals on psychology, psychiatry and anything else that might give him some insight into how the mind, his mind, worked.

One article he read described behaviour that sounded very similar to his own. It presented the concept of 'detachment', a condition that might manifest itself, apparently, in daydreaming and could extend to the extreme of dissociative identity disorder. He felt fairly certain that he had not reached that extreme, but as he read the list of symptoms, which included memory loss, he began to worry. Aphrodite often accused him of forgetting things – not just little things, but whole events. Like the time they had taken her mama out for her name day – he couldn't even remember the cafe they had gone to or the people they had met. Aphrodite said it was not normal and he had begun to worry about himself. Was his state of discontent a sign of something more sinister, he had wondered at the time. Were the things his wife (and mother-in-law) accused him of just the tip of the iceberg? Did he need help?

The more he worried, the more lonely and isolated he became, and the more isolated he became the more he worried. Then he too began to notice that he was beginning to forget things, simple things, like orders he was supposed to process at work on one occasion, and forgetting to lock the door when leaving home. He could never remember the names of Aphrodite's cousins, which both she and her mama used as proof that he was not interested in her life. For a while he thought he had fundamentally changed since he was married, that something inside his head had come loose, maybe. The world had become a vague, dreamlike place that lacked any real significance for him. He never felt alive as he had done when he was climbing, or as content as when he was picking mangoes in Israel.

He reached the lowest point in his marriage and began to feel completely separate, not only from his wife but also from his own physicality, his emotions and even his behaviours. The more Aphrodite nagged and complained, the more detached he became from his feelings. With some effort he managed to modify his behaviour to satisfy his wife and mother-in-law, but it felt like an act and he felt himself changing, disappearing, being replaced by a sort of hazy non-person who looked and felt like the old Miltos but who had no real substance and might disappear at any time … It was slightly better at work but he no longer identified with anyone there and he began to lump the rest of the employees into categories. There was his baba's gang of decisions-makers, the coffee drinkers, the workaholics, the proactives, the idlers, the geeks. But none of those groups had anything to do with him. He was alone, and unreal.

So when he found his wife in Augustinos's – the account manager's – office one day, drinking coffee, and his intuition told him that all was not as it seemed, he didn't know how to react; he was no longer able to trust his own judgement. His conscious brain argued that he was in no position to judge anyone. Who was he, anyway, to pass judgement on other people's actions? Hadn't it been pointed out time and time again by Aphrodite, or by her mama, that he didn't think straight? So he simply placed the memo he was delivering on the table between them and said nothing. As he backed out of the office, though, he felt himself sink further into himself and he retreated just a little more from reality.

The following Monday, six days later, at eight fifteen in the morning, Miltos was shaving, getting ready for work, when Aphrodite announced that she was indeed having an affair with Augustinos, and had been for the last two years, and that she was pregnant with his child. She stood in the doorway, making eye contact with him in the mirror as he froze at this news, his face half lathered, and then she calmly stated that she had never wanted a child with him and had taken precautions to ensure she did not. He put down the razor and stared back at her, not knowing what to do or say.

'I am leaving you,' she said, and at this he dropped the razor, turned and staggered towards her. She reacted as if she expected him to hit her but that was not his intention. He pushed past her into the bedroom, to sit slumped on the edge of the bed with his head in his hands as he felt his energy drain.

'Are you all right?' she asked, but there was no feeling in the question. 'Mama has already packed and gone,' she continued. 'She left when we saw the results of the pregnancy test.'

Through the fog that threatened to engulf him, this information, that her mama had already gone, gave him the slightest relief. At least it meant he would never have to see that old witch again, and he clung to this thought as he would have a buoy in a storm at sea. Aphrodite continued her narrative.

'Do you need me to get anyone?' But she was zipping up her suitcase as she said this and he did not bother to answer. 'You can find us at Augustinos's house, but there is no use coming over and thinking that we can talk about things or go backwards. It was over long ago, we just never admitted it.'

She paused and he could feel her staring at him. 'Are you sure you're all right?' This last question harboured a hint of concern but she quickly continued, 'You see, this is the problem, always has been. You don't open up to me. Everything goes on on the inside and you have never let me in, and nor have you ever come out. Goodbye, Milto.'

With this, she turned, grasping the handle of the suitcase, no doubt aiming for a dramatic exit, but the case was too heavy and she had to drag it along the deep pile of the rug. Then bump, bump, bump, she was down the stairs and scraping it across the hall floor to the front door. There was a man's voice; it could have been Augustinos's, or it could have been a taxi driver. Then the door shut and the car drove off.

Miltos sat for a while on the bed, not moving, absorbing the new silence in the house; then, slowly, he straightened, dropped his hands in his lap and looked up without seeing. In a flash he could feel! How he could feel! The world was real again, he was real again, and it was as though steel belts had been removed from around his chest and he could breathe again. He meant to just stand up but once his legs got moving he jumped on the spot until he found himself leaping on the bed and bouncing on it, knees to chest like a small boy. He only stopped when the phone by the bed rang, and he climbed down from the bed, smoothed his hair and answered the call.

'Milto, everything all right? Just that you are an hour late.' His uncle's voice was smooth, authoritative.

'Yes, fine.' Miltos's voice gave nothing away.

'So, you are coming in now?' His uncle's tone rose at the end, but it was not really a question.

'No,' he replied, and before his uncle could make any response he replaced the receiver, took his passport from the bedside drawer, grabbed his car keys and drove to the airport.

That was the beginning of his two-year walk-about in Thailand and Indonesia. He stayed in touch with his aunt and it was she who sold the apartment and put the money in his Thai bank account.

'I will make sure she does not get a penny, and I have told your uncle to sack Augustinos,' she spat down the phone when he called her from the airport in Bangkok.

'No, *Thia*, he is a good account manager. Let him stay. He will do his penance having to live with her and her mama.'

'You should never have married her,' his aunt began, but he cut her short. She had been just as keen as his uncle that he settle down, join the firm and have children. Well, his duty was done, and during

109

the time he was in Asia he phoned his aunt less and less until, finally, he stopped altogether.

On his return to Greece he found that they had moved and the factory had closed because of the downturn in the economy. He did not make any effort to get back in touch.

But all this was years ago and the only part of it that makes him sad now is that he has never had children.

He looks at the packet poking out of the home-made letter box. The lizard is back.

'What must it be like, eh, lizard?' He addresses the miniature green dinosaur. 'To have a home rather than a house, somewhere that you receive letters and not just bills? And, most importantly of all, where they don't make you feel crazy!'

But the lizard doesn't answer. It just sticks out its tongue.

Chapter 17

Miltos leaves the lizard and continues up the hill. The track is steeper further up and before he reaches the top he stops again to catch his breath. From this vantage point, the village looks as if it has been designed by a very young child who has just discovered the joy of drawing and colouring. Some of the houses are set along the curve of the roads, but others are at awkward angles and the road has been forced to meander around them. The church appears comically large compared to these orange-roofed dwellings, and the boys playing football in the open area in front of it are mere ants.

The fountain in the centre of the square has been painted bright blue inside and seems at odds with the sepia tones of its surroundings. From up here it looks as though it is full of water, but Miltos noticed earlier that it is dry and dusty. The outskirts of the village give way to orange trees that march in line, and curled and twisted olive trees that make use of any place where the ground is uneven. Here and there, low, barren hills push their way up out of this carpet of green and these are crowned with tiny whitewashed churches, some sporting garish neon-blue crosses. Overall, however, the plane is flat and the citrus trees dominate. Periodically, this emerald coverage is broken by clusters of orange roof tiles where the villages have sprung up. Saros town, away in the distance to the left, is mostly hidden by the hill Miltos is on, and just the very edge can be seen, where it dips into the sea, along with one or two white specks – boats that are anchored in the harbour. The bay is a wide, sweeping curve that extends a finger of blue all the way up to the edge of the village at his feet. High hills flank the far edges of the plain, a haze of purple, standing majestic.

'Beautiful, just beautiful,' he whispers to himself, and he turns his back on the sight to push himself on to the final summit beneath the pine trees. The sun is very hot and he is beginning to feel the need of some shade.

As he nears the trees the ground becomes springy with pine needles and the air takes on the scent of resin. He expects to hear only cicadas singing but there is another sound too. He could swear that in amongst the bugs' rasping calls he can hear a melody being quietly picked out on an acoustic guitar. He steps more lightly, reluctant to disturb whomever is practising under the trees, and as he rounds a fallen tree he is surprised to find the player so close.

'Ah, you are playing well,' he says by way of introduction, and then he takes a sharp breath at the sight of the familiar face.

'Yeia,' the young man with the guitar says, briefly glancing up. 'I am just picking out a few chords but nothing is coming.' He is sitting cross-legged in amongst the pine needles, with his guitar over one knee. There is an assured air about him.

'It is a good spot to spend some time in,' Miltos says.

'And you have come at the right time. I need to clear my mind, take a little break.' His smile is all teeth, even and white, emphasised by his deep tan.

Miltos steps forward again and sits down in the space the man indicates for him.

'I'm not mistaken, am I?' Miltos asks. 'You are Sakis, are you not?' There is just the lightest quiver to his voice. It has been a long while since he met someone whom he holds in such awe.

'Yes, I am Sakis.' As well as the assurance there is also, and unexpectedly, humility in the way he speaks.

'I saw you just last week at Lycabettus in Athens, and before that six months ago, in Thessaloniki.' Miltos makes a point of trying not to stare, but it is a shock to see one of his musical heroes so close and in the flesh. Sakis seems different here under the trees; his chin is lightly stubbled and he looks more youthful than he does on stage.

'I hope I entertained you.' Sakis flashes the smile that has graced his album covers.

'Yes, you did, thank you.' It is strange to feel himself struggling to know what to say. After all, Sakis is a man like any other man. Then a host of

113

memories of things he has read and heard about come flooding back to him. 'So this is the village that you disappeared to after winning in the Ukraine!' he blurts out, remembering the headlines around that time, when the papers tried to guess where it was that Sakis had run off to.

'Yes, this is it, but I would be much obliged if you would keep that to yourself.'

'Does the press really not know where you are?' Miltos asks, but Sakis does not answer. 'Or do they?' he adds lightly. 'Was it all just a way to get more publicity?'

Sakis continues to play as they talk, his fingers running swiftly up and down the frets: a gentle plucking just loud enough to hear. Miltos presses him. 'Did you really need more publicity after winning for Greece? I mean, the whole of Europe was singing your song.'

Sakis strokes the neck of his guitar now and chuckles to himself, but it is not a happy sound, more a reflective noise. 'No, I did not need more publicity. Let's just say it was a bad piece of management. I lost my voice, came to stay in the hotel by the beach – you know the one?'

'Stella's? I'm staying there.' Miltos's eyebrows lift.

'Yes, well, I was meant to stay there for a week, out of the limelight, to speed my recovery. During this time my manager was meant to sign me up to go to America but it all went horribly wrong, But as it turned out, it was all right in the end!'

'America! But all your stuff is so steeped in *rebetika*, traditional Greek music!'

'As I said, it turned out right.' Sakis plays a harmonious chord as if in triumph.

'Well, if you don't mind me saying, the music you've been releasing since you won has been on a whole new level. Really, it's amazing. Recently I have been driving a lot – that's my job at the moment, to drive – and I listen to all sorts of music, you know, to pass the time, but I keep coming back to your stuff again and again.'

'I am flattered.'

'But to change your style of music after your win, that was brave?' Miltos studies Sakis's eyes. Perhaps that is what he himself needs, a little more courage, to change direction and find himself?

Sakis takes his time, looking out over the village and then further, across the panorama. He seems very comfortable with silence and Miltos listens to the cicadas. Their volume has not yet reached its summer peak, and their rhythmic call is intermingled with birdsong from high up in the trees. Somewhere in the village, towards Saros town, a donkey brays, the end of its call wobbling and diminishing to a rasping wheeze. So lost does he become in the sounds around him that when Sakis finally speaks it makes Miltos start.

'Winning such a prestigious song contest was very flattering and I could easily have lost myself to the attention and the fame, the money, the prestige, all of that. Who wouldn't?' He breathes out noisily

115

through his nose before continuing. 'I am not sure I would ever have dared to change my musical direction at that time, had I not become ill. But it was not the illness that changed me. It was the influence of this village.'

He breathes deeply again, but this time it is a contented sound. 'Being here provoked a change in me and in my music. But you must know the effect of the village? You don't live here or I would have seen you around, but I take it you have family here?'

'Oh no – no one. Like I said, I deliver and collect rental cars. I just came to exchange one that was faulty. It is all just by chance that I am here, really.'

'Really.' The way Sakis speaks makes Miltos look at him to see if it is a question or a statement.

'Yes, really,' he says, but he is not sure if it was necessary. Then, feeling slightly uncomfortable, he tries to put the focus back on Sakis. 'So you blame the village, eh?'

'It had a strange effect on me.' He strums a couple of chords.

'I know what you mean.' After he has said this, Miltos wonders if he really means it or if he is just agreeing to smooth over a feeling of awkwardness that he alone seems to be feeling.

'Do you?' Sakis strums another chord and hums to it, which excites Miltos. It feels like a personal one-note concert from a man whom people normally only see from afar. 'In what way has it

116

affected you?' The musician speaks almost idly, but it makes Miltos think.

'Well, I have only been here for a day. I arrived last night, you see, but you are right.' He reflects, 'I have had so many conversations with so many people and the interesting thing about each of them is that they have left me thinking – you know, turning things over in my mind that I have not thought about for years.'

'Such as?' Sakis looks down at his fingers and plays a chord that makes a muscle under one of his eyes twitch as if it gives him physical pain.

Miltos looks up and out across the plain.

'Oh, you know – old loves, the ones that made me want to be a better person ... How all the girls I have known since then have not matched up to that first love. The ones that were fickle – or maybe that was me?' He lets out a short sharp laugh and then looks down at the ground. As he picks at the layers of the pine needle carpet, it changes from grey, where the sun has soaked out the colour, to sienna brown, and deeper still it is a burnt umber. Half a dozen tiny insects scurry away from the light as he lets the needles fall back into place.

'I had a conversation about controlling women,' he continues, 'and that made me realise that most of my life I have sought to be the dominant one, and I wonder now if this has been why none of my relationships have worked.' He pauses, and Sakis plays three notes very softly. 'I have talked about, or at least thought about, the fact that I have not had children, and I had not realised before how much this really bothers me.'

Sakis plays the three notes again and then rests his fingering hand on his knee. 'It did the same to me, this place. Made me ask what was important. That was why my music changed. It was not a brave move. My integrity was challenged, and it made me feel like I was dying. I had to find out who I really was.'

He plays the three notes again, and adds on a chord, then another. 'What do you think? I think I may have the beginning of something.'

The change in subject momentarily confuses Miltos until he realises Sakis is talking about his notes and chords. He is about to answer when Sakis changes tack again. 'It sounds to me like you are thinking about settling down, maybe?'

Miltos's mouth opens and hangs there until Sakis looks at him, and he quickly shuts it.

'I have met someone,' Sakis says bluntly. 'English, but she has a business here with Stella – not the hotel, or the eatery.' Sakis smiles as if he is about to reveal a secret, and Miltos wonders if he will get to meet this Stella before he leaves. She seems to be the centre of everything.

'Don't be fooled by Stella, she is dynamite! She has another business with this girl I have met. Abbie is her name. They have a candle-making factory over towards Saros. You know, traditional Greek candles, the type they use in the churches. They export them around the world.'

118

He strums his three notes again and, concentrating on the fretboard, he adds, as if it is a casual afterthought, 'They also make scented candles for homes and people who have beauty salons, that sort of thing.' He plays the three notes louder and adds the chords with confidence. 'I am even toying with the idea of asking her to marry me.'

'Congratulations!' Miltos's excitement comes through in his voice.

'No spilling that to the press, now.' Sakis says this with a quick glance at Miltos, and a quick grin. 'This is confidential stuff. I haven't even asked her yet. Just toying with the idea.' Playing a couple of chords, he sings the words 'Join with me', and then adds the three notes and lightly strums a harmony.

'What's stopping you?' Miltos asks.

'There is always that thought, isn't there, that she might say no? That terrifies me. That thought always leads on to thinking of all the girls in the world I have yet to meet, and then this holds me back from asking her.'

'Yes, there are always all the girls you have yet to meet!' Miltos laughs and leans back to rest on his elbows, stretching his feet out in front of him.

'Well, you have a few years on me, old man. You must have met an awful lot more than me.' Sakis laughs too. But Miltos stops laughing. Old man! Who is he calling an old man? He sits up so his chin is no longer on his chest, a position in which he could feel the loose skin from his neck gather. He lifts his head tall and pulls back his shoulders. Old man, indeed.

'Right.' Sakis gathers all his sheet music and folds it carefully into a small satchel that he slings over his neck, then stands and swings his guitar round behind his back. He opens the satchel again and appears to be looking for something. 'Ah, here you go,' He closes the bag and holds something out towards Miltos. 'That will get you into any of my concerts and allows you to come backstage to see me. But, you know what, I suspect I will see you again in the village before long.'

He chuckles and with a wave walks off down the hill, his hips rolling with each step, his knees turned out slightly as if he is a cowboy. There is no hurry in his movements.

'Old man, indeed.' Miltos looks at the card Sakis gave him. 'Guest pass, all venues, backstage,' he reads. The pass is valid for the remainder of the year. 'Generous,' he mutters, and then he stands and looks after Sakis. 'Old man,' he repeats. He waits a moment so he won't catch Sakis up and then he too starts off down the hill.

Chapter 18

Back down in the village square a reflex tells him to buy some gum from the kiosk. Not that he wants gum. What he wants is another glimpse of, and maybe even a conversation with, the coiffured woman who works there, to smooth his ruffled feathers.

Up under the pines, Sakis, intentionally or not, pulled a switch on him. One minute, he seemed like a mirror to Miltos – inside, Miltos felt exactly as the young musician looked: energetic, alive and full of vitality – and it was a real shock when Sakis suddenly and swiftly pulled that mirror aside and called him an old man. Even if it was said light-heartedly, that must be how he appears to the young musician. It jarred him, displaced his internal sense of self, and now he feels a need to re-establish how he believes others see him. After all, his muscles are still strong, his legs are still powerful. Who could not believe him to be young, or at worst middle-aged, when he still thinks nothing of walking for four or five hours for pleasure? Does he not spend long hours waiting for his next delivery helping the mechanics by lifting car tyres and lugging them around at the depot? It is just a game to pass the time for him.

'Hello,' he says to Vasso in the kiosk. He is aware he is flouting his own self-imposed rule of no more flirting, but to hell with it – he will flirt as much as he likes. He is not ready to be passed over.

'Hello.' She leans on the counter inside her wooden kiosk as if she has all the time in the world.

'Like a bird in a cage,' he says, and he watches her flutter her eyelashes. The reaction is flattering, but she is not a young women. Handsome, and giggly, but not young. 'I'll just take this gum,' he says, forcing himself to look away from her deep brown eyes. He needs to flirt with someone younger to feel himself again.

'Excuse me, papou.' A boy of about eight or nine pushes by his knees and takes something from a lower shelf. He holds it up to show Vasso, tosses a coin on the counter and runs off.

'Papou!' Miltos exclaims. First old man and now granddad.

'Ah, we all look old to the young, and the young all look like children to us. It is the way of the world.' Vasso giggles again. She doesn't seem to mind this fact in the least. But then, he reflects, how could she avoid the truth, sitting in the same spot day after day, year after year, watching the faces of the children as they grow up, marry, even have children of their own? Is this why he never settles anywhere – to avoid his own reflection? Maybe this is what is different about this village: the people somehow don't give you a choice but to see yourself, but at the same time they seem to completely accept you, just as you are. But who is to say they are giving him a true reflection? Well, he will not have a likeness imposed on him that he is not satisfied with, not by this village, not by young children or musicians, nor even by a comely kiosk owner. He looks over his shoulder at the corner shop and remembers the woman with mischief in her eyes, the lady in the blue dress. But she was a mature woman too. He pays for the gum and leaves without another word.

If the car was fixed and ready to drive he would be glad to leave right now. He takes the three steps up into the *kafenio* in a single stride, forcing a bounce into his movements. He chooses a table overlooking the village and sits with his back straight and his head up to appear alert, young.

'What can I get you?' Theo asks.

'A cola,' he says and then wonders if they still taste the same. He has not had a cola in years.

The man on the table next to him smells, but it is a comforting, warm smell.

'Goats?' Miltos addresses him. It's good to talk, to keep his mind from turning things over.

'Yup, just been trimming their feet,' his neighbour replies.

Theo returns with Miltos's cola.

'You want a drink, my friend?' Miltos asks his new companion.

'Thank you, I'll have another Greek coffee. *Sketo*, I don't think I could stand the sugar. Nicolaos, by the way,' the man says by way of introduction, and his face contorts in what could be pain. He is a big man, barrel-chested, and his eyes are half screwed-up and his lips tight.

'Miltos,' Miltos replies. 'You all right?'

'Toothache.' Nicolaos grimaces even more.

'Toothache – oh, I have a cure for toothache – shall I tell you it?' Miltos is glad that he has a chance to tell a tale, a chance to cheer someone up. It will stop him thinking about himself and will take him back to his younger days. 'Ah yes, toothache. Like all aches, if you concentrate on them they fill your world and there is nothing else in your mind. That is the worst.'

'But you have a cure?' The shepherd asks.

Theo brings the coffee and gives Nicolaos a commiserating pat on his shoulder before returning behind his counter to make crockery chime as he rinses it under the tap.

'Let me tell you. I was just out of military service.' Miltos looks up at the ceiling and it is as if he can see the exact day in the swirling cigarette smoke that lingers there in a hazy cloud. 'You would think that I would have been aware of the political tension in the Middle East. But I was young and, do you know, it didn't even occur to me to wonder what was happening in the world.'

He lingers on the feeling but considers that perhaps the wisdom of age has some advantages too.

He plays with his cola, turning it around and watching the ice stay still. His mouth twitches in and out of a smile as the sun reflects off the glass, lighting up the cola so it becomes almost red. 'So, anyway, I ended up in Israel, in a kibbutz, in the kitchen of all places. I was slowly pouring fourteen litres of oil into a hundred eggs, or something like that, making a sort of chocolate spread for something they called *matza im shokolad*. Do you know it?'

He pauses for a response but Nicolaos looks blank and a little confused. He is rubbing his cheek against his gums.

Miltos goes on. 'Anyway, I was sweating like a pig and through the open windows I could hear some of the other volunteers twittering and fidgeting and getting into a flap. The day before had been the last day of Jewish Passover, I think it was, and the PLO had infiltrated another kibbutz some distance away. It scared some people and now half of the volunteers wanted to leave.'

Nicolaos looks out across the square and then back to Miltos and settles. A story is being told and everyone likes a good story.

'The other volunteers at the kibbutz were from all over the world. There was a girl with flaming red hair from Scotland, Isla was her name, and I do remember that there were two pretty Australian girls. Oh, and a really beautiful French girl with her weasel of a boyfriend, and several Dutch. The French girl really was beautiful, but aloof, as only beautiful girls can be. This French girl and some of the others had even packed their bags and were ready to leave, but I didn't even think about it.' He pauses and takes a sip of his cola. It is sweet and sickly. He should have asked for a coffee instead.

'I don't know about you, but when I did my military service I think I fired a gun once, on a shooting range. I suppose I was lucky.' He grins widely. 'My first piece of luck was walking as tall as I do, the second was to have such broad shoulders.'

He sits up straight as if to demonstrate, but when he looks at Nicolaos to see if he is impressed he notices that his companion is nearly as tall as him and probably bigger round the chest. But he does not have the same straightness across his shoulders. Miltos pulls his elbows back to accentuate his advantage. 'And I was lucky enough to catch the eye of a visiting officer. Naturally, I didn't care if I was stationed in Kalamata, Thessaloniki or Thebes – it made no difference to me. But no sooner was I in my uniform than this officer shipped me off to Athens. He wanted me to be an *evzone* and guard the houses of parliament, in my *foustanella* and those shoes that turn up at the toes. Me!'

He throws his head back and laughs heartily. Other heads in the *kafenio* turn to see what is so funny, the infectious sound causing them to smile and chuckle. Nicolaos also laughs.

Chapter 19

'But why would you not make a good *evzone*?' Nicolaos asks as the laughter subsides.

'Oh, if only you knew how I cannot sit still. It is the story of my life. I have never stayed anywhere for long, and even when I am in any one place, to remain still there is impossible.' As if to demonstrate the truth of his statement, Miltos's foot starts tapping, and he puts his hand on his knee, forcing the movement to stop. 'And here was this officer selecting me as a presidential guard where I would have to stand motionless for hours at a time on Syntagma Square, for everyone to stop and stare at!'

His words roll into another laugh; all thoughts of age are forgotten and he feels young again. Faces around the *kafenio* look over with amusement.

'Is it true they never blink?' Nicolaos asks. 'They say the training is very hard.'

There is a clack of a wooden piece on a backgammon board and a chair scrapes. A game of tavli has begun at another table.

'I never found out. As I said, I was shipped to Athens, and the night I arrived this officer ordered me to drive him somewhere, to some function where he wanted to be able to drink, and that was that. The rest of my military service was spent playing chauffeur to the big guys. I got to drive limos, jeeps, Jaguars, Daimlers and, once, a really wide American vehicle.'

'But where was I with my story? Oh yes, listening to the volunteers on the kibbutz getting ready to leave because they were scared. The Israelis themselves seemed to take it in their stride. After all, the PLO had been around since the sixties, and they were used to these scares. In any case, where would they go? So there I was, mixing the eggs with the oil, and I could hear the bombs in the distance, and I distracted myself, thinking what if there was one bad egg in the mix? Would it be enough to ruin this batch of chocolate sauce? Would two be enough, three? As I considered this, I felt someone's eyes on me. I looked up to see the man who ran the kitchen, his name was Goddan, or something like that, and his eyebrows had lowered into an intense frown.

'"You not bothered about the bombs and the PLO?" he asked me.

'"What can I do?" I said above the noise of the mixing machine.

'He shrugged and his eyebrows rose. "You are right," he said. "I guess you either have the luck or you don't. Maybe you have the luck." And then he left.

'As it turned out, it seemed that I did have the luck. Later I found out that not only was that one of the safest kibbutzes, so close to the border, but also it was a pretty easy place as far as the volunteers were concerned. I later heard reports that some of the kibbutzes were run like slave camps, the volunteers being worked fourteen or sixteen hours a day, but I never saw any of that. We had big green lawns, a swimming pool, a room each for the volunteers, plenty of dope to smoke. It was a hippy's dream.

'But back to the story. The French girl did leave, and so did the Austrians. But Isla, the red-headed Scottish girl, she stayed on and for a while there was just me and her in the volunteer rooms, until more volunteers came, after the troubles calmed down.

'I don't know if you know your geography. I didn't before I went. The kibbutz was in the Negev desert, which is down in the south of the country, very close to the border. Just a few hundred yards from the kibbutz was a high fence, and beyond the fence the lush green grass ended and there was just the sand of the desert. It was the Gaza Strip on the other side of the fence. We would see the planes flying over occasionally. They had created an oasis in the desert, the Israelis. I don't know where all the water came from, but they must have used a lot of it, to get the desert so green.'

Nicolaos is sipping his coffee, sucking the dark liquid off the top, his eyes on Miltos, enraptured. Miltos knows he is a good storyteller. He puts energy into the telling, priding himself on his delivery. The two men on the next table have stopped their conversation and they too are listening. Even Theo has stopped clattering and loiters nearby, wiping the tabletops, straightening the chairs.

'I spent a couple of weeks in the kitchens, and then they moved me to the fields, to work with the bulls. They rotated us, and we would only work on a particular job for a short time. Some of the volunteers grumbled, but I found it interesting, to try new things. It was hot outside with the bulls, and dusty. We would round them up, and lead them from here to there. Sometimes we would have to give them injections, with big, thick needles. There was a knack to getting round behind the animal so you could stick your syringe in its rump and press the plunger before it ran off.'

Nicolaos chuckles but then nods, encouraging Miltos to go on.

'We spent a lot of time carting the hay about. That was hard work, heaving heavy bales of hay on and off the trailer. Built me up some fine muscles.' He lifts his arm and flexes his bicep, which is hard and round. Not as bulging as it once was, but there is enough meat there to make him feel proud.

'But the work was satisfying, too. There was an American guy who lived there full-time, and when he wanted the bulls to move out of the way or go in a particular direction he would throw a clod of earth at their heads. Boof!' Miltos jerks his head back and slaps the heel of his hand on his forehead to demonstrate. 'And it worked,' he continued. 'They would just move out of the way. I don't think they were bothered, they were so big and their skulls were so thick. But they were unpredictable. Sometimes they would just look at you and have no fear, and other times they would run off when they saw you near. I never understood them.'

'Ah well, at least with a goat you know where you are,' Nicolaos says. 'Even when they don't want their hooves clipped they are still gentle. They try to yank their legs out of your grip and occasionally turn their heads and lower them as if to butt you, but they rarely do. I find them to be really gentle creatures.'

'I have never trimmed a goat's feet,' Miltos admits.

'Nothing to it, the hooves are in two halves, just level them up, make them flat, and don't take too much off the heel else they rock back and it puts a strain on the tendons.' Nicolaos says this as if it is the easiest thing in the world.

Miltos leaves the last of his cola. He will not order another one. Not today, probably not ever. He cannot imagine how he ever liked the stuff. It is sickly-sweet and far too fizzy. Perhaps he will drink a coffee to chase the flavour away.

'You want another coffee?' He asks Nicolaos.

'I'll get you one.' Nicolaos turns his head to find Theo. 'One *glyko*, please.' He orders himself a sweet coffee. 'And what will you have my friend – another cola?'

'No. Coffee for me too, please. *Metrio*,' Miltos says.

'You sure you want it sweet, Nicolaos?' says Theo.

'Yes, why wouldn't I?' Nicolaos's eyebrows rise at his question.

'Because of your toothache?' Theo reminds him.

'Oh!' Nicolaos looks as if he has suddenly remembered something unpleasant. 'Oh yes, better make it *sketo*.' He looks sad. 'So what about this toothache cure?' He turns to Miltos.

'It worked very well until Theo reminded you otherwise,' Miltos says.

Nicolaos smiles at this. 'Ha! It did, didn't it?'

'Ach!' The grunt comes from the man at the next table. 'You may well have done Nicolaos here a service by taking his mind off his toothache for half an hour with your tales, but you have done me no favours. Look at that, half an hour late. The wife will never let me hear the end of it.' And the old man staggers to his feet, grabs his crook from the back of his chair and hastens from the *kafenio*.

Miltos also leaves a short time later, and he wanders up to the garage to see Aleko, on the pretence of a chat; the real reason, though, is to keep himself in Aleko's mind, to make his car a priority.

The mechanic assures him he'll be done tomorrow. This news gives Miltos a feeling of relief, although a part of him would have liked to stay for the baptism and the wedding, partly to see how the situation resolves itself but also because he quite likes Petta, and Ellie and Loukas too. But somehow liking these people unsettles him. He must move on.

Chapter 20

Down the road from the garage, across from the *kafenio* on the corner, a young girl is coming out of the corner shop with a bag of groceries. Miltos narrows his eyes, admiring her youthful posture, and recognises that it is Ellie, the English girl. She looks so young to be living here, in what is to her a foreign country, but then how much older was he when he moved abroad? About the same age, probably. Somehow the young seem so much more assured these days, with so much confidence. They seem to travel without a second thought, without any sense that they are doing something out of the ordinary. But then again, is he not the same now, always on the move? At eight months, this current job is something of a personal record.

He rubs his forehead. Is it realistic to think he can keep wandering from place to place and job to job until the day he dies? Is it not inevitable that one day he will feel tired, maybe even weak, and then what? He hand slithers down his face and he rubs his chin, feeling the stubble. He must buy some razors.

'Hello.' Ellie shades her eyes with her hand and stops on the steps of the corner shop, waiting for him to catch up. 'How is your day?' she asks. Her manner is easy and light. As he has no fixed destination he sees no reason not to go in the same direction as her. She turns at the bakery and, without thinking, so does he.

'I see you know this way back to the hotel.' It is not a question. Perhaps it is best not to say that he does not – she might think he is stalking her! – so he smiles and says casually, 'Thought I would go and have a quick shave.' It is such a relief to be with someone so full of life who seems to accept his company without judgement. His limbs move more easily, and he feels like smiling for no reason.

'That is my house, halfway to the hotel, there in the middle of the orange grove.' She sounds proud. 'Can you imagine anything more perfect?'

'Perfect,' he replies. Now, someone like Ellie, at her age, is too young for him, he knows that. And obviously, she would see him as much too old for her. It is easy to rule out the really youthful. But what sort of age group would suit him these days? His last brief relationship was in Bali, and she had been in her thirties. But how quickly conversation with her had petered out! She was excited about apps and social media, and he talked of the history of the island and places he had seen and had yet to see. She would enthuse, but only about the beaches and bars where they might pose and try exotic drinks. What was the point of travelling so far for a tan and a drink?

She will be thirty-five or thirty-six now. Does that mean he has to look for someone older than that?

Coiffured hair and a blue dress flash though his mind. He cannot deny the attraction he felt for either of the women in the village, but how would they see him? After all, he has nothing to offer. No farmland, no house, no business.

Ellie leads the way through the narrow streets of the village. The whitewash of the low cottages here is a stark contrast to the old mottled orange roof tiles, which sit low to the ground, almost hiding the small windows that are hunched under the eaves. Around cottage doorways, geraniums burst from brightly painted olive oil tins. Cats bask in corners, in every colour combination possible. Everything reminds him of places his mama used to tell him about, the places in which she grew up. He thought all such villages had long since disappeared.

Ellie turns down a narrow footpath between two old cottages where the paving stones are uneven. Up ahead there are no stones – just bare earth, trampled smooth by many feet. Ellie lifts heavy fruit on the branches so their thorns do not snag her hair as she winds her way around the trees. In amongst the shadows of the foliage ahead, there is a shock of white. It must be her cottage.

'It used to be a farmer's storeroom, and now it's my favourite place on earth.'

She speaks with such energy. Miltos squints at the building as they approach. The plasterwork has peeled off here and there but someone has painted the mud brick underneath it the same limewash-white as the rendered surface. The roof tiles are the old kind, like half-cylinders, one layer laid face up and a second laid face down to lock into the first. Age has distorted their colour; some are as dark as wet earth, whilst others are as orange as the fruit, and most are a combination of shades, mottled and covered in lichen. Here and there are patches of new tiles that look oddly out of place, and at one end, near the apex, plastic sheeting has been tucked under the ridge tiles – obviously a problem area. To Miltos it still looks like a storage barn. A chimney has been added at one side but its distorted and oddly shaped surface suggests that, although it appears to be an afterthought and recently built, old materials have been used. It is altogether a bit of a cobbled-together affair.

The only distinctly new addition to the place is the windows. The wood frames have sharp edges and they are newly, but thinly, painted. At one time it would not have bothered him to have lived in such a place. He would have seen the romance in it, but these days he does enjoy his comforts.

'It's lovely,' he says, reluctant to quell her enthusiasm.

'It's perfect. In an hour or two, Loukas will go to work. I have only a short shift this afternoon so when I'm finished on reception I will go and sunbathe down on the beach near him.'

She makes an absolutely contented sound, somewhere between a sigh and a hum. 'I love the summer, but winter was good too. The bar closed early and then we would watch the sunset together. Have you seen it?' She turns to look at him but an answer would spoil her flow so he stays silent.

'The darkness spreading over the water,' she begins, as if reciting a poem, 'the blue turning purple and then black.' Then her tone becomes livelier. 'It gets so dark we have to feel our way home through the orange trees some nights.' This amuses her and she gives a short, merry laugh. 'Then we can hear the night animals waking and scratching about, before we snuggle into bed together.'

She pauses as if she is remembering this more clearly; a slight colour comes to her cheeks but it is almost as if she has forgotten he is there.

In a moment she is back in the present and she reassures him. 'But summer last year was good too. So I expect this year will be pretty much the same. The guests don't seem to want to sleep. They often party through the night and Loukas can still be there at dawn. I love that too, but I do need to get up in the morning for work so I like this time of year best so far.'

As they draw nearer to her home she puts a finger to her lips. 'Shh.' Her eyes shine. 'Loukas is asleep.'

Her excitement at this thought is evident and Miltos feels a wave of jealousy for what she is feeling, the promises of her future. It jolts him into a decision.

He will quit this hire car delivery work, which is an old man's job. He will get a job that will make him feel young again and he will find himself his own true love. Someone young and energetic, smooth-skinned and full of fun. Maybe he could return to Dahab on the Red Sea. When he worked there as a diving instructor, did he not have the pick of every girl that came? Yes, that is what he will do.

'See you,' Ellie says, and she enters her house, closing the door quietly behind her.

He is now alone in the orchard. Alone with the sounds of a couple of thousand cicadas and a magpie that is somewhere in the tangle of branches, invisible. He peers through the foliage in every direction until he spots glimpses of blue and takes the path in that direction. His feet gain a little momentum at the sight of the water, and he hurries until he is out in the open and he can look to his left and see the sea all the way to the horizon. It is as deep a blue as he has ever seen it. A slight breeze ruffles its surface and each peak reflects the sun, making him narrow his eyes and put his hand to his forehead to lessen the glare.

From the sea's edge it is a short distance to the hotel, which is surprisingly well camouflaged from this direction by a screen of bamboo. He is tempted to take off his shoes, feel the sand between his toes, but as the distance to the hotel is not far he does not bother. When he gets back to his room he will call the centre in Dahab, if he still has the number with him. If not, it will have to wait until he gets back to Athens. But at least the car will be fixed tomorrow, and he can be in the capital the day after that, or maybe even the same evening.

Chapter 21

There is a dryness to the heat that wasn't there in Greece, and a heaviness, as if there is never any relief. The new airport at Sharm el-Sheikh is more contemporary and soulless than he had anticipated. Of course, he expected the country to have modernised to a degree since he was last here, but even so, the shining, glitzy shops and vast arches supported by a network of steel beams seem oddly inappropriate here in the middle of the desert.

He wonders if the shelters on the beach, with their roofs of palm leaves and handwoven rag rugs on the floor, where people would gather to chat and smoke out of the sun, have been replaced with similarly modern equivalents. He checks his breast pocket for his passport and his PADI licence and shifts his small bag more firmly on his shoulders. Once outside, he unzips the lower portions of his lightweight waterproof cotton trousers and stuffs them into his bag. The weight and bulk of his walking shoes meant he had to wear them despite the heat, and he reminds himself again to buy sandals as soon as he is in Dahab, or sooner, if there is an opportunity.

Behind him, a group of six or more girls in shorts lower their sunglasses from the tops of their heads and gasp at the heat, and then start talking all at once. An airport attendant in a long white *jelabiya* ushers them all off the tarmac.

Inside, there is a false coolness, and the overworked air-conditioning units hum in the background. As he moves towards passport control the girls are close enough for him to discern that they are British. In fact, if his ears do not deceive him they are Londoners. All except one, who is American. She stands out because she is taller, too, with long, straight dark hair and even white teeth, and a generally more polished look.

As he begins to tune in to their excitement he hears them say the name Dahab more than once, so he turns to smile at them. He could be teaching them the basics of diving tomorrow. They smile in return, but none of them makes real eye contact with him or allows the exchange to linger, and the icy finger of rejection touches his heart. But then he chastises himself and reminds himself he is not looking for a superficial fling any more. A more in-depth relationship will take time.

Outside, he conducts a harsh negotiation with a taxi driver over a ride into town. Once clear of the airport's sprawl, they travel across miles of flat, barren ground on the first leg of his onward journey, arriving at last at a town that springs from the desert.

The taxi driver drops Miltos off in a square that is edged with small lifeless shops. He stretches and surveys his surroundings. The unadorned square houses and minaretted mosques, along with hotel complexes, dominating the skyline on the edge of town seem at odds with the arid land; more than that, it seems odd that civilisation has prospered here at all. Not that it has prospered a great deal – many of the shops are boarded up. In fact, there is just him and a lone chicken, which struts around, scratching in the patch of dust designated as the bus station. As he hauls his luggage over to the waiting bus, he begins to wonder how many tourists there will be in Dahab. Still, if it's no longer a destination, it won't be the first time he has been stuck somewhere with no money and no work, and it does not worry him greatly. He always manages somehow. But the thought tires him a little.

The driver turns up eventually and climbs on board, the engine judders into life and the gears grind.

The bus climbs through barren hills, rocks and dust, and Miltos rests his head back and closes his eyes. When he opens them again they are no longer in the mountains, and the desert stretches away into the distance on either side of the bus, flat and featureless. Ugly angular concrete buildings begin to appear on both sides of the road.

Surely this cannot be Dahab! When he was here last the adobe buildings were sparse and small, and the hostels on the beach were the only sizeable complexes: eight or ten rooms clustered together, each made of sun-baked mud bricks. It was all so

142

basic, the windows just openings without glass, the beds nothing more than raised platforms with thin mattresses on top. Dahab was a small oasis, with the word 'small' more apt than the word 'oasis'. Of course, even back then, half a dozen shops had sprung up to cater for the tourist trade, and it was already questionable whether the 'genuine' Bedouin clothes and jewellery really were genuine, but the place still felt rural and remote and uncivilised, and that was what people loved about it. That was what *he* loved about it.

The bus driver assures him that it is Dahab and he steps down onto the dusty roadside.

Where before there was nothing but wooden goat pens, there is now a hotel three storeys high, and he is only on the outskirts. Further along there is another hotel, not as tall but just as shiny and new. After this, the buildings are lower, one or two storeys, and made of mud brick, just as he remembers them, but now the roads are full of shops that ooze their garish memorabilia, clothes and bric-a-brac out onto the dusty road.

To his relief the very centre of the village – or should he call it a town, now, he wonders – is much as he remembers. The buildings are the same, although some extensions appear to have been built between the originals. These are also shops, but somehow they look aged and as if they belong. They too sell baggy hippy trousers, mountains of beads, inexplicable things carved from dark wood, and wind chimes that hang silent in the still air.

With a hiss of air brakes and the throbbing purr of a well-maintained engine, a sleek new coach turns into the road ahead and stops. The doors glide open and air-conditioned coolness rushes out to mingle with the heat. The smell of sun cream **dominates as** a stream of young people climb off. The coach has come from the airport and it explains why there was no one on the local bus. The gaggle of youths climbing out is a very good sign.

The tall American with the long straight hair whom he saw in the airport is there, along with the other girls. The American raises her eyebrows when she sees him again. The girls are followed by a group of young men in colourful vests that display hairless chests: their eyes are concealed with designer sunglasses and cords run from their ears to music players too small to make bulges in their pockets. The girls give them a good deal of coy attention; earphones are removed and Miltos can hear names being exchanged and lengths of holidays being compared. That was the sort of conversation he had last time he was here. Back then, the girls had backcombed hair and wore over-sized sunglasses, and they had been impressed by the fact that he had no return ticket.

'You are a nomad. Like the Bedouins,' Crystal from Arizona had said. She had kissed him on the beach later that night, and they had been a couple until she left two weeks later, promising to write. Then there was Agnetha from Denmark – or was it Marianna from Finland?

Suitcases are taken from the compartment under the bus and the conversations become more animated.

'I'm going to learn how to scuba-dive while I'm here,' one voice says.

'They say the Red Sea is the most beautiful of them all,' someone replies.

'It's a diver's Mecca.' One of the boys tries to sound knowledgeable.

Miltos leaves their chatter behind him, and walks off up the dusty road.

Chapter 22

Where once the hostels were spaced out along the beach they are now crammed together, with newer hotels in what used to be spaces between the original buildings. It is in this direction that the group begin to drag their suitcases, and Miltos walks a few steps away from them with his small bag slung easily over his shoulder.

Most of the new hotels have grand entrances of tall mud-brick columns either side of the dirt roads that lead into them. Some are gated, some are open, and they all have signs hanging across these entrances, ranch style, displaying names that seem to Miltos to be no more than an arrangement of vowels with the odd consonant, spaces randomly breaking these groups of letters into words. Each complex looks as if it is built to fit the Western idea of an oasis in the desert, with palms dotted between buildings that have been smoothed over with a layer of mud. To his relief he finds the old compound easily, and not much seems to have changed. The place looks tired, with cracks in the adobe and a pile of very large and rather dirty cooking cauldrons piled up next to a tap behind the gate, beside which are not one but two men in dirty grey *jelabiyas*, lying full length on adobe benches against the wall, fast asleep.

The palm trees in the enclosure have dropped their dates and they lie like measle spots on the light-coloured compacted earth courtyard. Some have been trodden into the sand and their edges have dried and curled. The leaves of the palms cast hard-edged shadows, but as Miltos steps into these darkened areas he finds they provide no relief from the intense heat.

'Hello?' he calls. Neither of the sleeping men responds, although one does turn on his side with a guttural objection.

Between the buildings, tantalising slices of blue are visible and the promise of the sea draws Miltos further into the complex. The corners of the building are rounded and the doorways have no doors, except those to the rooms Miltos suspects are for guests, who would naturally demand some privacy. The few window openings are unglazed and form a repeating pattern of equilateral triangles; the walls, all of which bear the fingermarks of their maker, are undecorated and pale in colour. The intense blue of the sea, in contrast with the sandy walls, takes his breath away. The way it sparkles is almost the same as in Greece, but not quite. Having travelled the world, he knows there are many ways the sea can sparkle, or not; this particular sea view feels very familiar.

There is no need to call out again, as down on the thin strip of beach there is a large wooden structure with a fabric roof for shade and a low rickety fence around it, which is filled with both cushions and people. As he draws closer, the riot of colours that make up the clothes, the cushions and the batik patterns on the inside of the tent's roof jumble into one another and it is hard to make out how many people there are. At the far side of this oasis is a bar, with bottles suspended on optics and glasses shining in the sun. It looks jarringly out of place.

'Hello, my friend.' The bartender welcomes him with a wave of his hand and Miltos recognises the voice from last week's phone call. The bartender, Joshua, is younger than he expected. With a flourish Josh pours ice and a pink liquid from a large jug into a tall glass, lifting it high as he does so to create a brief cascade. As Miltos steps into the shade of the tent the Australian holds the drink out to him, grinning.

'Drink that,' he says, 'and we'll head over to the pool a bit later.'

Over a cool fruity drink it is agreed that a refresher dive or two would be a good idea for Miltos.

'I shoulda asked you before taking you on when you last dived. You'll be all right, it's like riding a bike. No worries,' Joshua drawls, and they head to the pool, where the equipment is laid out, all ready to be checked before the students head into the water.

'You've dived here before though, right?' Joshua says as they lower themselves into the diving school's pool.

'I learnt here, got my coaching certificate here,' Miltos replies. It seems strange to be in a wetsuit again, but familiar.

'Well, nothing's changed. The reef still falls away sharply, there are still the same dangers, and the same wonders, would be my guess.'

Joshua is gently treading water, waiting. Miltos tries to balance on one leg to put on his flippers, but after an ungainly fall he remains seated to finish the job.

'You probably won't need those in the pool.' Joshua states the obvious.

'Finding my feet.' Miltos makes a joke of it, but he knows he just switched to automatic pilot rather than thinking what he was doing. It does not make him look professional.

He is careful not to bash the tanks as he climbs into the water. What on land was a weight now provides buoyancy.

'Okay, so let's go down and then we can just run through the basics. We can do everything from emptying the mask to breathing from the same regulator and stuff. You know the lot – just to jog your memory about what you will be teaching first off.'

Joshua says it casually and then sinks under the water. The pool is so shallow he has to cross his legs for his head to become submerged and as it does it creates foam on the surface. Miltos watches the bubbles pop one by one and wonders if he is on trial.

The moment the water closes over his own head and his limbs lose their weight he relaxes. He had forgotten that feeling: the stillness, the sensation of entering another world. In open water he would flip his feet up, turn his head downwards and go deeper, looking for fish. But the pool is not deep enough for that.

Joshua is sitting on the smooth blue-tiled bottom of the pool. He is cross-legged with a hand on each knee in the 'okay' sign. As Miltos settles near to him Joshua gives a very clear signal for Miltos to move closer to him. He had forgotten that too – not the fact that divers use signalling, but the clarity of the way they use it, the balletic grace that hand gestures take on in the water.

They move closer together until he can see into Joshua's mask, see his eyes. The cheeky Josh of the surface is gone and before him is a professional. He points at Miltos and then, with the same hand, points two fingers at his own eyes and then a finger to his own chest. Without words and with complete simplicity he is saying you, watch, me. This followed by further clear signalling: remove mask, clear mask, replace mask.

Miltos lifts the mask from his eyes and it immediately fills with water. He leans forward, exhales bubbles to fill the mask and as he rights himself performs a careful refit. The glass is clear now and it feels as if he last performed this action only yesterday, his muscles remembering the movement more than his brain.

With smooth gesticulations Joshua leads him to practise clearing the regulator of water using the purge button.

Time slows down until it no longer has any relevance and the graceful movements of signalling and performance become a silent symphony, and he can see the smile in Joshua's eyes, which is no more than the reflection of his own delight at being in this world and watching his own expertise return to him.

Eventually, after running through the remaining skills, they bob to the surface, pulling out their regulators and pulling off their masks in unison.

'You're a fish,' Miltos says, and he slaps a hand on Josh's shoulder. The sun is hot after the relative cool of the water.

'If that is true then you are Old Neptune himself,' Joshua replies.

Miltos tries to accept it as a compliment, but the word that lingers in his ears is not Neptune: it is the word 'old'.

Chapter 23

After refreshing his memory in the pool, Miltos heads back to the beachside with Josh. The multi-coloured roof of the tent mottles the sunshine that lands on the girls sitting in one corner, who talk quietly, with the occasional loud giggle. Miltos rubs the back of his neck with a hanky. The boys from the bus lounge in the opposite corner pretending to be cool, listening to their music through headphones, trying their best not to glance too often at the girls.

Josh sits between the two groups with a clipboard in one hand, making notes. 'Listen up,' he calls out over the murmur of voices. 'This is Miltos.'

Miltos puts a hand up, in a gesture that is almost a wave, to those assembled in the tent. Some nod in response. Most just look up at him blankly. The girls continue to giggle, but to themselves, rather than in response to him.

'Right, Miltos is our new instructor,' Josh tells them, and then he stands to address Miltos directly. 'You'll be taking these newbies in the pool this afternoon.' He indicates the girls, who have stopped giggling now and look up at him – a little scared, or nervous at least, of what they have signed up for.

Miltos is relieved when the American girl takes the initiative and introduces herself as Virginia. 'And this is Paula, Jess, Rosy and Polly,' she drawls, pointing to her companions in turn.

'Ladies,' says Miltos with a wink, and they smile now, and the awkwardness that was there is dissolved.

'After the girls' initial lesson,' says Josh, consulting his clipboard, 'you'll be taking Bryce, James, Skinner and Grace for air sharing and weight belt removal. They've done some before but they need to be reminded of all they know in the pool, and maybe later in the week we'll go into open water.'

Three of the boys look up from their phones with a 'Yo', 'Wotcher' and 'Hi' and then resume their private worlds. Grace sits apart, reading a book. There is grey at her temples, and smile lines around her eyes and her clothes are an odd assortment of tie-dye and batik. She is probably in her mid-forties, or older perhaps, but still younger than Miltos. Nevertheless, she looks old to him and he responds to her warm smile with a curt nod.

'But until then there is still the night.' Joshua leaps to his feet and heads to the bar. 'Shots all round, I think.'

The girls giggle and the boys look up once again from their electronic devices.

It is not long before Rosie, Paula, Polly, Jess and Virginia are deep in slurred conversation with Josh and the other boys. Grace, on the other hand, is still sipping her first shot as if it is an aperitif, intent on her book. Miltos is keeping up with Josh drink for drink but, although he too is now laid amongst the cushions, he doesn't quite feel part of the group. Maybe this is because for him this is not a particularly novel event. Certainly it is not the first time he has been tipsy in a group like this one, not by a long way. For these young people, though, this could be an adventure of great significance – maybe the first time they have had such experiences. Their conversation is about diving, and travelling, and although it is not particularly stimulating he reconciles himself to it by thinking that he is here now, and may as well make an effort to join in, become a part of the group.

'There was a time once,' he begins, noting with some satisfaction that he has their attention, 'when I was diving out in Thailand, at Koh Dok Mai, when from nowhere–'

'Fake,' one of the boys says. Miltos stops mid-sentence and blinks.

'The whole of Thailand, so fake.' It is Skinner who is talking.

'Really?' Rosie says. 'I loved it.'

'Me too,' Polly agrees. 'Did anyone go to Ayutthaya?'

'So peaceful.' Virginia says, nodding.

'Did you see the Buddha head in the tree roots?' says James in a crisp English accent. He has broad shoulders and a muscular physique and, judging by the way he twitches his muscles, he is well aware of it. His blond hair is cut short and shaved up the back of his neck and his clothes all look new and of good quality.

'But Bangkok is so fake,' Skinner insists. His loose clothes do not hide his thin frame and his white skin has already reddened on his shoulders. He moves in jerks and every motion seems to scream his discontent with the world.

'Nah' – 'No' – 'Get out of here!' the others chorus.

'Way too Western, anyhow,' Skinner concedes. Miltos does not recognise the name Ayutthaya, or know what this Buddha head is they are talking about, and he is somewhat relieved when the conversation flows on, leaving the rest of his tale untold. The others seem just as well travelled as he is, if not better, and they begin to compare notes on Cambodia and Burma, and the places they name are unfamiliar to him, as if new places have been discovered or the old ones renamed. Grace looks over and smiles, her eyes rolling, as if to say 'The young today!' He smiles briefly in return but looks away again.

Josh jumps up to make more drinks and the conversation becomes both more animated and less coherent, and there is much laughter. Grace, who has been sitting apart from the main group and not really joining in, picks up her book and wishes them all a good night. Shortly after this, Miltos finds that he too is tired and he stands to go. Unfortunately for him he does this just as the portable CD player Skinner is fiddling with starts to blare out music. In a single bound the others get to their feet to dance. Rosie and Paula make eye contact and nod their heads to let him know that 'his idea' to dance is a good one, and now it feels too awkward to explain that he was in fact getting up to go to bed. James says he will make a cocktail he has invented. The rest of them whoop, arms in the air, and Miltos stifles a yawn as he shuffles his feet in time to the music.

'Where's the toilet?' he asks Josh in a quieter moment.

'The dunny's down there,' says Josh. ''Fraid your room's right next to them till we clear out the bigger one, but that one's even nearer the kitchen.' Josh is slurring and speaking loudly.

Miltos heads for the toilets. In the dark he cannot step between the fallen dates and his feet squish them repeatedly. At one point they cause him to slip, his arms reaching out to regain his balance. Righting himself, he finds he has lost his sense of direction. The buildings all look the same in the half-light, and he is not sure he can remember where Josh said the toilets were anyway. He steps into a room and switches on the light. It is bare, with no adornment at all. A thin foam mattress on a concrete plinth takes up half the space. He backs out and finds the toilets, just opposite. The water pressure is high and as he washes his hands his trousers are splashed. He tries to wipe them dry but his hands are wet too and the dark stain spreads. He will need to wait before he goes back to join the party, let the warm air dry him off.

The mattress in the bare room is as good a place to wait as any. He lies down, just to test it.

Miltos does not stir until a clattering of pans wakes him. As there is no door to the room, with one eye open he can see a man in a *jelabiya* pouring the remains of something into a toilet to be flushed away. The sun is already high in the sky and, bleary-eyed, he wanders to the tent on the beach. The glare off the sea stabs his retinas and he puts up a hand to shield them. Across the water, Saudi Arabia looks like it would be close enough to swim to, if he had any strength at all, which he doesn't.

Josh has set up a blackboard in one corner of the tent, and half a dozen or so of the youths staying at the compound are seated in front of it, lounging on the cushions. Josh is explaining about air pressure, and he looks up as Miltos approaches.

'Ah, here you are,' Joshua greets him. He is standing by a whiteboard with *200 bar/3000 PSI (there are 15 PSI per bar)* written across the top. Then there is a smiley face, and underneath are the words *At what depth will you read 2ATM of pressure?* Miltos's head may be fuzzy and he may feel queasy but the answer jumps into his mind automatically.

'So, tell them the answer, mate?' Josh taps the board with his lidded felt pen, encouraging Miltos to become part of the teaching team with him.

'Ten,' Miltos grunts. 'Is there any coffee?' Josh and the others are fresh-faced and show no trace of last night's partying.

'And as your prize ...' Joshua turns his back on the class, goes to the bar and returns offering Miltos a plastic cup. He smells the coffee and does not care if it has sugar and milk or not. It burns his tongue, scours off the furry coating, and within a minute or two the caffeine hits and his brain begins to wake.

'So, hit them with a question, Miltos, any one you like.' Joshua appears to be enjoying standing at the front, being in charge. The girls are wide-eyed, the boys looked impressed. Grace has her pen paused over a notebook. Hands in pockets, Miltos broadens his stance next to the Australian.

'Okay, so who can tell me the most common reason for the cylinders slipping in the nylon tank bands?' he asks, hoping to lure a little of the awe in his direction.

'Oh yeah, good one,' Joshua says, and he takes Miltos's coffee cup. 'You want a refill?'

'Can you put sugar in that?' Miltos asks as the students scribble their answers on their clipboards. The second hit of caffeine helps him to stand straighter. He is taller then Josh, broader too. But when everyone has scribbled their answers it is to the younger of the two that they all look.

'You've missed breakfast, mate,' Joshua says. 'This lot are ready for the first practical.' The students seem excited at the prospect of their first venture into the sea, and a buzz of conversation starts up.

'Skinner, James, Bryce and Grace – you are with me. Open water for you guys today.' Rosie and Paula look disappointed at this announcement. Paula sucks her tongue loudly; Jess nudges her with her elbow. Neither of them takes her eyes off the tanned Josh.

'I think I would like more practice in the pool before going into open water,' Grace says quietly but distinctly.

'Okay, you are with Miltos then.' Josh is already moving away, keen to get going.

Miltos heads towards the pool and the girls awkwardly find their feet amongst the cushions and follow him like ducks.

Grace catches him up. 'How long have you been diving then?'

Chapter 24

The pool is perfect for teaching: shallow enough so everyone can stand on the bottom with their heads above water. They scull their hands in the cooling water for no purpose; they seem confident that they are not going to drown or even have any reason to panic. None of them had any difficulty in checking their equipment or putting it on so the morning promises to be an easy one.

Miltos invites them all to dip beneath the surface, and the sudden silence and calm takes him once again. If he could find this feeling somewhere on land, or maybe – and this would be a longer-term solution – find a person who could create that feeling within him, how happy he would be. Then he would settle down without even being conscious of doing so. But this is such a futile thought. His need for this feeling makes him restless and this keeps him moving. As long as he is moving he believes he will find this feeling. But permanently globetrotting means he never stays anywhere long enough to find a person who could create this long-term solution – but then staying somewhere for any length of time makes the feeling unbearable, so he has to move. It is circular, relentless. So, best keep moving. At least then he is in control.

The group are sitting on the bottom waiting for him to begin. With a clear hand movement he invites the first to come close to him. It is Grace. She is trim for her age and looks no different from the other girls in her diving gear. He signs for her to release and retrieve the regulator, which she does with ease, and he gives her the 'okay' sign. He can tell that she would not be the sort to panic easily and he wonders why she did not go for her first open-water dive today.

Next he calls up Polly – only, as she draws closer, he sees it is Virginia. They are of similar build and in their masks it is difficult to tell them apart. Her movements are jerky and hesitant, and she is clearly not comfortable in this watery environment. She'll need more practice time in the pool.

Once they have all released and retrieved the regulator and have surfaced for a quick debrief they submerge again, this time to shed and replace the weight belts. Virginia's tendency to panic shows again. Polly is remarkably calm, and Paula very agile. The morning proceeds well, and when they have practised a few other important skills they take a break, at which point Miltos finds a light meal all prepared and waiting in the tent. There is no sign of Joshua and the others, who are presumably eating on board the boat.

After lunch, his group practise buddy breathing, changing every three seconds. He teams

Virginia with Grace and they make a good diving couple. Everyone is making good progress. Another day in the pool and he would be happy to take them for a brief open-water dive.

By the time they have finished it is mid-afternoon and everyone seems physically spent. He too feels tired – it is a long time since he concentrated so hard. As he sits on the cushions in the tent he is glad of the rest, and his mind goes blank watching the sea and the gulls.

Plodding slowly along the narrow beach, kicking up a little sand dust, comes a man with a team of three camels. The animals' short fur fluffs out in the slight breeze and they generally look well cared for; they have no sticks or rings through their soft noses and their multi-coloured halters are tasselled and unrestrictive. The driver, wearing a pristine white *jelabiya*, stops just level with the tent and strokes the lead animal's nose. The blue sky behind them throws them into high relief. With a slow movement the lead camel blinks its long lashes and makes a low grunting sound before nuzzling affectionately at its owner's ear. In response, the man's hand finds the shaggy fur at the top of its neck, under the jawbone, where he scratches. This seems to delight the camel, who pushes its chin out, elongating its neck and growling gently in appreciation. After a few minutes the man adjusts his *keffiyeh* and looks into the tent with a broad grin. Polly, Rosie and Paula are wriggling with excitement. Virginia is taking a photograph on her phone.

'You want to ride?' the man asks with an easy gesture, inviting them closer. The skin on his face is bronzed and clean and glistens in the sun. Rosie is on her feet without hesitation, followed by Paula and Polly, and by the time they are out of the tent and down at the water's edge the camels are kneeling in the narrow strip of sand, ready for them to climb aboard.

When the animals stand again the girls sway from one side to the other, giggling and squealing as they grip the animals' humps, hanging onto tassels and ribbons as the beasts begin to walk. They make their way along the sands, all of them laughing and shrieking at the unfamiliar motion.

Miltos first came across camels by the pyramids in Cairo. He tries to remember the name of the girl he was with but it doesn't come. Nice woman, rather young, but just a little too spiritual and naive for him. It was in the early days of running the hotel in Cairo and he was eager to please all who stayed, and he had brought her to see the pyramids. The girl's pale skin and blonde hair made her a target for every seller of wares or provider of services as they made their way to Giza. They had only just arrived when a boy, not much more than thirteen or fourteen, approached them with his camel. The woman made it clear that she had no money to pay for a ride, but the boy did not seem put out in the least.

'Just sit,' he offered, 'only photo.'

And it was agreed that if the camel did not move, that would not count as a ride, and there would be no charge. So up she climbed, and no sooner was she on top than the boy tapped the animal's rump and away he and his animal ran. Miltos knew he was expected to run after them, but instead he lit a cigarette and waited, listening to the babble of voices all around him: Egyptian men smoking and passing the time of day, and Americans adjusting cameras and comparing the sights to what they had seen the previous day or what they planned to see the next day. He can remember thinking that the roar of the city in the background was so at odds with the stately grandeur of the pyramids here at the edge of the desert, and that the whole experience seemed too surreal to be true.

Eventually the camel driver halted his beast, turned it around and headed back, but the boy still would not allow the camel to stop and kneel to let the girl off.

As he drew near to Miltos he said, 'Ah, so she had a ride after all, so you pay.' He grinned as spoke and Miltos could see that he had done this a hundred times before to a hundred other tourists with, no doubt, profitable results. The woman was demanding to get down, and the owner waited for Miltos to pay him.

Miltos had continued to smoke calmly. 'I think, perhaps, my friend, that I will sue you for kidnapping,' he said to the boy, also smiling. At this the boy swallowed hard and tapped the animal to make it kneel, and the woman slid down and hurried back to stand as close to Miltos as she could.

'A joke, my friend,' the boy said, straightening his *jelabiya* where it had become caught in the reins. 'A joke.'

As Miltos and the woman moved on to get a closer look at the sphinx, she clung to his arm as if danger was all around them.

'Have you ever ridden a camel yourself?' Grace asked, bringing him back to the present.

'Yes,' Miltos replies. 'In Morocco. It made me a little seasick if I'm honest.'

'Oh, I think you are brave to go on one in the first place.' Grace puts down her book.

'A bit high for me,' Virginia joins in, and Miltos feels relieved that the conversation is not exclusive.

'Not as high as an elephant,' Grace says, and she is about to continue when Joshua and the boys return looking animated but tired.

'So, who wants to take a day out and go to Petra tomorrow?' Josh collapses into the cushions. 'Where are the girls?'

'On camels.' Grace sounds scathing.

'Oh, okay, I'll tell you when they get back. No point in repeating myself. Is there any food?' He looks around for one of the men that tend the camp, cooking the food, tidying the cushions after them. 'Hey!' he calls to a man who is hanging out grubby-looking cloths on a line. 'Any food?'

The man nods and hurries towards the kitchens. Miltos narrows his eyes at Joshua, who has closed his own as he lies back in the tent.

'I feel sick,' Rosie says. The camels are back, and their owner is grinning. The girls look a little stunned after their camel ride.

'Me too,' says Paula.

'I need a drink,' Polly exclaims, and no sooner have their feet touched the ground than the camels and camel driver are forgotten.

'Hello, you beauties.' Joshua sits up a little. 'I was just suggesting that we take a trip tomorrow, to Petra, in Jordan. What do you say? We drive from here to Nuweiba and take the ferry across to Aqaba, and then I can arrange for a minivan to take us to Petra. We can stay overnight, and I have a friend in a hotel who will give us a very good deal, and then back the day after. Who fancies it?'

The level of excitement in the camp grows and they all talk at once until Joshua shushes them and demands a headcount of who is in.

'Miltos? You coming? It would be your official day off but you're welcome.'

'No, I've been before,' says Miltos. 'You guys go and have a good time.'

The boys put their heads together and talk amongst themselves.

'Nah, Miltos, you should come,' Skinner encourages.

'Yeah!' Bryce agrees.

Miltos is surprised by this invitation and looks up to see them nodding and smiling at him. They want him to go. It is very flattering, and he gets just the slightest sense of belonging, which feels nice, even if it is a little unbelievable.

Chapter 25

The afternoon fades into evening and the sky is awash with stars. Between the pinpricks of light are more distant glows, and Miltos leans back against the cushions, looking out past the edge of the tent roof. He stares into the relative darkness between the stars, picking out another layer of stars or glowing planets.

The men who work in the kitchens come out with a cauldron of ful medames, aromatic with parsley, chilli, garlic, onion and lemon juice, all competing for dominance. More large metal dishes are brought out, piled high with flatbread, fried eggs and curd or yoghurt, and the guests gather round hungrily. Miltos is not particularly interested in how the camp is run, but he notices Joshua writing in a tatty book, each page curled and dirty. He is close enough to read what is being recorded: who is eating and who has had drinks from the bar. Josh catches his eye.

He leans over and whispers close to Miltos's ear. 'The trip to Petra is a good little earner. I make the money on the hotel, the hotel makes the money on the minivan. That leaves you, if you want, to

168

make a markup on the crossing. It's easy to haggle the price down for a party of five or more, and easy to tell this lot whatever price you want. Don't overdo it though – else they might complain and find out how much it normally is. Still, haggle hard when you buy the tickets and it will give you room to manoeuvre.' He nods encouragingly, grinning.

'The bar is yours as well?' Miltos asks.

'Sure. Buy a bottle, sell it by the glass, keep everyone happy with shots. It's a win–win.'

'Who owns this place then?' Miltos suspect the owners are in Cairo, or further away still.

'Him.' Joshua points to the man in a dirty *jellabiya*, who is taking a pan from the kitchen to wash. 'Him and his brother, but they don't speak a word of English. So I book in the tourists, give them the price for the rooms and the food, and everyone is happy. Before me it was a man called Davie, but he went off windsurfing in South America and left me in charge. When I get itchy feet I guess you'll be in charge. That's the only rule, you have to leave someone in charge or you can't go. It's just polite, you catch my drift?' With this, he closes his notebook and rolls to his feet to get some food.

After they have all eaten, the group lie in various states of repose, hands on stomachs.

'I think I might burst,' Skinner says.

'Hey, James, man – I think we need a little after-dinner toke,' says Bryce, and James busies himself, taking things from the pouch that is tied around his waist. Miltos recognises the familiar ritual. He must have seen the men in the Cairo hotel perform this ceremony three or four times a day – or more, even – and it no longer interests him. When the performance is complete, James hands the carefully rolled oversized cigarette to Skinner, who accepts it and applies a lighter. It's a long time since he was in Cairo with those two jokers, running the hotel – around thirty years now – but the smell of tobacco and herb that begins to fill the tent takes him straight back there, as it always does.

The girls sit up and take notice of what is going on. The boys grow increasingly languid as they pass the herb between them. Bryce takes a long drag and offers it to Grace, who curls up her nose and becomes even more engrossed in her book. He passes it to Virginia instead; she takes it with little interest, and after a couple of puffs she passes it on to Rosie and Paula and Jess who are sitting upright, waiting. They giggle as it makes it to their quarter of the tent. The joint then travels round to Josh, who offers it on to Miltos. Miltos shakes his head. The world is an amazing place; why would he want to cloud his view? He leans back to look at the stars again.

'Told you,' Skinner says, but it is not clear to Miltos what he is talking about or to whom, and nor does he care. He has eaten well, his eyes are full of stars, and the night is as warm as the day. He wants for nothing.

As the cigarette makes a second round, the girls start to giggle uncontrollably, and Joshua uses this moment to move a little nearer to them. If Miltos

170

were to hazard a guess, he would say Josh is interested in Paula. She is feisty and just a little unpredictable. Following Josh's lead, James and Bryce move in as well. Skinner is flat on his back in the corner, staring up at the roof of the tent with a blank expression on his face.

'I think I'll say goodnight,' Grace says, getting up, but no one acknowledges her except Miltos.

'Goodnight,' he offers but makes a point of not looking at her, keeping his focus on the stars.

'There are ten billion galaxies in the observable universe.' Virginia moves so she too can lie with her head back to see beyond the roof of the tent. She swallows audibly before adding, 'And in each galaxy there are a hundred billion observable stars. Which is a heck of a lot of stars, but I can't do the math for you.'

'That *is* a lot,' Miltos says. 'It puts my life into perspective.' He chuckles a little but it is not easy to laugh lying like this on his back, with his neck extended and his head too far back.

'Makes me think how unimportant my little day-to-day choices are. At the time, they seem so important. There is not one star out there that cares if I wear a blue T-shirt or a green one. It does not alter anything at all in the universe, so why do I struggle with such a decision for half an hour each day?'

'Ah well ...' Miltos starts slowly. 'The thing is, if you wear the blue T-shirt when the moon is new and it rains in the night, then you will marry someone who appears to be the love of your life but will actually wear you down to nothing, and you will give birth to the person who eats the last ever fish to swim in the sea.'

'Oh no!' She sounds genuinely horrified and Miltos hurries on.

'But if you wear the green one when the moon is three quarters full and the wind blows to the west, you will meet the love of your life and bear children, one of whom will save the world from global warming.' He pauses for Virginia to release her tension by laughing, which she does. 'So …' – he draws the word out to pique her interest – 'it is very important which T-shirt you wear.'

'Ah, how well you understand the world,' she replies. 'How wise you are. I think I might throw away my blue and green T-shirts and just wear white from now on.' Virginia seems to be enjoying the conversation.

'Ah, but if you wear white a wise man will whisk you away on a round-the-world trip to see all the sights and you will have the most amazing time.' Miltos wonders if he is being too obvious.

'Then my decision to wear white could be a good one.' She does not miss a beat with her reply. He would like to look over at her now, to see if he can tell how much of this is fun and games or whether they are really connecting. It is all in the timing. He must appear to be uninterested, let her think she must do a bit of running, but all the while he will be carefully reeling her in.

172

'Yes, it might be very daring to wear white – tempting fate, perhaps?' He continues his theme.

'Are you going to come with us tomorrow then?' she asks.

'You think I should?' Reel her in, little by little.

'Why not? It will be fun.' With this, she scrambles to her feet and wishes everyone an easy goodnight. Skinner is now snoring and Rosie is staring at the back of her hand, but the rest wish her peaceful sleep.

Miltos waits a suitable length of time and then he too goes to his room. It is nice that they are all asking him to come with them tomorrow, and he is looking forward to the day ahead. He falls asleep quickly.

Usually an undisturbed sleeper, tonight, in his dreams, he is back in the village. The car is still not fixed and before him are Marina from the corner shop and Vasso from the kiosk: they are reaching out to him, trying to grab him, pull him back to the square where a party is being held. A woman with golden hair, obviously not Greek, is holding them back, protecting him. He wakes, sweating slightly.

Chapter 26

The next day comes too soon and the group gathers in the yard by the main gates half-asleep. Only Josh is full of energy as he directs a minibus that is backing into the compound. The owner, the man in the dirty *jelabiya* whom Miltos had seen asleep on his first day, begins to deposit boxes and canteens near the van.

'Food for now and for later. We sell it,' Josh explains as he begins to load the food into the minibus, pushing the boxes under the seats. Polly, Rosie, Paula, Jess, Skinner, James, Bryce, Virginia and Grace all climb on board, where all of them, apart from Grace, who is reading, close their eyes and wait, drifting back off to sleep.

As the bus leaves the town, the open, featureless desert valley stretches before them; the road, flat and straight as far as the eye can see, is bordered by arid stone mountains. For a second Miltos experiences a rush of excitement at the thought of the journey into the unknown. But then he remembers he was on this same road thirty years ago, when he was as young as these kids around him. There is nothing here that he hasn't already seen. The road meanders through the barren hills without break or change. Where is the excitement in that? Isn't he just repeating himself?

Josh grins at him and lifts one hand off the wheel to rub his fingers together, miming the word money. He, at least, seems excited by the possibility of what the day will bring. Miltos could make a tidy sum too, but for him money lost its charm long ago, when he realised he would always be able to make what he needed, but would probably never be rich.

That realisation came to him in Tel Aviv.

After he left the kibbutz he moved to a work hostel in the capital. Phone calls offering work came in to the hostel every morning, and if you were up early you had the pick of the jobs, which ranged from labouring to washing up, to painting and decorating.

Miltos's first job was washing up in a fancy restaurant. After a week there, working long hours late into the night in the heat of the kitchen, he came down with a fever that made his head spin and his bones ache. He struggled through till the final sitting but could not manage to stay any later than that. A day or two later, when the fever had subsided somewhat, he returned to the restaurant, but they had a new man in by then and it was clear that he was not going to be offered wages for the week he had worked, on the basis that he had not worked till closing time on his last day. The owner ignored his pleas and continued with preparations for the evening ahead. When Miltos hassled him for his money the man became irritated and told him to leave and pointed to the front door.

Miltos's sense of right and wrong was offended, and although he really needed this money in order to pay for his bed at the hostel, it was the principle of the thing that really got to him – added to which, the amount they were arguing about was trivial, and the owner could take it out of his back pocket and not notice the difference the next day.

The first customers were beginning to file in, taking their places at tables that were bedecked with starched linen tablecloths and red candles. The conversation buzzed gently, and Miltos stood there in a rage, trembling from head to toe at the injustice of it. The owner stood by the front door, waving him out with a dismissive gesture. What could he do? His story would be dismissed if he called the police, and besides, he had no work permit. As he made his way reluctantly to the front door, he passed a little stage where musicians would sometimes play, serenading the diners from the grand piano, or softly strumming acoustic guitars. Before the thought had a chance to form in his mind, and almost before he knew what he was doing, Miltos hopped up onto this stage and sat cross-legged in the centre, with his arms folded across his chest.

'Get off, go – the customers are here,' the owner hissed, holding the door open for him, but Miltos did not move. He could see his actions were causing a stir. Some of the customers looked up at him, perhaps anticipating an act of some sort.

'Will you go?' the owner hissed again, but Miltos did not say a word. 'If you don't go, I will get my brother.' The owner's brother was a big man and was usually kept out of sight, doing the menial jobs that required strength.

'If you get your brother this will become a much bigger incident. Right now, if you pay me I will slip away and no one will be any the wiser,' replied Miltos.

What could the owner do? The money Miltos was asking for was peanuts to him, and he had the restaurant's reputation to consider. It was the most precious money Miltos ever earned because with it came the conviction that he was valid: that his time, like everyone else's in the world, had value and he had every right to stand up for himself. He knew in that moment that he would always get by in the world.

The hills, towering on either side of the trundling minibus, stand in front of more hills; it's a place where a man could easily become lost. The valley bottom is compressed sand, the road nothing more than compacted dust and pale-coloured shale. Skinner is snoring. Paula is laid across Rosie's knees, her hair hanging over her face. Virginia's head rests against the window. She catches Miltos looking at her and smiles, and he notices for the first time that she is wearing a delicately embroidered white blouse, and last night's conversation is brought suddenly to mind. For a moment he thought he had dreamt that conversation, but her prolonged look confirms it was real. He gives her the biggest grin he can and then turns to look out of the front window.

Up ahead, in the middle of nowhere, are a woman, a child and a goat. As the bus approaches they stop walking and move to the side of the dust track, the woman's hand on the child's chest to stop it running in their path; her gaze follows the progress of the bus as it rumbles past. The sight of these figures standing alone in the middle of this endless desert brings back the dream of the woman with the golden hair holding back Marina and Vasso. It comes to Miltos with such clarity that it suddenly seems more real than everything around him. His hand finds the shell in his pocket and he rubs at its edge.

The authenticity of the Greek village lay in the longevity of people's relationships there. Neighbours who worked side by side had gone to school together, and their mothers before them had grown up together, as had their parents, back and back into times forgotten. That was what united the village and made it so real. How must it feel to be a part of that? The longest relationship he had ever had, apart from with his baba, was … He stops breathing and sucks on his bottom lip. Who? With whom has he had the longest relationship? There was the girl in Thailand – he met her the day after he arrived, and he was there six months. What was her name? Chunlian, was it? A sweet girl, but she never voiced her own views, and that had grown tiresome. Then there was Fleur in Holland, but that had been more intense than long-lasting. Oh, the times he had wished her back into his life, only to unwish it moments later when he recalled the reality. She had been too much. Beautiful, hypnotic, but too much.

'What are you sighing about?' The road ahead is so straight and flat that Josh is only half concentrating on the driving and takes the time to look at him as he speaks.

'I was just thinking about the girls I have dated.' He says it quietly, not wanting to be overheard by Virginia in her white blouse, but even as this goes through his mind he looks out at the desert and sees sand and rock and more sand and rock, and the landscape feels as barren as his life and it all seems a little pointless. He pulls down the passenger-side visor to see if there is a mirror, and adjusts it so he can see Virginia. Even she seems pointless. He could continue to gently court her, and maybe he would succeed, and then maybe they could go off and explore the world together. It would be nice to see everything fresh again, through her eyes, but then would that really be living or just a second-hand experience?

He shifts in his seat, which is not very comfortable, and begins to wonder why he came. He could have spent the day floating in the sea or sleeping in a hammock. It is a bit sad that at his age all it took was the flattery of an invitation to make him go on a journey he would normally have avoided. And by Skinner of all people – not even

Virginia. What on earth does he have to prove to Skinner?

He rests his head against the door frame and tries to sleep. The rattling vehicle is jostling and bouncing over the holes in the road, and he does not expect to receive any relief, so it is a surprise to him that he is woken by the bus juddering to a halt.

A sign tells him they have arrived in Nuweiba, but he can only think it must be mistaken.

Chapter 27

Last time he was here, Nuweiba was little more than a collection of windowless concrete buildings, the ground around them compacted sand, dust and dirt and bits of mortar with the occasional brightly coloured plastic bottle. Around the outside walls three goats had played follow-my-leader – stunted, black, long-haired creatures scratching in the corners of the abandoned buildings for food. At first glance, the place had seemed clearly deserted, and Miltos can still recall the surprise he felt when he discovered that inside one of these cuboid shells, upstairs, was a bank, and in another was the ticket office for the ferry across to Jordan.

All this has changed in the years that have passed, and expensive-looking hotels have sprung up where the abandoned concrete block buildings used to be, with well-tended lawns in front of them and neat plastic signs directing the visitor here and there.

Josh starts the bus again and they drive through the streets of the town, where colourful wares spill from shopfronts that were previously abandoned but which are now adorned and brightly painted in an attempt to compete with their neighbours to lure the passing tourist inside. As for foreigners – back then only Miltos and a Swiss couple were waiting for the ferry. They had had to wait a long time, watching the speck of a boat slowly making its way across the water from Jordan. Now, as the minibus approaches the water's edge, a high-speed catamaran can be seen, moored in the new, purpose-built harbour. Over on the other side of the harbour, cargo ships are lined up where containers and haulage lorries are waiting to cross.

'Well, this place never had much charm, but what it had is gone.' He speaks his thoughts aloud.

'When were you here before?' Josh asks.

Miltos opens his mouth to reply but then stops to consider. Was it in the early nineties? Josh probably wasn't even born then. Best to stay quiet, so he shrugs instead and mutters, 'a while ago.' Vague.

'Right, so if you go get the tickets, we'll wait here, or maybe have a look around the town.' Joshua turns around to see who is awake as he fumbles in a plastic bag. 'Here are all the passports. You'll need them for the visa stamps. If you are lucky you could be back in an hour. You have two hours before the ferry "officially" leaves but – well, to be honest mate, they seem to choose when they leave on a whim so don't worry if it takes you longer.'

Miltos takes the proffered passports and frowns, wondering, as he climbs out into the burning sun, why it should take him two hours to buy tickets.

Josh lies down across the bench seat, eyes closed. He is not going anywhere.

Raising a hand to shield his eyes from the sun, Miltos feels obliged to trot to avoid being exposed to the heat for too long. For some reason the glare feels harsher here than back at the camp. Maybe it is all the concrete that surrounds him. Every few steps someone tries to sell him something or pull him into their shop. He shakes himself free repeatedly and it is with relief that he finds the visa building.

There is a long counter down one wall, with arches cut out of the protective glass separation. The arches are so large there seems little point in the glass being there at all. Several men are working away at their desks behind this counter and a few people are milling around in the central area. The air is hot and stagnant, and there is no air conditoning. The windows are small and if there was any breeze to be had it would struggle to enter the room. Strip lighting hardens the daylight. Miltos approaches the first arch and places the passports on the shelf. The man takes the top one, looks it over, and asks, 'Jordan?'

Miltos nods his affirmation and the passport is stamped. The room echoes with the noise, but no one pays any attention. Each man is absorbed in his own duties and it is too stiflingly hot to show interest in anything beyond that which is necessary. Miltos is the only man not wearing a *jelabiya* and *keffiyeh* but the intensity of the sun has already darkened his skin and he might almost pass for a local nonetheless. He

183

watches the man taking each passport in turn, inspecting it and then stamping it. There seems to be very little formality in the process and at one point the man stops to accept a cup of tea from a colleague. A pound or two would be sure to speed the process, and the man behind the counter gives the impression that he is waiting for something, but without asking. If he is to make any profit from this venture, however, Miltos feels he will have to avoid bribery. He waits patiently and when the teller sees no money is going to be passed he drains his cup and finishes the job.

The ticket office is a different matter. The room is almost identical in size and shape but the walls have not been painted and it is much hotter here, and there are a great many more people. Here, tourists and locals jostle, each wanting to be served first.

At this point, Miltos realises he has been manipulated into doing the job that someone must do but no one would want. It would be a disaster to bring the whole group in and let them try for themselves, and it now makes complete sense that Josh would offer him such a role, to avoid it himself. Maybe this is why the Australian was so keen he should come along.

With his sleeves rolled up he enters the fray and, with a few choice Arabic words, and using his height to his advantage, he makes some progress. It is oppressively hot and each of the other men in the throng exudes his own distinctive body odour. As time progresses, the air appears to become more dense and less breathable. The scrabbling and pushing gets worse and Miltos can feel his patience reaching breaking point. He does not often lose his temper, but in this heat and stench it may be beyond his control. With elbows out, he pushes harder and then something in him snaps. He no longer sees the people around him as human and his regard for them is gone. Not caring about the toes he steps on or the ribs he digs his elbows into, he slides between people, physically pushing them out of the way. This is met with shouting and hand-waving but he narrows his eyes in response and increases both his speed and force. Once at a booth, he grabs the man in front of him under one arm and by his collar and lifts him out of the way, and fills the space he has created with his broad shoulders. The man issuing tickets raises his eyebrows at this technique but Miltos ignores this and demands tickets. Meekly, the man tears off the number required and names a sum.

Miltos tuts a very Greek 'no' and then in Arabic says, *'Aqall.'* The price is too steep. The teller looks even more surprised at hearing Arabic spoken but this one word has its effect and Miltos is offered a lower price. An elbow digs in his back and his anger is ignited for a second time.

'Anna aihmab?' He might have said it wrong but he thinks he has just asked the teller if he thinks him a fool. The teller now looks fearful and hands over the tickets, asking for a very modest sum. Miltos pays and then turns to face the sea of people; he is given a relatively easy passage to the door, with

annoyed muttering following him as he goes. Outside, the hot, still air is refreshing by comparison. The decision is already made; there is no way that he will be buying the tickets on their return. He has already done the maths, and even with the cheap price he has negotiated and with the price he intends to charge the clients, he will not make enough to justify such an unpleasant experience.

Back at the bus Josh is still asleep, but there is movement by the ferry. In the back of the minibus Skinner is awake and shaking James and Bryce, who yawn and open bleary eyes. The girls stretch and Grace takes her book, which was laid over her face to keep out light and flies, and closes it.

During the process of getting onto the ferry, their passports and visa stamps are inspected no fewer than five times, but at least they are allowed to board first, before the locals, so for a brief moment they have an empty ferry to themselves. For Miltos, the relief is energising.

They find a place to sit and then they wait. The boat is meant to have left half an hour ago but still people are pouring on. After another hour's wait they are underway and it seems, from the whoops of joy and general uplift in mood, that this is an unexpectedly quick departure. The crossing itself takes just over an hour on tranquil seas, and with the sun lowering the sky is now tinged with pale yellow and pink at the horizon.

The calm is broken as they dock in Jordan, and then the process of boarding is reversed as they all stampede off. Again, the heat takes Miltos by surprise, even though the sun is sinking, and he makes a note to buy a hat. The line of people in front of him filters through passport control, all visas being checked again. As they draw close to the uniformed officials he finds Skinner is by his side.

'Oh, hold this man, my shoelace has come undone,' he says, and holds out his pouch, on a belt that is usually around his waist. 'Don't lose it, man, all my wealth is in there,' and he crouches to tie his lace. 'I'll catch you up,' he adds when he sees Miltos waiting, trying to hold his ground against the force of the crowd.

It is easier to move with them than to stand still, so Miltos allows himself to be swept through passport control and waits on the other side. The group come through in ones and twos and reunite around Josh, who leads them to a yellow van with a very happy man smiling away in the driver's seat. He has one arm leaning on the open window, his other hand resting on the wheel.

'This is Khaled,' Josh says, and they climb aboard.

'Where's the pouch, man?' Bryce asks Skinner.

'Oh yeah, can I have my belt, man?' Skinner says to Miltos.

Miltos hands over the money belt, at which point Josh shakes his head and looks at him as if he has done something very wrong.

The look dries his throat and he feels distinctly uncomfortable.

Chapter 28

The Orient Hotel, if Miltos's memory serves him correctly, is just a short distance from the narrow, dusty path that makes its way through the canyon to Petra – the Rose City. On the side of the path there used to be a man selling water from a cart at inflated prices. The last place to buy a drink before the mile-long trek through the canyon, he would warn.

Now, the way is lined with new shops and hotels, and there is even a visitor's centre. Miltos looks around, half expecting to see the skinny dog that sat in the shade and scratched at fleas, but the road has been paved now, and there are no dogs. When he was here last he set out early and the shadows kept him cool – he seems to recall that there were very few areas further in where the sun was unavoidable. But even so, the air was hot and the walk was long and some of it was at quite an incline. That cannot have changed.

The bus pulls into the hotel's car park as the sun casts its last rays upon the day. The hotel appears to be only partly completed, as though the builders got as far as laying the concrete blocks that make up the walls and then cleared up their mess, packed up and moved on. The walls have been neither rendered nor painted and the ground outside is no more than compacted dust. The owner hurries out, eager to greet them and seemingly unaware that his establishment is little more than a concrete shell. He bustles them inside, along corridors with tiled floors and no windows, to a variety of rooms where the beds are made up with cheap red-and-blue chequered sheets, and the cabinets are topped with vases of plastic flowers in faded tones. On closer inspection, it appears that these are lightly covered in dust; blowing the dust off reveals vibrant colours beneath.

Skinner, James and Bryce dump their bags in one room and themselves on the beds, leaving the door wide open. Miltos's and Josh's room is across the corridor, and the girls are taken further into the darkened building. Miltos flings himself onto his own bed and watches across the corridor as James takes from Skinner's pouch his illegal herbal tobacco and the paraphernalia to roll it into a cigarette.

'Whatever possessed you?' Josh flings his own bag in a corner. 'Do you know the laws for bringing that stuff into this country? They still have the death penalty here, you know?'

'I can't believe he did that to me!' Miltos stammers.

'What did you think? That he needed to tie a lace that was already tied? Come on, man, you are not that naive.' Josh seems genuinely annoyed at him. 'Can you imagine how that would have reflected on the camp? They would investigate all of us,' he says, looking shifty.

'Don't call me naive,' Miltos barks, and he slams the door shut. 'If I have to look at that little halfwit rolling his herbs after what he did to me, I might go across there and do something to him I would regret.'

'Er, I wouldn't do that, man,' says Josh, looking Miltos up and down. The inference is clear: Skinner is tall and muscular, and, although Miltos is also well built, Josh does not fancy his chances in a fight between the two of them.

'Surely you knew he was up to something when he asked you to come with us?' Josh asks.

This hurts. As he waits for the anger to subside, Miltos watches Josh take off his boots and pour trapped sand from them into a wastepaper bin in the corner of the room. The bin is made of wicker basketwork and the sand spills out through the holes to form small hills on the tiled floor. Miltos studies the expression on Josh's face. The tanned young Australian is intent on draining the desert from his boots and it is very clear he is not joking.

For Miltos, the offence lingers; in his heart he is wounded. A pain goes across his chest and, just for the briefest of moments, his bottom lip quivers. He has always prided himself on letting other people's behaviour, no matter how personally directed, or how hurtful, slide past him like water off a duck's back, and this reaction takes him by surprise. He quickly controls himself and his upper lip curls into a sneer. He could be back at camp, taking a day's rest, in the peace of the empty compound. Instead, he is sharing a room with this arrogant stranger, on a lumpy bed with cheap ruched cotton sheets, with a day in the blazing heat to look forward to, as well as the uncomfortable and prolonged return journey. And all for what? Because his ego got a little boost from being asked by the young and oh-so-effortlessly-trendy Skinner to go with them?

What an old fool he is.

He is not sure whom he is angrier with, Skinner or himself. But more than that, he wants to know why Skinner chose him? Why not Grace, Virginia – or even Josh? He swings his legs off the bed and flings the door open, digging the handle into the wall behind it, indenting the hollow that is already there a little deeper. The aroma of the weed fills the windowless corridor but there is no one around to mind, except him. Their door is half-closed now, and with a nudge of his toe it swings open. The window is open and the evening air brings with it the smell of spices cooking. This does not mix well with the remaining stale herbal fug.

'So why me?' he demands. 'Why the hell did you choose me as your possible sacrifice, me to be your drugs mule!' Miltos can see no reason not to be straight.

Skinner, Bryce and James are lying on their beds, all with their ankles crossed, Bryce with his hands interlocked on his chest, James with his

191

hanging over the edge of the bed and Skinner with his behind his head. They look up and blink like tortoises at Miltos's sudden entrance, slowly, and with no comprehension showing in the depths of their pupils.

Miltos steps to the end of Skinner's bed. 'Eh?' He does not bother to ask the question again. Skinner is grinning as if what he is saying is funny and this infuriates him. James is the weakest link, so he turns on him, kicks the leg of his bed to rattle the frame. James's eyes open a little wider at the unexpected movement.

'What?' he asks, sounding as if he genuinely didn't hear the question the first time, or he has already forgotten it.

'Why me? The pouch?' Miltos demands.

Skinner sniggers.

'No one was going to look at you?' James slurs.

'What?' Miltos frowns.

'It's true, the risk was minimal, no one was going to check you out,' Skinner drawls.

'What?' Miltos turns to Skinner.

'You were great,' Bryce adds. 'The harmless old man routine.'

'Don't worry, bro, I'll skin one up for you. Take a chill pill, man,' says Skinner, struggling to sit up, and reaching for the pouch on the bedside table.

'Better not make it too strong, man,' James drawls. Bryce seems to find this very funny, and starts to laugh uncontrollably.

Skinner says something more, but Miltos has not yet got past the description of him as a harmless old man. He looks from Bryce to James to Skinner, all sniggering. Their lithe bodies are taut under tight-fitting T-shirts, their sagging jeans with designer tears held up by expensive, cheap-looking, worn leather belts, and he suddenly feels a world away, and bile rises in his throat.

'I would never have done such a dreadful thing ...' He is about to add 'in my day', but already the beginning of his sentence has James muffling a giggle and the gulf between them opens into a chasm, and in that divide arises a pride. Pride that he is himself, that he is not one of them, that he is not of their generation. Pride that his generation at least has a smattering of integrity. His lower lip pushes up into his curled upper lip and he narrows his eyes and looks at each of them in turn, condemning them for being who they are, and cursing them for playing with his life with such flippancy and disregard. His disdain churns acid in his stomach and when he can no longer bear to look at them he turns on his heel and walks out and along the corridors, eager to get away from the boys and Josh.

Downstairs, through a doorway opposite the unmanned reception desk, is a small room with a dark wooden bar at one end. It looks distinctly out of place in Jordan, more like something that he might have found in London thirty years ago, or maybe even in one of the smaller bars in Astoria a while back: all brown wood, and dingy. But, of course, what is most surprising is that it exists at all in a Muslim country.

Khaled is behind the bar, smiling, one hand resting on a beer pump and the other on a bottle of something as he talks to his only customer – Virginia, in her white blouse. Miltos stops in his tracks. A drink would be nice, but he is not in the mood to flirt or even converse with a woman.

'Sir, what can I get you?' Khaled flashes a grin, showing a mouthful of teeth. Virginia turns and smiles, and this helps his dented ego a little, but he would still be better off alone right now.

'Let me buy you a drink. A real alcoholic drink,' she says, and she pats the bar stool next to hers.

If he could think of an excuse, he would. He stands without moving, racking his brain, but nothing will come.

'You are Greek, right, so how about a metaxa? Do you have any metaxa, Khaled?'

'Ah, such a shame, no metaxa, but we have beer.' He nods his head vigorously.

'What happened to the law of Islam?' Miltos strikes out. 'Has no one any integrity around here?'

'It is not such a strong beer, but very refreshing.' Khaled's smile remains intact and from under the counter he produces a can with Arabic words printed on its shiny metal surface. Miltos steps forward to look at this anomaly more closely, and sure enough it has been produced and canned in Jordan. He shakes his head in disbelief and scorn, but he cracks it open anyway and takes a long hard pull of the cold and slightly fizzy liquid.

'Horrible, isn't it?' Virginia says. Hers is in a glass with ice cubes.

'It's not the best,' he admits, but he drains the can. Before he has replaced it on the bar top Khaled has produced another, and without a thought Miltos snaps the ring pull and drinks again. The beer has the desired effect and Skinner and his little boy cronies no longer have the impact they did ten minutes ago.

'So, are you tempting fate, or did you run out of clean T-shirts?' He allows his finger to touch the hem of the short sleeve of her white embroidered shirt, inviting her to recall their last conversation.

'Well, it did occur to me that I could do with a bit of wisdom in my life.' She lets her eyelids flutter a little. The obviousness of the gesture highlights just how young she is.

Chapter 29

It is tempting to flirt back, and it would be familiar ground, somewhere that feels safe. Her youth would make it so easy to impress her. He had guessed at mid-thirties, but now he is talking to her, looking at her up close, he sees she could be even younger than that. She is a good twenty years his junior. A touch of guilt flits through Miltos's heart. Would releasing his well-practised charm on her make him any different to Skinner and his gang, who took advantage of his naivety, his stupidity, his own subconscious need to be accepted, for their own ends? Not really. Both their actions and his, if he chooses to flirt with Virginia, are a form of manipulation of another person for personal gain.

'Well, that depends on what you call wisdom.' He answers her seriously but does not meet her proffered gaze. Instead he looks at the bottle in his hand.

The beer might taste better cold, in a glass with ice cubes, but Khaled has left the bar area and is arranging the room keys on the board behind the reception desk. The hotel owner is whistling a

Western song and seems to be in a world of his own. Miltos chooses not to disturb him.

'Oh, I think wisdom comes from experience – maybe we call people wise when they have knowledge others don't possess? Something that can only be gained with time and age.' She uncrosses her legs and crosses them the other way. Miltos is reminded of a film he once saw, in which the protagonist used this same movement to distract the policemen who were questioning her. It does not distract him. If anything, he feels a twinge of boredom. Her finger traces the rim of her glass and Miltos tries to remember the last time he saw someone behave towards him with such cheap clichéd moves. He wants to laugh, but her actions seem sad, and it would offend her, so he just smiles as if he is interested in what she is saying. Then the words she just used make their impact.

'What do you mean, "age"?' He tries to keep any edge out of his voice.

'Well, there's the thing, isn't it? My pop was about my age when he left home. Just walked out, never came back. He had the wisdom, even at that age, to realise what a loser my mom was. Yeah, wisdom.'

She gazes out of the window into the darkening night. 'It took me twenty years to catch up with him and realise that there was no saving that woman, and I was damned if I was going to go down with her. I tried to help. Oh, believe me, I tried. From my last year at school until the day I left her, I had a job, I earned the money to pay the rent – but in the early days I gave the money straight to her.'

She laughs – a dry, harsh, lifeless sound. 'Course, the rent never got paid. She just drank it away and we moved from neighbourhood to neighbourhood. So then I wised up, and I paid the rent direct. I bought the food direct and I tried to get her to rehab. That was my life, aged sixteen. Keeping life together and getting her to rehab.'

Virginia drinks her beer and looks around. 'Khaled?' she calls, and he scuttles around the reception counter, across the mop-streaked brown-tiled floor and, with a theatrical flourish, pulls two cans of beer from below the counter. Miltos waves his back underneath. The stuff is not nice and he has no desire to get drunk. What for?

Virginia doesn't seem to notice that she is drinking alone. Khaled leaves and she continues her story. 'I wish I had been wise enough to leave sooner, but wisdom comes with age, this is my point.'

Her words are slightly slurred and the hand that she had been using to fiddle with her room key on the bar top – number twenty-two, he notices – comes to rest on his knee.

'So …' She leans towards him, her chin down so she is looking up at him, all fluttering eyelashes. 'A little age and wisdom in my life would not go amiss.'

And there she is, half drunk, with tanned skin and shiny hair, her chin now lifted and her lips pursed ready for the old man to kiss her. He is being lured into being her lover, but what she really wants him to be is her protector and wise father. Is the offer for a night, a week, until she leaves the scuba camp? Or is she looking for more of a commitment? There is no doubting her beauty, her clear eyes and glowing, youthful skin. But where is the mystery, the experiences that have moulded her as a person, the interesting angles to her personality?

Back in that Greek village, the woman in the kiosk had a majesty about her that told of the struggles she had overcome and the depth of her character. The other woman, the one in the blue dress in the shop, had a twinkle in her eyes that told him she had learnt to be resilient in life, that she could take a tough situation and find the humour in it to keep herself buoyant. She would never be reliant on anyone. How much more attractive those attributes appear compared to a superficial beauty and a sad story.

Virginia isn't just a blank canvas. She has struggled, as she has just told him, with her mama, and no doubt with her baba. To walk out and leave her to survive and cope with a drunk mother! What a swine. But Virginia's struggles manifest themselves in her as a needy quality. She gives off the aura of someone waiting to be rescued. That was what was so intriguing about those Greek village women. They did not want rescuing; instead, they gave the impression that they wanted to play, to have a bit of fun. And thinking about it now, isn't that what has been the problem with his more recent relationships?

None of them worked on a level that allowed fun! Nearly all of them were with younger women, and they all wanted to be rescued, one way or another.

Take Lana from Iceland, whom he had met on a plane some ten, maybe fifteen years ago now. The plane was delayed five hours so it was natural that they talked to each other, and she had given all the appearance of being independent: she owned a business that involved international travel and was financially independent. But she was an only child and it was not long into the relationship before it became apparent that she wanted to be rescued from her loneliness and a future in which she imagined herself left on the shelf, a carer to her elderly parents. Kim from England, on the other hand, was really searching for financial rescue. Her credit cards were maxed out, and she was on the run from rent she owed. How was it possible to run up so much debt on credit cards? That's right – hadn't she been using new ones to pay off old ones? What she originally owed had tripled, she said, from the interest that she could not pay. He had done what he could, but he could not change her exuberant nature. Kim would likely always be in debt, and he left her, knowing it was pointless to stay – he could not change her.

But those village women! The more he thinks of them, the more he wishes he was there with them now, flirting with one, then the other. Who knows, maybe one of them could be "the one". With this thought, he is taken back over thirty years to Saros, to his first love. How sure his emotions had been, intensified by the threat of military service looming in the near future. It makes him sigh, and his sigh becomes a yawn.

'Well, I'll tell you what is missing in my life right now,' Miltos says, easing off the bar stool, slowly enough for her to retract her hand without embarrassment. She looks at him with eager anticipation. 'Sleep,' he concludes, and with a touch of his finger under her chin he walks out of the bar.

'Oh sir, sir, your name for the bar bill?' Khaled is quick to ask as he passes the reception.

'Skinner,' says Miltos without hesitation. 'Room fourteen. And put the girl's beers on my tab too.'

Chapter 30

The sun shines through the flimsy, coarse weave of the hotel's curtains and Miltos rolls over to see that Josh's bed is empty. He levers himself over the edge of his own mattress, letting his spine straighten as his feet hit the cold tiles. With a yawn and a stretch, it occurs to him that if they are to see all of Petra they should have set off before the sun was even over the horizon. Immediately after this conscious thought comes a heaviness that he recognises as boredom. It is a sensation that was not there the last time he visited this part of the world and it catches him by surprise.

He blinks and rubs the palm of his hand across his face. The nearest bathroom is down the hall, by the girls' room. After pulling on his trousers and shirt, he steps out of the natural light in his room into the dimly lit, windowless corridor and pads to the open door. Just as he reaches the bathroom and the smell of chlorine hits him he sees Josh come out of another door, along the corridor, closing it gently behind him. Room twenty-two.

He sighs. He is not so much disheartened by her fickle nature, but, rather, experiencing a general disappointment, not only for Virginia but also for Josh, Skinner and his buddies, for all of the younger generation who are so busy grabbing at the thrills and spills close at hand that there is no discrimination. They will take whatever is offered, whatever is available. Surely there is no pride in that?

As he releases the cheap beer of the previous evening and then swills his face in tepid tap water, he is almost at the point of just walking away, leaving this group to itself. The boredom has grown into a disillusionment, and everything he is doing, the whole reason for his journey here, seems shallow and futile. But despite the urge to abandon this path, his own sense of decency dictates that he must complete this trip, at least – ensure that everyone gets back to camp safely. He must play the part he has agreed to, even if he has no respect for the others.

Back in their room, Josh is spraying aftershave into his unwashed armpits. He is grinning to himself and casts a sly glance at Miltos, obviously waiting for his roommate to ask where he was the night before so he can spill out the details of his conquest. Miltos is not sure who he feels more pity for – Virginia or Josh.

'We should have set out earlier,' he says. 'It will be past midday by the time we reach the Temple of Dushares, and it's a hard uphill walk to the monastery. It will be too hot.'

Josh is stuffing things into his bag, his grin gone now as the reality of his role for the day is brought into focus.

It's another hour before they set off, and as soon as they reach the visitors centre their pace slows and they lose first one and then another of the group into the shops there. Burdened with cheap keepsakes, they finally enter the canyon, but here, even in this late hour of the morning, they are in shade. The canyon walls are so high and they are like ants following the trail.

Miltos breathes a sigh at the sense of freedom that the huge rock walls on either side give him. It is the boldness and magnitude of nature that has this effect on him, like the sea, and like the plain of orange groves outside Saros, around that little village in Greece. The canyon echoes the childish calls and shouts of Skinner and his friends. They catch up with and overtake other groups of tourists who are walking the same way, some of whom are stopping to photograph every rock, others just struggling to walk in the heat, rolling from foot to foot and wiping sweat from dripping brows. They are easy prey for the local men who are leading their camels and offering rides. Miltos anticipates the first glimpse of the Treasury, the first and most impressive of the facades that have been dug out of the rose-coloured sandstone. So large, so grand, it took his breath away when he first saw it.

Another curve of the path and then, there it is! A slice of ancient wonder visible between the high canyon walls. Startlingly bright in the sun after the shadow of the canyon. It is larger than he remembered it, the edges of the carved pillars and doors sharper than his recollection. It towers regally above them.

'Oh yeah, got to get a picture of me with that!' Rose exclaims. Grace is a little apart from the rest of the group, her nose in her guidebook. Jess has glanced briefly at the incredible facade and is now petting one of the camels. At least Josh is staring at the sight before them: four tall columns, carved to give the impression that they are supporting the ornate triangular lintel that is one with the rock. The doorway is set back and it is possible to walk behind the central columns into the cool, dark interior. The last time he was here, Miltos expected the grandeur to continue inside the carved monolith and was a little disappointed to find there was nothing more than a small, unremarkable chamber beyond the entrance. The stone itself, however, is a beautiful mix of colours – pink, purple, maroon, in stripes where the different strata were laid one on top of another.

He wants to remark on the age of the sculptured stone, the design of the architecture, the magnificence of the location, and he moves towards Josh a little to make him his confidant.

'Got any painkillers?' Josh may be facing the Treasury but his eyes are glazed. 'I have the hangover from hell.' He swallows and his Adam's apple bobs.

Miltos steps away to find that Grace is staring at him. She colours as their eyes meet and then she looks down at her book.

Is it so much to ask to have someone to share this with? Someone who understands the history of these remarkable carved buildings, someone who can appreciate the architecture, the stone, the stunning location?

With this thought, he steps away from the group and continues his discoveries by himself.

Chapter 31

'So, what you are saying is that they left you?' The taxi driver's right hand rests idly on the wheel, and he appears to be paying remarkably little attention to the road ahead. Bouzouki music plays softly on the radio, and the scent of pine trees and dust drift in through the open windows. In a couple of hours they will be in the Peloponnese, and then in Saros. The taxi driver offers a cigarette to Miltos, who shakes his head, and then lights one for himself, during which operation both hands leave the wheel. Miltos is glad that the road is empty of other cars.

'Yes,' he confirms, looking out at the olive trees that stretch away towards the hills on one side. On the other side is the sea, shining, sparkling, darkly blue and promising adventure.

The relief at being back in Greece is greater than he expected. In the hospital bed in Jordan he became obsessed by the idea of returning home, and it shocked him to realise that he felt this way. Even though he had been born in Greece and lived there for the first twenty years of his life, it made no sense: given that his numerous adventures and escapades had been spread across so many locations, why decide Greece was home? Was it just because he was born there, or was there something more about the country?

'*Aman*!' the taxi driver exclaims. 'So how long were you in the hospital?'

'Only a few days. They wanted to keep me in for two weeks, in case I had a reaction to the antivenom.'

The taxi is an expensive indulgence but his priorities have shifted to such a degree that getting back to the village speedily seems more important than anything.

'Did this Skinner man not even thank you?' The taxi driver asks.

Miltos grunts his answer. 'They got me back down the track to the visitor's centre, and by then I was shaking and my arm was numb so they called an ambulance. Some man said to keep my hand below my heart and to take slow breaths, so I was concentrating on that – you know, to stop the venom working its way through my system.'

'Scorpion stings are common out there then?'

Miltos begins to wish he had not started telling his tale, which is diverting the driver's attention from the road again. 'I don't think so. The locals, and the hospital, seemed pretty surprised.'

The car veers slowly from one lane to the next; even so, Miltos's thoughts drift back to Petra in Jordan.

Skinner seemed to be in so much pain, his ankle wedged at an awkward angle after his fall. Miltos had already warned him that it was an unsuitable place to run about – there was so much loose rock that far off the track – but there had been no stopping him and Bryce once they understood that the monastery was the highest and last of the carved facades. Their youthful energy needed an outlet and off they ran, and Skinner fell, wedging his ankle between two rocks and twisting it badly.

Bryce raised the alarm but he seemed to go into a sort of panic, in which he was unable to process the situation in front of him. All he needed to do was lift the rock so that Skinner's ankle was released, but instead he just stood there with his mouth open and a blank expression. Miltos did not hesitate, thrusting his hands under the rock and lifting it clear. Skinner eased his foot out and sighed with relief, but there was no word of thanks.

As he released the rock, Miltos felt the sting like a hammer blow; he withdrew his hand quickly and saw the red mark. It is funny how some things you just know; even though he did not see the creature, he knew what had happened.

Initially it caused him no alarm. Most scorpions are not very harmful, he had once read. So they started the walk back down the track from the monastery with everyone's attention focused on Skinner, who demanded support, mostly from the girls. Miltos had expected the red mark on his hand to have stopped stinging by the time they got to the visitors centre, but instead the inflamed area had grown, he was sweating, his arm was tingling and his tongue had started to feel numb.

'Well, thank goodness they knew what to do, eh?' The taxi driver makes a last-minute swerve around a slow truck and Miltos grips the dashboard.

'Come on, man, I don't want to survive a scorpion sting only to be killed in a road crash.'

The taxi driver stares intently through the windscreen, both hands on the wheel, and Miltos decides he will not tell him any more details. The story is distracting him. They continue the journey in silence but his mind is replaying the conversation he had as he was being loaded into the ambulance.

'You never said there were scorpions.' Jess was holding onto Rose's arm as if it was she who was bitten, Virginia looking on.

'They are mostly harmless,' Josh said with authority.

'Well, that's not the case, is it, else we would not be watching him being loaded into an ambulance?' Virginia pointed out.

'Well, of course the old and the young are vulnerable.' Josh stated, waving his hand in Miltos's direction. 'People our age wouldn't be bothered by such a bite,' Josh concluded.

Josh and Grace had gone to the hospital with him, and of the two Grace had seemed more concerned. But nothing much was happening after the first antivenom injection, and neither of them stayed once the minutes turned to boring hours.

Josh mumbled something about visas expiring and patted Miltos awkwardly on his shoulder. 'Here's my number, man,' he said, 'and you know I would stay if I could, but the guys are already complaining that they've paid for a diving holiday. You know how it is, bro, but here's my number, and call me if you need anything.'

He had twittered on for a while, and Grace had nodded her agreement but she looked tired. Her compassion was exhausted and he had given her nothing in return, not even a smile.

It was the same in the hospital, where the younger nurses were over-sympathetic and talked at him more loudly than was necessary and then, moments later, just a short distance away at the nurse's station, they spoke to each other about him as if he could not hear.

So he lay there in that alien bed waiting for the antivenom to take effect, for some sensation to return to his arm, for the swelling in his hand to go down. For a while he watched the nurses, compared the room to the hospital he was in when he broke his collarbone climbing. But this time he had no visitors, nor any clinging women wanting his attention. He was alone.

Lying there for hour upon hour, time was the only thing he had. The day drifted into the night, and finally, almost through boredom, he used the hours to face the chasm between himself and people like

211

Josh or Skinner. This naturally led him to contemplate the fact that he was over fifty, which in turn led to the harsh shock of realising how little he had to show for the years he had been alive. Nothing except a heap of memories that he had churned out to entertain people so many times they had lost their vibrancy and become stagnant snippets of his glory days. He had nothing of material value, but, worse than that, he had no friends – not a single person he had kept in touch with over the years, no one who had witnessed his life. This awareness crushed him, because he realised that the free spirit he had always prided himself on had reduced his life to such a state that if he did die of a scorpion bite … Well, first of all no one would know, but more importantly no one would care.

He discharged himself the next day, following a sleepless night chewing over these revelations. The course of antivenom had finished and it felt like it was working. He comforted himself with the knowledge that if he lived to be ninety, which seemed like a reasonable estimate, then he had forty years of life left, and he resolved to make better use of them.

That was when he knew he wanted to return to Saros, and to the small village with the woman in the kiosk and the woman in the blue dress in the corner shop. It was time to do the one thing that terrified him. It was time to settle down and stay in one place. With this decision came a calm, a peace, as if he were underwater and his limbs were loose and nature was surrounding him like a blanket, tucking him in and keeping him safe.

Chapter 32

'Are you sure you want to walk from here?' The taxi has stopped at the edge of the village.

'Thank you.' Miltos pays the man and watches as he pulls away, mounts the kerb, overcorrects and drives on the wrong side of the road for some distance.

Maybe he should get a taxi licence? After all, he can drive better than that!

He rubs at his hand, which is still a little swollen, and with his small bag over his shoulder he passes the brightly coloured railings around the infant school, suddenly nervous, doubting his earlier resolve as he heads up the street that leads to the square.

'So, Milto,' he says to himself under his breath. 'This is home. Where you will let life wash over you, let your branches bend with the wind but keep your trunk strong and encourage your roots to grow. A job and a house will come. It always has, only this time you are playing for keeps.' The thought both thrills and terrifies him.

Single-storey whitewashed cottages line the road on either side, and from the one with pale grey-blue shutters, he can hear the sounds of an acoustic guitar. Perhaps it is Sakis; he relishes the fact that already he has some history in the place, some knowledge, even if it is very little. He can see the kiosk up ahead now, and for the first time he wonders if either of the women who have so occupied his thoughts recently is married. The one in the kiosk was wearing black, so she could be a widow, but the other had a blue dress on. Perhaps her husband is still alive. That would be a shame.

He immediately rebukes himself for such a selfish thought, but cannot help feeling a little disappointed. On the plane from Sharm el-Sheikh he found himself dwelling more on her than on the woman in the kiosk.

As he approaches the square, the thought creeps up on him that he has no plan – not as such, not about what to actually do next. He has presumed he will spend the first night at Stella's hotel, where he stayed before, in the same room if possible, but who knows what tomorrow will bring? The narrow entrance of the sandwich shop on the left is closed, but the eatery on the right is open and his stomach growls. His flight this morning left before breakfast and the hours have spun away since. Did he eat on the plane? Some nuts, perhaps; he cannot remember. The noises from his stomach are too loud to be ignored. He will have a plate of something and sit and contemplate this village that he is to call home.

Out on the pavement, under a thin tree whose trunk and branches are wrapped in fairy lights, is the choice table. As he sits down, he can hear talking and laughing inside, but for now he wants to be on the pavement, to take stock of everything and feel the pace of the place. The pharmacy on the corner is shut, but there is a light on in the upstairs window. The bakery opposite looks dark both downstairs and up. No doubt they will have an early start, and they might be in bed already, even though the sun has not quite set. There is a pinkish glow to the houses and everything is softened in the gentle early evening light. The *kafenio* at the top of the square seems fairly busy, with the chairs out on the square itself facing a large flatscreen television that is propped up on a table against the floor-to-ceiling windows. Adverts are showing and the men are chatting, but soon the football is on again and their attention is regained. Tomorrow he will have a morning coffee there, get the feel of who is who, see if anyone wants a worker, ask around about a room to rent, maybe.

'What can I get you?' A slight woman with thin legs, wearing a sleeveless floral dress, appears by his side. She seems familiar. Her hair is shoulder-length and he suspects its frizz comes from working over a hot grill all day.

'Chicken, sausage, chips, Greek salad. Not the greatest choice in the world, but what we have is good, hot and served with a smile.'

She rests a hand on his shoulder and he takes this as a sign that he is already accepted.

He immediately likes her and takes a longer look, trying to judge her age. Then heat rushes up his neck and into his cheeks as he catches himself slipping into this old habit.

'What is it?' she asks, 'Have I got charcoal smudges on my face again? It happens all the time.'

The woman pats self-consciously at her face and Miltos shakes his head.

'So what will it be? Or maybe you just want a drink – but you look hungry to me.'

She is lively, about his own age, a bit thin, perhaps, for his liking, but what a smile!

'*Yeia sou.*' A man with one arm saunters out from inside, wearing an apron.

'*Yeia sou,*' Miltos replies, and he watches. The man excuses the interruption and talks to the woman about ordering more charcoal with such familiar ease and such admiration in his eyes that there can be no mistake – he is in love. The way she moves her hips towards him, turns her body to face him, makes it clear that this is not a one-way romance.

The one-armed man returns inside, calling as he does to Miltos, 'You want a beer?' The way the man addresses him, it is as if he has lived here all his life and he too is part of the family.

'Oh yes, please,' he calls. 'And chicken and chips, please.' He addresses this last request to the woman.

'Okay.' She turns and is gone and he is left listening to the laughter coming from inside, the hub to the village.

'So, you are back.' The woman is quick to return and she sets a plate of food before him. 'I put lemon sauce on it. I hope you are all right with that?'

'It smells amazing.' Miltos hears the unintended surprise in his voice, and immediately feels heat in his cheeks. The impressions he makes and the relationships he develops will have long-lasting significance if he is to settle here and call this village home. This thought both excites and scares him at once.

'Couldn't stay away, eh?' The woman is fishing. He kind of likes this – at least she is showing an interest in him. His instinct is to say nothing: that has always been his way. Tell stories, keep people amused, but always stay at a distance and wind up with nothing. Well, that needs to change for a start, if he is to stay.

'No. Couldn't keep away. You know what? I've decided to make this place home.'

It sounds ridiculous. He takes up his cutlery so he does not have to meet her gaze. It is strange how vulnerable he feels knowing that he is not just going to walk away tomorrow, or the next day. But what if he cannot make it? What if it all feels too scary, too intense, and he feels compelled to run? Maybe it is his destiny to always be apart. Maybe it is something over which he has no control. He stabs at the chips with his fork, forcing his doubts to recede.

'Good a place as any,' the woman replies, organising the napkin holder and the bottles of oil and vinegar on the corner of his table. 'Best you

218

know our names then.' She pulls out a chair, uninvited, and sits down. 'I am Stella, and in there is Mitsos, my husband.'

So this is Stella. Stella of the hotel and Stella who runs the candle factory with Sakis's girlfriend. He should have realised, and now she tells him it is so obvious; here she is, running the eatery. She is much slighter than he imagined but he feels a thrill to finally meet her, as if he is meeting the mainstay of the village.

'Theo,' she continues, 'he owns the *kafenio* up there. Yes, there he is.' Stella looks across the square and nods her head at a man carrying a tray across the road. 'That man with the bouncy hair. And in the kiosk is Vasso.'

'She married?' he says before he can stop himself.

'Was. Widowed now.' Stella is just as abrupt but she is searching his face now, and a little smirk plays around her lips. She continues, but her eyes are on him and she speaks more slowly.

'In the corner shop' – he looks across to the corner shop, keenly aware of her gaze – 'that's Marina, was married, but has been widowed for many years, one son and a grandson. The baptism is this weekend. It was meant to be a while ago but the priest got ill and then the church was double-booked. But one way or another it has worked out better. So there's a baptism the day after tomorrow and a wedding the day after that.'

'Oh yes – er, what was her ... um, Ellie. From the hotel, and the barman,' says Miltos, happy to be able to add another slim connection to this place, this new home. 'They were getting married. I met them.'

'Yes, that's right. Loukas,' says Stella. 'If you are still here I guess you'll get to know everyone!' And, as abruptly as she sat, Stella now stands as someone calls her name from inside.

Chapter 33

Miltos eats slowly, savouring the food in the way that only a really hungry man can, and watches with interest the activity in the *kafenio*, outside the corner shop and by the kiosk on the square. He recognises faces from the last time he was here and the familiarity feels good. The lemon sauce is divine and the food is better than at Stella's hotel, and he makes a mental note to eat here often. Stella comes out with another beer without him having to ask and returns inside.

'Hello.' The greeting, in English, makes him start. The speaker's golden hair is striking, and he remembers her from the corner shop. 'I thought you had gone,' she says in Greek as she draws closer.

Not sure which language to use, Miltos finds he does not answer at all.

'Is Stella around?' she says, maintaining her Greek. She sounds fluent, and her accent is good, but she is obviously not Greek.

'Inside,' he says finally.

'Oh, you speak English.' Her eyebrows lift and she smiles.

'I spent some time there, and in America.'

She stops walking and stands by the tree, looking into the eatery.

'Where?' The question is in English but the directness of her delivery and the inflection are all Greek. She must have been around Greeks for a while to pick up the mannerisms. Maybe she lives here.

'*Pandou*,' he starts in Greek. 'London, Leeds, Birmingham, Glasgow, Bradford …'

'Bradford?' the woman interrupts. 'I was born there.' Her attention is no longer on the eatery.

Her hair is a mane, thick and slightly curly, and Miltos imagines she spends hours trying to tame it. Her dress is long and clings to her figure in places, but without seeming obvious or cheap. It is what his aunt would have called classic. He takes her all in with a quick, well-practised glance. Her toenails are not polished, but they are shaped and trimmed, which delights him: he likes all those little things women do to themselves. She has already slipped one of her flip-flops off and the toes of her bare foot rest on those of the other. Her attitude could pass for Greek but there is something about her that could only be English.

'Nice town,' he adds non-committally. 'Er, you want a drink? It's nicer not to eat alone.' He looks down at the remains of the chicken.

'Actually, I was looking for Stella.' She looks inside again.

'There are some fine mills in Bradford,' he says.

She gives a little laugh, easy and light. 'They're all being converted into flats now, and the town has a new energy. Business capital of the North, they call it. It was a dying town when I left.' She seems to have lost interest in finding Stella and she takes a step towards his table.

'Please.' He pulls out a chair and she sits with a grace that he hadn't expected.

'Juliet.' She offers her hand and they shake.

'Miltos. I'm pleased to meet you.'

'What were you doing in Bradford? Business?' Juliet asks.

'I suppose so, in a way.' He is reluctant to tell her that he was just wandering about, aimlessly, picking up work where he could. Perhaps it will be better to tell her a tale about something that happened to him whilst he was there. Something that will highlight his strengths, paper over his weaknesses, flatter himself in her eyes. He tries to bring something to mind but as he looks out over the village he reminds himself that it is his intention to stay. Whether he likes it or not, the villagers, including Juliet, will get to know him, warts and all. However scary or unnatural it seems, it's time to do things differently.

'Well, no, actually I was just travelling,' he says. 'I was a bit lost, perhaps.' His words sound awkward to his own ears.

'Oh,' she says.

He cannot tell if there is any judgement in her voice, but her gaze is steady and she remains leaning

223

towards him, which suggests she has not judged him negatively.

'I had come back from the Middle East and I couldn't settle,' he explains. 'I had this sort of urge to keep moving, as if I had to find something.'

'And have you found what you are looking for now?' Juliet asks, a smile playing around her mouth. Her easy manner inspires confidence.

'I've travelled much of the world looking for this thing, whatever it is, and I have come to the conclusion that either it does not exist, or it is right here under my nose and it has always been there but I cannot see it.'

'Intriguing.' She leans back now, her gaze steady. She has kicked off both flip-flops now, and her legs are outstretched, crossed at the ankles. 'So, what do you think it might be? Tell me more.'

'There is nothing to tell, really. At least, I think there is nothing to tell. I don't know exactly what it is, but I have a sense of a few of the pieces, and a feeling that if I could get them to join together it all might make sense.'

'Oh,' says Juliet, and the way she settles deeper into her chair gives the impression that she is waiting for more information.

Her responses make him feel brave, and he feels inclined to continue. In his stomach is a flutter of excitement, which feels strangely pleasant, and a thrill at doing something he would normally avoid. It feels energising, as if he is taking a risk that could reap him a big reward.

'Well, the only time I have really loved with all my heart was before I went into the army.' He speaks slowly, lazily, savouring the moment and the changes he is making, 'Since then, whenever my life feels like it might be on the wrong track I judge where I am against that love. If what I am doing fits with that love then I am doing okay. If the two feel worlds apart or if they seem opposed to one another then I know I am on the wrong track and I need to get out. Does that make sense?' He does not feel like he has expressed clearly what he is trying to say, but Juliet's attention is focused on him, and she nods as if she understands.

'Hmm, I like your thinking.' Juliet's words encourage him. She brushes her hair from her face.

'So, perhaps love is the first piece. The second is a feeling I get when I go diving, or if I walk in magnificent scenery, or study nature. It is a sort of calm, a peace that tells me all in the world is well, that the world will keep turning despite my existence and not because of it. I need to do nothing to ensure the world's continuance and it gives me such a sense of peace. So, peace is the next piece.'

'Better and better,' Juliet replies.

'Oh, *yeia sou*, Juliet.' Stella comes out. 'You want another beer?' she asks Miltos.

'Juliet, may I buy you a beer?' he asks.

'Oh yes, why not,' says Juliet, and Stella trots back inside, returning with two beer bottles but no glasses.

225

'Do you want a glass?' Miltos asks, but Stella is inside again, shaking the oil from the potatoes, banging the mesh holder against the deep fat frier.

'No, the bottle's fine.' Juliet takes a serviette from the holder and wipes around the top before drinking, as if she is well practised at swigging from a bottle, which surprises him.

'So, any more pieces?' she asks.

'Did you not want to see Stella about something?' Miltos reminds her.

'Oh no, it doesn't matter. I just needed a break from my work, and there was something I wanted to say to her but I can't remember what it was now. But never mind that – tell me, are there any more pieces?'

'Well, I don't think there are, apart from something that does not fit.'

'Ooh, what's that?'

The way she speaks makes it so easy to reply. There is warmth in her voice, as if she understands, or at least wants to understand.

'As I have said, it doesn't fit. It is something about excitement, the waiting for a pleasure to come. A waiting that can often be even more enjoyable than the experience itself.' He sighs and then takes a drink. His plate is empty, knife and fork neatly pushed together. 'But maybe that is to do with something else.'

'Humm.' Juliet rubs one foot against the other. 'So we have love and peace and anticipation. Where was the love you had before the army?'

'Here. Well, there.' He points down the road. 'In Saros.'

'Ah, so maybe what you are saying is that you have come back for her, your love, because the anticipation has been long enough, and now you want peace?'

Chapter 34

Miltos blinks and swallows hard, trying to maintain his composure, but Juliet's eyes are on him and he feels exposed. He lifts his bottle to his mouth to create a barrier between them with his arm.

'Are you from Saros then?'

She continues as if his vulnerability is not visible to her. Maybe it isn't? There is a tiny part of him that wonders if she is setting a trap to make him reveal his personal details. He blinks. But why would she do that? Is he being paranoid?

These thoughts are pushed into the background as the urge to tell her more overpowers him. Now he has started along this road he wants to continue; all he is feeling is fascinating. He is astonishing himself with how easy it is to be so open and honest.

'My mama was born in a village around here,' he begins. 'Up in the hills. It is very similar to this one.'

He stops. He has not thought of that village in years. She used to talk about it often, telling him stories at bedtime, but he has never actually been there. She had talked and talked until it became a mythical place in his mind. But it is a real place; it must have actually have been somewhere.

'And you?' Juliet's response startles him.

'Yes, er … yes,' he stammers. 'I was born in Saros. Moved to Athens when I was five, and came back when I was gone seventeen. Then I was enlisted for my national service at eighteen and I haven't been back since.'

'Ah, so you are a local.' Juliet laughs her light and easy laugh again. 'Is your family still there?'

'No, Mama died when I was almost five, and that was why we moved. My baba needed my yiayia to help with me and she lived in Athens. But then my yiayia died, and he moved back here.' He is on a roll, there is no stopping him! 'He was ill, and he didn't want to die in Athens. It happened soon after, but I was in the army so …'

He trails off now, reluctant to think about the funeral, and he hopes Juliet will not press for more details: the brief leave he was allowed, the corner plot they put his baba in, the mess of rocks that the gravedigger shovelled on top and the fact that he has never been back to erect a proper headstone. He hangs his head and looks at his feet.

'And your girl? Do we know if she is still in Saros? Married, single, divorced?' Juliet releases him from the corner plot and leads him to a more pleasant place. He accepts the invitation and looks up again.

'No, she was not from Saros town. She was visiting from a nearby village.'

229

'This one?' Juliet asks with great animation.

'You know, I'm not sure.'

'What was her name?'

'Ah.' He tips his chair back and laughs. 'Now you'll think I am making it all up! You see, I don't know her name.'

'You loved her from afar? How romantic!' Juliet sits up a little, puts her elbows on the table, interlocks her fingers and rests her chin to look at him.

'Actually, we got pretty close, but, well, names, they did not matter.'

Juliet lifts her head abruptly.

'What?' he asks, laughing again, lightly, easily.

'I think I know who she is – or, well, actually, I think she may be one of two people. Oh, how exciting.'

'How can you know who she is?' He sits more erect.

'It came up in a conversation. Two of my friends here in the village had true loves, but I don't know if I can tell you. One of them at least keeps it a secret.'

'If it helps' – he pushes his plate to one side and mirrors Juliet's position, leaning towards her – 'I am very good at keeping secrets. After all, who would I tell? And isn't it half my secret as well?'

'No, it would not be right, but maybe I can tell you about the other one. She had a lover, before she was married, and everyone cannot help but know because ...' Juliet suddenly shuts her mouth and turns red.

'Are you all right?' He leans towards her, touches her forearm.

'Yes, yes ...' Juliet is stammering. 'Just, well, no one expects an old lover to come wandering back, do they? I was just wondering how either of them would feel if you really were him.' She looks across to the corner shop; her cheeks are flaming red and she is blinking rapidly.

'Are they single?'

'Neither of them has a partner.' Juliet's pupils have gone very wide and dark and she turns to stare at him like a hare caught in a torch beam.

'Can you tell me the name of the one you think it might be all right to tell about?'

'I could, only now I am not sure.' She murmurs the name under her breath, but he cannot make it out. 'But it might not be her, there is another possibility.' Juliet exhales.

'And you don't think she would want you to tell me?'

'Well, like I said, I am not sure it would be right to tell you.' Juliet looks away, towards the kiosk.

'What harm would it do?'

'Well, she has kept it a secret from all the village.'

'Not all the village. You know.'

'True, but – well, I don't think she would want it to be common knowledge.'

'But the first woman, you could tell me who she is?'

Juliet looks up to the corner shop. Miltos follows her gaze.

'Is that a clue, the corner shop?' he asks.

Juliet looks away sharply and picks up her beer.

'The woman in the blue dress?' Miltos leans back in his chair again and takes a drink from his bottle.

'Phew, it has calmed down in there. They always seem to want their food at the same time. How are you guys doing? Do we need more beer?' Stella comes out wiping her hands on her apron, but stops when she sees Juliet's face. 'You all right?' she asks.

Miltos puts his hand on his chest to try to calm his racing heart. It was one thing telling Juliet his story, revealing his love, but the direction things have gone in is quite another. And now here is Stella. He does not want the whole village to know his business. He should never have started this conversation. If Juliet says one word he will run, just as he has always run when emotions get too high.

And with this realisation, his dreams of staying in the village evaporate and, already, he finds himself going through a mental list of where he will go to look for work next. Perhaps he should go to England; it has been a while since he was last there. He has distant cousins with a restaurant in Bradford.

'I am fine.' Juliet responds to Stella's question and the colour in her cheeks begins to subside. 'Just chatting.'

But she says no more, says nothing about his lost lover, does not mention that his family are from around here. His relief is expressed in a big exhalation of breath.

'Does that big sigh mean that you have had enough? I have more chips ready if you want them?' Stella says.

'No, I am fine, thank you. Just fine.'

'Miltos is thinking of staying in the village. You know, to live,' Juliet says.

'Yes, he said. I told him it is as good a place as any.' Stella picks up his empty plate.

'I think for him it might be the best place of all,' Juliet replies, looking him in the eye, and then she stands. 'I'd better get back and finish off the translation I was working on. I only came down here for a break. Now, what was I going to say to you, Stella? Oh yes …!'

It seems Juliet has many jobs, and one of them is teaching Greek at the hotel. She tells Stella that tomorrow's lesson is cancelled, unless new clients arrive, as her last student left today. Stella asks her to stop by for coffee and a chat and they both agree that would be nice.

Miltos takes out his wallet to pay.

'Can I walk you home?' he asks Juliet quietly.

'I only live round the corner,' she says.

'I will walk you to the corner then.' He hands Stella a note and waves away the change she offers. Then he and Juliet take the first slow steps to the corner.

Chapter 35

'So, Marina, eh?' he says, looking over at the corner shop. The unshaded bulb inside the Aladdin's cave of household goods glows orange. Its light seeps out through the window and door, casting long orange rugs across the road to the square to meet the white splashes of harsher light being thrown out of the *kafenio*.

'But maybe not,' Juliet says quickly, and she glances at the kiosk.

'And the other person – you feel you really cannot tell me?'

'I must have a word with her first, you understand? Also, I am not so happy that I have told you about Marina.'

'Well, you didn't, not really. I guessed,' he answers, and the tension he often holds across his shoulders relaxes a little. If she is discreet one way she will be discreet another. He may not know all he wants but she will not tell all his secrets either. He concludes she is a trustworthy person.

'So, I will wish you a good night,' Juliet says. 'Perhaps it would be best for me to have a quiet word with Marina too, you know, before you talk to her. Smooth the way as it were, clear the path, prepare her for any possible shocks.' It is said lightly, with a giggle at the end.

He can tell that she wishes she had never mentioned Marina. If his meeting with Marina were to go wrong, she might blame herself. Well, he is fine with waiting. It will be easy for him to do nothing – after all, that seems to be what he is best at. But it is delicious to know that Marina could have been his love. So warming to think that the shy young girl might have grown into the curvy woman that Marina is today, with the mischievous glint in her eyes.

'Perhaps, if you feel it is right, you could have a word with the other lady too?'

'If the right situation arises,' Juliet replies.

'I understand.' They shake hands again and then give the customary kiss on either cheek and wish each other a good night.

As he walks away he is not sure if it was he or she who lingered slightly on the second kiss, or indeed if it was his imagination. He turns to look at her once more but she has turned the corner.

To go to the hotel he will have to pass through the square again. He could have a coffee at the *kafenio*. He could be really naughty and go into the corner shop and buy something, although he is not sure what. But that would not be fair to Juliet, and he promised, so he must wait. There is time for all of that.

What he needs to do is think about work and a place to live. The buses into Saros, he has gathered, are very infrequent. Maybe he should hire a car for a day or two so he can get into the town when he likes. There will surely be a better chance of finding work in Saros.

'So, that's a decision then?' he says to himself. 'An early night and then in the morning hire a car from Aleko and start looking for work in Saros.'

He heads for the hotel.

Waking in the same room he stayed in before gives him a further sense that he is home. He stretches his limbs before sitting up, and then he pads to the bathroom, where he lets the hot water run over his face and down his shoulders, using a whole mini-bottle of shampoo in one palmful. The flow of water slowly restores his senses, and he recalls his conversation with Juliet.

'Marina!' He greets the morning with the word. Wrapped in a towel, he goes back through to the bedroom and catches sight of himself in the dressing table mirror. He sucks in his stomach and tenses his muscles. There is still evidence of a six-pack, and his biceps are tight and lean. He still has it! He relaxes his tense muscles and his skin hangs a little soft in places. Of his chest hairs, one or two are white. He runs his hands through his thick hair, trying to smooth away the grey at the temples. Then he smiles, and his reflection reminds him that life is what you make it: finding joy, being grateful, making others happy, and now, his own personal quest – finding love.

'So Milto, welcome to the first day of the rest of your life! Now everything is different. You must stay open for things to come to you and you must not, on any condition, run, okay?'

He nods at the mirror. 'Okay,' he confirms.

Aleko is not surprised to see him.

'Life has stopped surprising me now,' he says. 'I gave up being surprised when my wife had triplets five years ago at the age of forty!' He laughs and hands over the car keys to Miltos.

'*Po, po, po*! Triplets!' Miltos exclaims, and he looks critically at the rusty vehicle that Aleko has assured him is safe, and reflects that at least the rental rate is cheap.

He only gets as far as the square before he notices the engine temperature is rising too rapidly. It would probably be wise to take a bottle of water with him, just in case the radiator is leaking. But for the meagre sum Aleko has charged, even if the car only takes him one way and stops working he will have saved money over taking the bus! Mostly he thinks Aleko just wanted it out of his yard, to give himself some room.

'*Kalimera!*' he greets Vasso in the kiosk.

'And a good morning to you too. Is that Aleko's old car?'

'Just borrowed it to go into Saros.'

'You are going now?'

'Yes.' Miltos smiles, the day is warm, the sun is bright, all is well with the world.

'Good.' She picks up the telephone receiver and dials. 'You wait, I'll come,' she says to him and then turns her back, talking rapidly into the telephone.

When she has finished she turns back. 'Right. Your change.' She starts to count out coins and as she does so a young man, lithe, runs with little effort from the house by the side of the kiosk.

'Ah, Petro, I will only be an hour or two. I am going to the market in Saros.' With no further exchange she comes out of her wooden hut and Petros takes her place. She tidies the magazines as she passes, and the empty bottles that have been left by the drinks fridge. Petros sits slumped inside the kiosk and takes out his phone, holding it with both hands. His thumbs start working and soon he is lost in his digital world. Vasso turns to Miltos and points at the car.

'Right, let's go,' she says. 'You will be coming back, yes?' She has given him no choice but he is not in the least put out by her presumption. A little amused, perhaps – and he looks with fresh eyes at this woman who can ask directly for what she wants. They climb in the car.

'Maybe you can help carry some bags.' She is smiling now and patting her hair. The coy looks she gives him tells him she is playing a game, pretending she is still young enough to flirt in such an obvious way, asking him to carry her bags. It makes him smile.

She drops the pretence just as quickly as she adopted it. 'Ach, you men, you will do as you like.' And she smiles to show she forgives him anyway. The smile is accompanied with a light tap on his knee. 'But if you have a muscle to spare,' she says, eyeing his biceps, 'which you clearly do, then you can help if you like.'

She rests her hands in her lap and looks out of the windscreen and nods, indicating that the journey may begin.

Miltos grins and tightens his biceps as he puts the car in gear.

Chapter 36

The orange trees are a blur as the two of them speed their way to Saros. The car splutters once or twice on the way, and the exhaust backfires, making them both jump and laugh, but they arrive in one piece and Miltos finds a shady tree to park under by the *laiki* – the farmer's market.

The market stalls themselves are lined up on either side of a main road in Saros town, which is closed to traffic for the morning. Each stall has its own tarpaulin roof of white, faded orange or pale green. Cars are parked adjacent to the road, on a patch of disused ground where the old train tracks still run, and self-seeded pine trees tower overhead, providing welcome shade.

From the car, the two of them can hear shouts and banter from the stallholders and shoppers alike. Miltos holds the door open and waits whilst Vasso takes her time to adjust her hair in the mirror. She accepts the hand he offers, stepping out gracefully. She is lighter on her feet than he expects and he makes a quick visual reassessement. She is a large-busted woman with good legs and shapely ankles. He catches himself and looks away before she notices. She thrusts at him a bundle of plastic bags that she has brought with her, and she leads the way amongst the stalls that are piled high with mountains of colourful fruit and vegetables. He accepts the role with some amusement and follows dutifully in her wake, watching her as she goes. She walks tall, and the way she moves is lovely to see.

The throng of people closes around them, and the sound of the stallholders calling out their prices and describing the exceptional quality of their wares dominates the general hum, which resonates under the canvas-covered stalls. Vasso, now almost lost in the colourful jostle of people, stops at a table that is piled high with tomatoes. Miltos follows, trying to keep up, watching her mannerisms. She picks up one tomato and her fingers make an impression on the surface; small dents on the smooth red skin.

'They are very tasty,' the stallholder tells her, raising his voice above the clamour around them. A short lady wearing a black headscarf elbows her way past Miltos to get to the stall and grabs at a tomato. Her fingers break the skin and she discards it, pushing past again and off to another stall.

'They are a little soft,' Vasso replies and the stallholder begins to select them himself.

'These are good,' he says, holding out a handful, and Vasso takes them from his hand to feel them. Miltos cannot remember the last time he was in a Greek market. At one time he had a creased black-and-white photograph of his mama choosing fruit at such a stall, his little hand in hers, showing a time he could not remember. He wonders where the photograph has gone, or when he last saw it, or thought about it even.

'Can you take this, please?' Vasso fishes in her purse for change, and Miltos takes the bag of tomatoes off the scales. He feels in his bag for coins and pays the stallholder before Vasso has finished counting.

'You didn't need to do that,' Vasso chides him as they push their way into the throng of people again, but she is obviously enjoying the attention. The next stall is piled high with artichokes, large and with long stems. She tests one of the stems to see how well it bends before selecting six.

Miltos takes this bulging bag. He can smell fish, and looks around to see a stall half covered in melting ice, water dripping onto the pavement.

'Right, we need fish next,' Vasso says.

Miltos watches where he steps, avoiding the fishy water. They pass stalls piled high with strawberries, a man scooping them into paper bags with a metal shovel, women waiting with hands that grab and pay; a stall of vine leaves, small piles of them with a stone on top to stop them fluttering away; an olive stall offering every variety imaginable. Towards the end of the pavement are smaller stalls displaying vegetables with the soil still clinging to them, fresh from some back garden in one of the villages surrounding Saros. Miltos and Vasso are near the harbour now. Maybe he can take her for a coffee, sit and talk for a while. He is exhausted from the bags he has been carrying but also flattered that she is taking it for granted that he can manage to carry such heavy loads.

'I like to have something ready for Thanasis when he wakes – you know, a good meal.' Vasso says, stopping at a stall displaying watermelons. She taps one to test its ripeness. 'And Stamatis doesn't eat much these days but I want what he does eat to be good,' she says.

Miltos tries to disguise the brief frown that crosses his forehead. Had Juliet not said she was single? No, it was Stella who said she was widowed.

'Thanasis, Stamatis?' he asks, trying to sound casual but leaning in towards her to make himself heard over the din of the market. He can smell her perfume: something light and flowery. It suits her.

'Thanos,' she says, abbreviating his name, 'is my son,' and her face takes on such a young look. Her eyes sparkle and she chuckles to herself. 'I have the pleasure of living with him and Stamatis, my father-in-law,' she says. 'They run a taverna together, but they never get a chance to sit and eat, it is so popular, and they are so busy.'

Her hips start to swing as she walks. 'So I make them eat before they go. It may not be Spiros's own amazing food but what I cook is nourishing.' Her chin is lifted. 'And they always eat it.'

'And your husband?' he says, even though he knows there is no longer any husband. He does not get any sense that she is lonely, though. Quite the opposite, in fact: she sounds as if she is very content with her life.

'Ahh.' It is a sad sound. 'Spiros was such a good man. There was nothing he loved more than cooking.'

'How long have you been alone?' he asks, gently. They have stopped at a cafe just past the last of the market stalls, with chairs and tables arranged on the pavement. He deposits the bags around one of the tables and pulls out a chair for Vasso, and even before they are seated the waiter takes their order for coffee.

'Occasionally,' she says, 'just for the briefest of seconds, it feels like I have been alone forever. But as soon as I feel that, he is there again, in my head and my heart, so close to me.'

'Are you lonely?' There, he has asked her.

'Oh my lord, no.' She crosses herself three times. 'No, no, no.' She repeats herself and he wonders if she is protesting too much. 'For a while, when Thanos and Stamatis were in Athens, and it was just me in the house, then I was a little lost, rather than lonely. Now they live with me and I could not ask for more.'

He studies her face, unsure how to respond. She is a fine-looking woman – human, warm – and her voice always seems on the point of laughing, even when what she is saying is sad.

'My friends in the village were teasing me the other day, suggesting I needed a new romance, which I don't, but ...' She stops to thank the waiter for her coffee before continuing. 'I thought about it for just a second and then I decided to surprise them all! Ha!'

'You surprised them?'

'People often think they know you, do you know what I mean? Just because they see you every day. But we all have secrets, so I let one of my secrets out and shocked them all. Ha.'

She laughs again, the sound of a mischievous child. She sips her coffee and then lifts her head to show him her coffee froth mustache Miltos laughs but a heat comes to his cheeks at her behaviour.

'You like to shock, I see,' he says. She takes the serviette he offers and wipes the froth away, laughing again.

'I like to laugh,' she says. Miltos smiles. She is strange one, with not the slightest hint of malice in her – nothing but softness and kindness but definitely different.

'So, what was this secret you told your friends, and how did you shock them?'

'Ah, well.' She lowers her gaze for a moment, as if deciding something, and then looks him full in the face. 'Why not!' she declares, and he is quite excited by the fact that she has obviously decided to take him into her confidence. He can feel himself warming to her personality. She is more than just a pair of good legs.

Chapter 37

'A while ago … No, let me start again.' Vasso clears her throat. 'Back when I was just a string bean of a girl, just seventeen, I saw this boy in the post office.' She pauses but does not look at Miltos. She is watching a teenage gypsy with a child on her hip, begging for money. The dark-skinned, dark-haired woman wanders out into the road as if she is immune to the laws of physics, as if the cars could not impact on her, in her invisible bubble of agitation. Her technique makes the drivers slow and as they do she approaches their windows, hand held out.

'In the post office of all places. Oh, the sight of him, and the way he stared at me,' Vasso says.

Miltos is looking at Vasso, images coming into his mind, the past racing into the present. His deep ability to love, which he has suppressed all these years, surges to the surface unshackled, in boyish, free emotions. Vasso! Could it be that the girl of his dreams is sitting right here with him? His heart races and he wants to reach out and take her hand. Is it really true, is this the person for whom he has held back from other relationships all these years? Or is

247

she talking about another post office, another boy? Perhaps it is best to take this situation very slowly. He interlaces his fingers on his lap, holds his breath and waits.

'But my mama was with me so I could not speak to him then. But I saw him later, on his–'

'Moped.' Miltos cannot restrain himself.

'How did you know?' Vasso says sharply, looking up at him amazed, as if he has just performed a clever card trick.

'Just a guess.'

He cannot stop looking at her. She looks nothing like the young girl he remembers from thirty years ago … But of course she would not look the same, any more than he looks as he did then.

'Well, we hit it off, but I was going away to Orino Island to work and he was due in the–'

'Army?' Miltos says, wondering if he recognises the curve of her neck. Does she not recognise him?

'Yes, the army.' Vasso seems to find his pre-empting her funny and she laughs again, but the focus of her eyes is not on the present. 'So we only had two days together. We went swimming, we walked, we talked. Well, when I talked about this the other day, Stella could not believe it of me. She thought that Spiros was the only boy I ever kissed, but let me tell you, this young man, wow, he was quite a kisser.'

Miltos shuts his mouth, which has hung open of its own accord. He remembers it all: the post office, the chance meeting, the day swimming in the sea … and then his memory fails him a little, as there seems to be a jump ahead to the night, to that wonderful night on the beach when he fell in love and it changed his life.

'There, I have shocked you too,' she says, and her merry chuckling begins again.

'What was his name, this fantastic kisser?' He leans towards her.

'Ah, well, you see, I never found out his name. We just called each other "my love".' She sighs and leans back in her chair, gazing towards the blue sky.

The throbbing in his temple increases and a cold shiver runs down his spine, making the hairs on his forearm stand on end.

'My love, eh?' He can hardly speak, his throat feels so tight, and his tongue sticks to the roof of his mouth. 'And you spent the night on the beach, slept under the stars?' He cannot hold himself back from that moment when his heart opened and he was in love.

'Oh no! Oh my goodness, no. That would never have been possible, but we did swim in the sea.' Her face takes on a dreamy look.

Miltos's eyebrows gather. The pictures in his mind dance. He remembers their eyes meeting in the post office, and he remembers the night on the beach with the girl he loved. This is her: Vasso is that girl. But then she cannot be, since she is denying their night on the beach.

'Surely, with such passion between you, you would have taken a night under the stars together – but I can understand you not wanting people to know that.' He tries to make it easy for her. Perhaps she is just shy.

'No, really, there was no night under the stars. At the time I wished there had been, but later, when I met Spiros, I was glad there hadn't.' She turns her thin, worn, wedding band around her finger.

Then this cannot be his girl, because that night under the stars is all he has dreamt of for years. But he remembers the post office meeting, the girl's mama being there, their meeting later by chance when he was riding around on a borrowed moped. Could his memories be so flawed?

So much was happening back then.

As soon as they arrived in Saros, his baba began shouting at him about his attitude, his lack of help with the unpacking of all the household items they brought from Athens. He shouted back too, his baba hissing at him to quieten down, worried about the impression they would make on their new neighbours, but he didn't care.

'This is your idea, your move – you unpack!' Miltos shouted, before storming out, slamming the door of the tiny rented apartment.

He had not wanted to move from Athens, leaving behind his friends in the city, his life there. But he was not quite old enough to survive on his own, and so they had arranged to move together.

And, as if this was not enough, just before the move he had been called up to join the army, for two years, to complete his military service.

When he returned after their argument, his baba bawled at him, 'Grow up now, Milto, this is your home too,' as if he had never left, as if the argument was all that had been going around in the old man's head since his son had slammed the door five hours previously.

But in that moment, all Miltos could think about was how much the two-roomed apartment smelt of damp. He went through to the small kitchen and opened the window. There were black mould spots on the ceiling in the kitchen, and the paint around them was discoloured as if these spots had arisen before and someone had tried to wipe them away with a damp cloth.

'No, this is yours, Baba. Your dream, not mine.' He kicked through the carpet of old newspaper that his baba must have unwrapped from around the plates and cups lined up on the chipped formica-topped table.

'But you were born here in Saros, it is your birth town.' His baba looked so small and weak as he leant on one of the large suitcases they had brought with them from Athens, as if his legs could not take his own thin weight.

'I won't be here. I will be wasting my time doing national service.' He spat these words in the old man's face and then took the curled-up enlistment papers from his pocket and threw them on the table, where they lodged against a cup, a corner of them through the handle. He looked at them and thought that he could not have done that if he had tried – a thought that struck him as rather bizarre; he seemed to float outside of himself and watch until the whole world was spinning, and then he covered his face with his arm and wailed.

'It's only the army.' His baba was probably disturbed at his son's response, but his words just seemed callous. 'What kind of attitude is that? Are you not proud of being Greek?' the old man ranted.

'Oh stop,' Miltos retorted, 'Greece is a third-world country with greedy politicians and old men like you in their fantasy worlds.'

Calling his father old was intended to hurt. Then he watched his baba cough, a spasm that racked his lungs and made him double over. How cruel his youth had made him, because, instead of offering help or showing concern, Miltos opened the door and stormed out again.

It was later that day that he had seen Vasso going into the post office with a woman he had rightly presumed to be her mama. Three days later was the night on the beach, and the fourth day was the last time he saw his baba alive, his old man's face fixed in a scowl as he forced his son onto the train that took him off to do his national service.

'How many days did you have with him?' he asks Vasso.

'Just two.' Vasso smiles as she answers and then looks down at all the bags from the market. 'Oh,' she exclaims. 'I didn't get courgettes. I was going to make *kolokithokeftedes*.'

So, the third night – had he dreamt it? How does he remember it? Go back a little, before the train, before his last sight of the old man.

'Where are you going?' his baba shouted between coughs.

'Out,' Miltos replied, but although he did not show it he had been concerned about the hacking sound his baba had been making. It sounded bad, worse than the previous week.

'I need you to help unpack before you go. You could be posted to the other side of the country.'

There was a whine in his baba's voice that had annoyed him, although no doubt it was intended to rouse his sympathy. It felt like his baba just wanted to make use of him in his last hours of freedom, and he was not about to waste those.

'No, it is you who needs to unpack,' he retorted. 'I don't. After all, I'm going to be shipped to the other side of the country, aren't I?'

After this, their arguments lost all reason and they resorted to insults. His baba was probably irritable due to his ill health, but Miltos did not know that then. Or did he? Was that what made him so angry at that time? Had he known that his baba's desire to return to Saros was so he could die in his hometown? This period of his life is just a blur of feelings and sorrows and melancholy. None of the images in his mind seems to run in order or make sense. To him, Saros was the town where he lost his mama. The sight of the buildings, the lie of the land, catapulted him back to being five years old and feeling alone and vulnerable.

As for his baba, this was the town where he had met and lost his soulmate. Only, this time was not his baba's time. This time, his baba had returned with the cough that would kill him. Was his youthful anger a precursor to the loss of his baba? … Or was he cross that his baba was ill and would neither talk about it nor take any remedy for it? He does not remember any doctors or hospital visits at that time.

Or was his anger all about his unspilt tears for his mama, and Saros town had just brought them to the surface? Or maybe it was because the country would soon stifle his youthful energy in drill and order and being told what to do, when his youthful blood carried energy through his veins that would have moved mountains.

Such a waste. Now all the memories melt into one another. His sadness over his mama's death, his desperation over his baba fading away before his eyes. His powerlessness to do anything about any part of his life. The girl, that night, had lifted him from his misery. They met in the post office, they swam in the sea and they spent that wonderful night on the beach. That is the way he has been remembering it all these years, but here is the girl and the girl denies the warmth and intimacy that made him fall in love.

Then suddenly, a spark of memory! His sudden intake of breath causes him to cough. He struggles to speak.

'Meli?' He says.

'You okay?' Vasso asks and she slaps him on the back, quite hard.

'Meli?' he says again as the coughing subsides.

'Did you want honey?' she asks, glancing back at the market stalls, looking puzzled.

'No, you – Meli?' he says, his eyes growing wider as he recalls the pet name they had used for each other.

'No, I don't want honey,' Vasso answers, and as she blinks the image of her separates from the image of Meli, or was it Melissa – the girl he spent the night with on the beach. A totally different girl.

Chapter 38

Could it be that all these years he has combined the two events, the two girls, into one in his mind? Why? Why would his mind play this trick on him? But even as he asks himself this question, his heart provides the answer. He had just said goodbye to friends in Athens in order to return to Saros town, the place where he said his final goodbye to his mama years before. He never wanted to have to say goodbye again, not to anyone, ever.

For that matter, when had he ever really had the chance to say goodbye to his mama? He was only five, and they had left for Athens almost immediately. It was as though she had deserted him. For years it had given him comfort to believe that she was still alive in Saros and that they would return one day and she would be waiting for him. It was not as if she had prepared him for her leaving. That was what it had felt like: one day she was there, warm and loving and close, and the next she was gone, leaving him alone, so alone. He had felt the pain, the loss, so strongly at night when he was alone, it was as if he would suffocate and not wake the next day. That was what he had wished for, for so long: not to wake the next day, not to be alone at night listening to the strange sounds of Athens.

Now he snorts in derision at how soft he was. That night on the beach in Saros, with the girl, the one Vasso is claiming is not her, was the first night he had really felt in control of his life. His closeness to the girl's warm body, her love for him, their intimacy – he really felt that his life meant something, that things could go well and that he was important. He knew when the dawn light came that she was his future and that he must run away with her, that they must make their own life. When the first fingers of dawn lit up the hills, he had already decided that he was not going to do his military service and that he was going to elope. It would not be so difficult to escape the army, ducking and weaving through life without his discharge papers. It would only have to be until he was forty-five, anyway – they could keep moving until then. It would be an adventure. And after that he would not be eligible. They had almost got away that first morning too. Had they not been at the bus station, ready to leave, when his baba had caught him and dragged him away? Away from his Melissa, his sweet little honeybee.

Melissa – that was what he had called her: his little sweet bee. He sighs.

No wonder he had merged sweet Vasso with Melissa in his mind. If he had not done it, he would have had two girls to mourn the loss of, when one was bad enough. And isn't that what he has been doing ever since: merging one girl in his life with the next so none of them was distinguishable from the others, so not one of them would ever be in a position to leave him, like his mama did? He has ensured that he has had just one, never-ending relationship all his life – 'my love' merged into 'Melissa' merged into Isla, into Lana then Chunlian and Virginia, and all the girls in between.

His stomach churns.

'Are you tutting and sighing at me? Did I say I wanted honey?' Vasso asks, presumably doubting herself.

'My mistake, I was thinking about something else.' Miltos shrinks little.

'Something not very happy, by the look of you. Are you all right?'

Vasso stares at him with such concern he can feel tears pricking. The same tears he often cries when he is alone, when he sees lovers, watches weddings, thinks of his life. The tears of someone who has never been cared for, who has a nagging feeling that something isn't right, and that when it comes to women he keeps repeating the same mistakes, which lead to the same conclusions. He puts his hand in his pocket and rubs at the shell's worn edge.

'I am fine,' he lies. 'So, your amazing kisser, your lover who you never spent the night with. What would you do if he were to turn up again?' He forces himself to ask this question. He needs a conclusive answer, although he can almost guess what she is going to say.

'Ah, ha ha.' Vasso's light laugh is so charming he cannot help but smile. 'He would not know me, but then I would not know him,' she says. 'Age changes people. How would we recognise each other?'

'Well, let's just say you do. Then what?'

Vasso loses her smiles and looks serious for a second as she contemplates his question.

'I would thank him, both for what we had and for what we didn't have.'

She gives him a little sideways look, and colour comes to her cheeks – presumably at the thought of all they didn't have. 'But he opened my heart, and I think it was because of this that when I went to Orino Island the next day and met Spiros, I was ready. Yes.' She brightens. 'I would thank him.' Her smile returns.

'And you would not entertain pursuing a romance with him?' Miltos asks.

'Oh, *panayia mou*, now why would I do that?' She crosses herself. 'I like good company for sure, and I would never say no to another friend, but anything more than that, no thank you. I have had many good years with the love of my life. I can ask for no more. I am happy as I am. Of course, I still have hopes that Thanos will find a wife and I will have grandchildren, but as for intimacies for myself, my life is rich enough without it and I enjoy the freedom of being single, my own boss.'

She pats her hand flat against her chest to emphasise her contentment. 'Right. My coffee is finished. The shopping is done. Do I take a taxi back or are you going my way?' she asks.

'How could I refuse such a gracious request?' Miltos stands and puts his hands on the back of her chair.

'Ah, a gentleman. Now, I have no objection to having a few more of those in my life,' she teases, and she reaches for the bags, but Miltos is too quick and he gathers them up, waiting for her to take the lead and head back to the car.

'So, what were you coming into Saros for?' Vasso asks as she settles in the car. 'All you have done is help me around the market.' The car coughs as it starts.

'And a pleasure it was too, and far more fun than looking for a job.'

'Oh, you are after a job. Are you any good with your hands? Have you asked Stella? I think she needs a general person to fix things around the hotel. But I am not sure, you will have to ask her.'

'I will have my lunch at the eatery and see what she says.'

'You could,' says Vasso, 'but I am making *kolokithokeftedes*. Come and eat with me.'

It is a strange feeling to be sitting next to a woman whom he is neither ignoring nor to whom he is trying to make love. It is almost like she is a man but with all the assets of a woman. And she can cook, and she clearly likes to nurture. He concentrates on

260

the road and wonders at himself. How can he have
got to such an age and not experienced having a
woman as a friend?

'I would love to have lunch with you,' he
replies. 'I did not expect to find friends in the village
so quickly.'

'Ah, well, you see,' says Vasso with a laugh in
her voice, 'all strangers are just friends we have yet
to meet. But now we have met!' And her light
laughter fills the car.

Chapter 39

The morning sun peeks over the top of the courtyard wall, lighting up the jasmine that cascades down its undulating whitewashed surface. Along the bottom of the wall, on three sides of the courtyard, are geraniums in pots, the dark green leaves contrasting with the bright orange flowers. Tables laden with food are lined up along the fourth wall, on either side of the arched doorway that leads back into the hotel. A gecko scurries up the wall above a terrine of thick and creamy goat's yoghurt.

Miltos is the only guest left breakfasting, and he has refilled his coffee cup and helped himself to a second helping of toast, enjoying the moment and letting his mind go blank as he chews. Lunch with Vasso yesterday was a most pleasant experience and they talked longer than he had expected. When she returned to her kiosk to relieve Petros, he wanted to think over his new friendship so he wandered into the hills and became lost, and dusk was falling by the time he found his way back to the hotel. Consequently, he missed the evening meal on offer there and this morning he is hungry.

'I wondered if I might find you here.'

The voice, so close, startles him out of his reverie. The gap between the large white umbrellas, where the sun slices through, causes him to squint and put up a hand for shade so he can see who is addressing him.

'Good morning, Juliet,' he replies in English, and smiles at the sight of her.

Without hesitation he puts his linen napkin by his plate and half stands, inviting her by a touch on the chair adjacent to his to join him: a gesture he learnt in Italy.

'I cannot stop as I have a group this morning,' she replies. 'Basic Greek. It will be all "a ferret's toes" – *efharisto* – and "parrots' claws" – *parakalo* – until lunchtime.' She speaks with amusement, as if she will enjoy her morning ahead.

'I remember doing the same, with Russian, and French. Are you sure you do not have time even for a coffee?' He is still half standing, now smoothing back his hair, which is already almost dry from his morning shower.

'I'm afraid not,' she says, but her stance relaxes and she rests one hand on the back of the offered chair.

He sits and puts his napkin back on his knee but leans back and to one side to create a triangle of space between himself, his breakfast and Juliet and waits for her to say whatever it was she came to tell him.

'I just came to say that I happened to have had a word with Marina and, er ...' She hesitates, seemingly unsure how to continue. 'Well, initially she was shocked, obviously. But then I got the feeling that she doesn't really think you are the man she once knew. I mean, we don't really know yet, do we? But she was also nervous – you know, in case you are him. Either way, the point is, what I am trying to say, is that she would like to meet you.'

She finishes this last sentence rather quickly, and then regathers her composure before continuing. 'The other lady, however, I have not spoken to yet.' Now she looks at him.

'And nor must you,' Miltos is quick to reply. Juliet gives him a quizzical look. 'I think I might have misremembered one or two details. It's possible that I knew Marina. Yes, possible. But impossible that I would know anyone else.' He does his best to sound emphatic.

Juliet looks at him intensely for a second, and then with a light dismissive wave she says, 'Great, I wish you luck then. Will you wish me luck with my class?' And she turns to leave.

'Good luck,' he calls after her, but she is already gone, through the arch and into the hotel building.

If she had lingered for a second more he might have asked her to have dinner with him tonight. But as soon as she is gone his thoughts return to Marina, the woman in the blue dress, who may be his little Melissa. He spreads honey on his toast and takes a bite. The honey is runny and the smallest drop falls to his trousers. He wipes them clean but it leaves a mark. Concentrating on this, he becomes aware of how old his clothes have become, without him even noticing. They are faded and the stitching around the pocket has gone. He runs a hand through his hair again. Perhaps it is time for a haircut as well.

The courtyard is a suntrap, and the wind cannot disturb the air within the walls. The only sound that can be heard is that of bees buzzing around a rosemary bush that grows in one corner, and Miltos, full of breakfast, sighs contentedly and settles back into his chair, half dozing in the calm, soothing warmth, and his mind wanders. Who might he have become if he had had Marina by his side all these years? Maybe they would have a house together. No, that is for sure; he would have ensured that they had a house. Children! Maybe they would have had children. That is also almost a certainty. What sort of baba would he have been? In what ways would it have changed him? He is aware that his years alone have made him unintentionally selfish, at least to a degree. Maybe he would have become more stable, more … He struggles for the word and settles for 'adult', and the vastness off all he is contemplating begins to feel overwhelming. He turns his thoughts back to the woman his little honeybee has become.

Has she had children? He should have asked Juliet, prepared himself. But then, how does he prepare himself for meeting her? – the woman who showed him care, showed him how to love, became the object of his devotion over all these years and, to

265

a degree, became the obstacle between him and any new love. Obstacle! How can he refer to her as an obstacle? It sounds as if he is blaming her for getting in the way. He must not blame her for that. Oh no – that was his doing!

He drinks the last of his coffee and wipes his mouth, leaving the napkin on the table.

So when should he meet her. Tomorrow? Today? This afternoon? This morning? Now? He should have asked Juliet when she was expecting him. Maybe he should wait until Juliet's class is finished, get more information. But there is no way he can wait. He has waited years already. In fact, he is not prepared to wait another second. His chair scrapes across the courtyard's fine pebbles as he stands.

His easy long strides are more hurried than they have been for years as he takes the road from the hotel to the village. It crosses his mind to take the way through the orange grove, past Ellie's house, but he is not sure he would want to stop and talk if he saw her, and not to stop would be rude. His excitement is bubbling in his stomach, churning his coffee with his toast until he wonders if in fact he might be sick. As he turns onto the road to the village the feeling subsides, but then he wonders why he has not brought the car. Maybe he could take Marina into Saros, go for a coffee, maybe revisit the beach, just to remember the spot. No, he must not suggest that; it might give the wrong impression.

He falters, suddenly unsure, until a puttering sound takes his attention. A tractor emerges from under the last row of orange trees in the orchard opposite. It pulls out onto the road with a grinding of gears and the farmer nods and calls 'Kalimera'. A brown-and-white dog runs behind it at a steady pace. Miltos watches as the tractor draws level with the church, putting a temporary stop to a game of football being played there.

He can come back for the car if he needs it. The village is a stone's throw away and there, beyond the church, on that corner of the square, only just visible, is the shop where his Marina sits. His Marina-Melissa in the blue dress.

A blue dress! That means she is not in mourning. Surely Juliet would have said if Marina was married, and he feels quite certain that Marina would not want to meet him if she was. That would be very awkward – unthinkable, even. But then again, it seems unlikely she has stayed unmarried all these years. Even he has gone down that path. These things happen. But hadn't Stella said she was widowed and single?

His steps quicken as he draws nearer to the village. He stops and rubs his chin, feeling a few hairs by his left ear that the razor missed this morning. He takes a deep breath and continues to walk. The excitement, the potential, the reality of meeting his Melissa rouses a sea of mingled emotions within him. There is elation, love, fear, defencelessness, sorrow for the years that have

267

passed since then and also an overwhelming urge to protect her. As he draws level with the first houses he pulls his shoulders back, remembers how tall and broad he is and that he is still strong and has only a few grey hairs. It gives him courage. Above all, he must still appear attractive to her; nothing would be worse than if she rejected him.

The boys playing football by the church see him and the ball comes his way. It is a long shot and it curves off towards the edge of the road so he breaks into a run to stop it, halts his momentum and kicks it back. The boys jostle to be the first to kick it again and the ball comes back to him once more. His age drops away as he dribbles the ball and as it does his concern over Marina turns from worry to joy. He is eighteen again and he is going to meet her.

He reaches the three steps that lead up to the corner shop a little out of breath, and he steadies himself, putting his hands on his knees. Then he straightens himself to his full height and walks into the shop.

Chapter 40

Marina puts down the pen she is holding and turns to replace the box of cigarette lighters that she is halfway through pricing on the shelf behind her.

'Yeia sas.' She addresses him formally and politely, and faces him, resting her hands on the counter between them for a moment, then nervously smoothing out the wrinkles down the front of her blue dress. Miltos notes the gesture and wonders if it indicates that she knows he is the man Juliet spoke of.

He clears his throat, unsure of how to return her greeting. He holds out his hand to shake hers, mirroring her formal tone.

'Miltos,' he says, with no further explanation.

'Marina,' she replies.

They stand, looking at each other in silence for several seconds. It seems like a long time to Miltos, but he is reluctant to break the silence, unsure how to begin.

'I mentioned to Juliet that I once knew a girl from here,' he says finally. Best to start slowly. He clears his throat and Marina shifts her weight from one foot to the other, resting her hands lightly on the counter again. 'It was a long time ago,' he continues, 'and I know things change, but this girl has kept such a special place in my heart.'

He could say more but what if it will feel like pressure to her? There are packets of nuts on a shelf by the counter, two of which have fallen sideways in the tray. He puts his hand out and sets them upright. 'So, I thought it would be lovely to meet her again and thank her for such wonderful memories …'

The minute he has said this he worries that she will think he is referring to their night on the beach, and of course he is, partly, but he is also talking about much more than that. He looks at her but her face is unreadable.

'I want her to know that I have never forgotten her kindness, her gentle nature.' That's better, but he is now aware that if he says anything more he will be speaking for the sake of making a noise, and that he must stop. But he is not sure he could stand the silence if he did so. Maybe he could buy something, to make it seem like a more normal event. He looks around, hoping that there is something that would be the right sort of thing to buy in such a situation. Boxes of women's tights, packets of condoms, brightly coloured sweets, and behind the counter a picture of the man he talked to in the square. What was his name? Ah yes, Petta. A picture of Petta and a woman and a baby.

'Is that your son?' he asks. 'I met him in the square, a very nice man.'

Up to this point the conversation felt as if it was loaded with danger. It is a relief to now be on such safe ground. After all, does he not have a conversation every day or two with some stranger about their children whilst in a bakery, in a taverna, at the checkout at the supermarket or at a kiosk? Family is a safe topic, guaranteed to be a positive, polite and easy conversation.

Marina's cheeks drain white and just as quickly flame red.

'I have three children,' she states directly and with no expression of pride or horror. Her voice is flat. It is not said unkindly, but it is made clear that it is not an opening for a conversation.

'*Na sas zisoun* – may they live!' He offers her the time-worn phrase whilst trying to hide his surprise at her reluctance to talk about them.

'*Efharisto*,' she replies in a tight voice, and Miltos's mind reacts to the tension of their exchange by conjuring an image of Juliet's Greek class, with ferrets' toes and parrots' claws, and he starts to giggle, he cannot help himself. The muscles around Marina's mouth twitch and she breaks into giggle too. They both know that they don't know what they are laughing at, but it is a way to ease the tension. As they laugh, the air between them clears, the atmosphere in the shop lightens, and they look at each other less cautiously, almost as old friends do, with love and kindness and openness, until Miltos feels fully confident that, even if they are not who he thinks they are to each other, they at least stand a

271

very good chance of becoming firm friends, or perhaps even more than that.

They stand in silence and he searches her face for all he thinks he remembers about her and all the unknown things that must have happened since.

'So …' Marina breaks the impasse.

'So. I was wondering …' Miltos cannot stop staring as he speaks, knowing that at any moment he will find out if this is the girl of his dreams.

'Hi, Marina. Hello, Milto.' Stella bursts into the shop full of good cheer and smiles. 'A lighter please, Marina.'

Marina turns and passes a hand over the box of half-labelled lighters, selecting a colour.

'I understand you are looking for a job, Milto.' Stella pushes her frizzy hair back from her face. Marina looks up sharply at this.

'I have two vacancies at the moment but both of them only need a few hours a week.' Stella talks as if she is in a hurry. 'I need a general fixer of things in the hotel, and I need someone to drive the minibus. It's not much, I know, but, well, if you're interested we can see how it goes. Have a think and let me know. Right – thanks, Marina.' She puts down some coins to pay for the lighter and bounces out of the shop.

Miltos watches Stella leave, and when he turns back it is with a certain amount of surprise at finding Marina staring at him.

'A job?' she says quietly.

'Ah, er …' he stammers, aware of how it may seem to her. The possibility of him being her first lover is one thing, but him moving into the village and making it his home must feel to her like something else entirely. Maybe he has been too hasty. Perhaps he should have resolved his relationship with Marina before broadcasting that he has made the decision to live here permanently.

'Marina,' he says, 'can we go somewhere so we can talk?'

She does not answer for a moment. Then with a sudden burst of energy she makes her way from behind the counter, past the barrels of rice and spilt peas, pushes aside the shepherd's crooks that are hanging from the ceiling and opens a small back door that he had not previously noticed. Light floods in through the doorway and dust specks dance in the sun's rays. The groaning shelves, whose boxes, cartons, tins and misshapen goods have been in shadow, now come alive with splashes of sunlit colour.

'Like a peacock's tail!' he cannot help exclaiming. Marina turns back to look at him. His cheeks begin to grow hot, but something that could be merriment dances in her eyes before she hurries through the door into a courtyard and across to what must be her home. He waits with his hands in his pockets, trying to remain calm, keeping his mind blank, his fingers worrying the shell. He looks straight ahead. On the top shelf are various ouzo bottles: Mini, Dodeka and Plomari, each with a handwritten label showing the price. Probably Marina's writing, curly and intriguing.

'So, come!' Marina is at the small back door again. The girl from the photograph with Petta slips into the shop behind her and sits behind the counter. Marina waits for Miltos to follow her lead into the courtyard, and they each pull a chair from around a wooden table into the shade of the large lemon tree that grows in the middle of the walled garden, and they sit, at a slight angle to one another, but close enough to talk quietly.

The sun filters through the branches of the lemon tree and dapples her face, a shaft of light brightening her hair over her right ear. The scene is like a Renoir painting he saw once in the Musée D'Orsay in France, the model mature, voluptuous, passionate and beautiful in her innocence, unaware of how attractive she was. It was what fired his appreciation of impressionist painting. If this is his little Melissa, then he chose well.

Chapter 41

'No, there, the piece of string,' Aleko shouts over the din of the engine.

'You cannot be serious,' Miltos exclaims, raising his voice above the engine. The whole vehicle is shaking and there are cobbled-together bits of wire and tubes where Miltos is sure there were once regular connections.

'It should have an electrical cut-off but – well, this was just a quicker option until I have time to get around to it,' says Aleko. 'Just pull the string and the engine will cut. Diesel, you see. Much easier.'

Aleko points repeatedly to a dirty bit of twine tied to a lever in the depths of the throbbing engine, the other end hanging limply over the fender. This end has a loop knotted into it. Miltos pulls at the string and the noise of the engine is replaced by the gentler sound of the crickets and cicadas in the orange orchard next to Aleko's house and yard. He rubs his dirty finger in the palm of his other hand.

'Noisy when it's running, isn't it?' he comments.

'Only with the hood open.' Aleko lets gravity slam it shut. 'So, you feel all right with all that? I know it has idiosyncrasies and some of the fixes are not ideal, but if you bring it back here after you've used it I will work on it when I get a chance. Keys.' He drops the keys into Miltos's hand.

'Right, I have to sort out this tractor. Grigoris is here every hour, hassling me to make the damn thing go. Does he not realise I have a rent-a-car-business to keep running?' And with a quick grin he walks away, leaving Miltos to face the minivan alone. On the surface it looks new and shiny; the seats are all clean and tidy, and it has been resprayed in the not-too-distant past. But closer inspection reveals that the seats only appear new because they have covers hiding the original, worn fabric. Tiny rust bubbles have poked their way through around the wheel arches, which have been discreetly touched up, and it makes him wonder what more might be wrong that is not showing.

He climbs up into the driver's seat and adjusts it so it is the right height and distance from the wheel and starts the engine as Aleko instructed. Cautiously he steers the lumbering van out of Aleko's yard and then down to the square, where he turns right by Marina's shop, heading towards the hotel. As he passes he tries to glance in to see Marina but the interior of the corner shop is too dark. Perhaps it is best to leave her alone for the moment anyway. She has a lot to think about.

Checking his watch, he estimates he just has time to put a new handle on the door that leads from the hotel kitchens to the outside bins before he must make the pickup. The door has been yanked open one too many times and the internal mechanism no longer works. He knows what the problem is and has found some bits and pieces in Aleko's workshop that might do to fix it, but if they do not work he will have to advise Stella that she will need a new one.

Since two days ago, when he took on the position of handyman at the hotel, he has been busy with an endless list of things that needed fixing, or painting, or replacing. He has been amazed at how much there is to do around the hotel to keep everything running smoothly. Already it looks like it will be far more than just a part-time job, and now that he has agreed to drive the minibus as well he won't have an hour to himself. Stella was delighted when she found out he spoke so many languages.

'Ideal pickup man,' she said and laughed, and Miltos saw a chance to flirt with her, but for some reason he did not feel the need to do that sort of thing.

The hotel's air-conditioning units have kept him the busiest so far. When Stella showed him the first, a big unit in the dining room, he swallowed hard and made some knowledgeable sounds, but the truth was he didn't have a clue.

Stella saw through his bluff immediately. 'You have no idea, do you?' she said. He expected her to get cross or at least a bit short but she seemed to take it as if it was a joke.

'I don't think I ever said I knew about air-conditioning units.' He was aware he was being a

277

little defensive but he smiled as he spoke, softening the edge in his voice. Stella put her hand on his shoulder.

'No I don't think you did,' she said, encouraging him to laugh with her, and they stared at the unit, now their mutual enemy. 'But I know where you can find out everything you want to know.'

She showed him to an office, clicked on a light, and led him to a desk with a computer. 'Your desk,' she said, and showed him how to get online. She seemed to find this even funnier than his reaction to the air-conditioning unit and she left the room laughing even harder. Stella seems to have a knack of making work into fun, and he is not surprised that she has achieved so much in this small village.

Once seated at what was now his desk, he brought up page after page of diagrams of air-conditioning units, which he was surprised to find were so easily available online. He even found the manual for the very unit he was to work on. He became so engrossed that when Ellie came in to turn off the lights at the end of her shift she did not even realise he was there.

They said a cordial goodnight but he remained, grateful that Stella had given him a deal on the smallest of all the hotels rooms as this meant he could continue to read long into the dark. The next day, armed with his new-found knowledge, not only did he manage to fix the unit but, according to Stella, he made it work better than it had before. Since then, the internet has been useful in helping him deal with other jobs around the hotel and, so far, he is loving his new position. As for air-conditioning units, he now feels confident he can fix most of the more common issues without having to refer to the diagrams.

He pulls the van into the hotel car park and parks round near the kitchens. He will fix the handle and pick up the group from Saros, and then he will take a look at the filter system on the pool. Now that is an interesting project. He had never really thought how much chlorine you need to put in a pool, or how to keep the water clear – never appreciated that the water could cloud over or that he would have to keep an eye on the pH level. Until a couple of days ago he had no idea what a pH level even was, until he had started to read up about it after Stella asked him to hoover the pool. He thought she was joking at first, asking him to hoover the water. But sure enough, there was a brush on a very long handle, with a tube that sucked all the dirt, leaves and unfortunate insects off the bottom.

There is so much to learn, but at least he knows he is in the right place to do so. He cannot imagine being anywhere else but the village now, and in a few days – he can still hardly believe it – he will be in the church with Marina, who will be wearing her best dress.

'Can you fix it?' Ellie asks as she comes into the kitchen holding her coffee mug.

279

'Done.' He stands and pretends to try the handle but really he is showing Ellie his handiwork.

'Right, I'd better go and get this group.' He looks at his watch. 'Twenty Scandinavians! And all studying Swedish massage, no doubt …'

He grins and Ellie rolls her eyes at him.

Chapter 42

'So what are you saying, Marina? Is it him or is it not?' Vasso asks.

'What?' Marina's eyes widen, but the corner of her mouth twists into a smile.

'Irini told Frona that there was a stranger talking to you in your courtyard. Tall, broad, good-looking,' Vasso explains, her eyes narrowing.

'You lot gossiping again?' Stella steps into the shop and Juliet, Frona and Vasso shuffle back to make room for her. There are crates of beer stacked up where the women normally sit and the corner shop feels overly full.

'Yes, about your handyman,' Frona explains.

'Miltos? He's a good worker, such a nice man. He and Mitsos are thick as thieves.' She nods her head in approval. 'Do you know he speaks Italian and French and a bit of Russian?'

'And English,' Juliet adds.

'He can speak any language he likes to me,' Frona says and she tries to lift her head but her back is curved with her years so she chuckles to herself instead.

'Frona, shame on you!' Vasso chastises her in an affected voice. 'Anyway, he is not like that. I cooked him *kolokithokeftedes* after he took he took me to the market and he was an absolute gentlemen. Carried my bags, bought me coffee. Intelligent too, as if he knows what you are going to say before you say it!'

Juliet casts her a quick look.

'You know he once lived in Saros? Apparently he had a girlfriend from here, from this village,' Stella says, looking quickly from Vasso to Marina. 'That is what he told Mitsos.'

'And that is the impression I got from Irini, Marina. That you were talking to this man like old friends.' Frona says the last two words in English, or rather in an American drawl, reminding them all that she has seen more of life than most.

'Oh, that Irini.' Marina looks to the open back door and smiles at her daughter-in-law, who is hanging out the washing, nappy after nappy strung across the courtyard, white, crisp and clean against the greying whitewash of the house.

'So, come on, Marina,' Vasso urges. 'Is it him? Your lover?' She too says her last word in American-English, but, rather than suggesting that she is well travelled, the mixed accent sounds like she watches a lot of films.

'It was a long conversation,' Marina says. The women find a place to lean or perch, ready for the tale to be told. 'We started it in the courtyard.' She points to the back door where Irini now leans against the frame, a bag of clothes pegs in her hand. 'Then he went and got his hire car and we drove to Saros. He chose a place where we had coffee and we talked some more. Then we walked around the edge of the town, along the harbour.'

She sighs dramatically and looks at the ceiling. 'Time seemed to fly and before I knew it we were having dinner together.'

'So were you the girlfriend?' Stella is almost hopping from foot to foot with this news.

'Well, it's more complicated than that, isn't it?' Marina takes the picture of Petta from behind the counter and wipes it with a bit of tissue before replacing the golden frame on the nail and dropping the tissue in the bin. 'I swear he was more nervous about us breaking the news to Petta than anything.'

'So it is him!' Vasso shouts and then puts her hand over her mouth, her eyes wide as she looks from Marina to Frona, to Stella, to Juliet, and then she locks gazes with Irini.

'It's him,' Irini says, and her joy shines from her face.

'Oh Marina, congratulations,' Stella says.

'I'm not sure what you are congratulating me on. It is lovely to see him again and I am so very pleased for Petta to have both his mama and his baba, but congratulations?'

'Aren't you and he …?' Frona sounds disappointed.

'Let me tell you,' Marina begins, to prepare them for her story, and the women settle for a second

283

time. The hotel minibus drives past but she does not look quickly enough to catch a glimpse of Miltos driving. She returns her attention to her waiting audience.

'It was when we were walking along the harbour and the sun was setting. The colours on the water were lovely – you know, when the sea is as still as oil. I had noticed the colours, I really had, but I see the sunset every day, and just at that moment I was feeling a little hungry so I was thinking what I might have to eat when we had finished our walk, when he said, "If only Turner" – I think that was the name – "had come to Greece, he would have lost the coldness from his canvases. Gauguin, he could capture the heat." He had spoken almost as if he was talking to himself and, well, I was at a loss as to what to say, so I said, "Stella's got a lovely picture of a donkey in a hat on her eatery wall, but I don't know who painted it." Of course, I knew what I had said was stupid the moment I said it, and it made us laugh so hard we both had tears running from our eyes and he looked at me with such love and I looked at him with all the love I felt for him. I remembered all the times when things were bad with my husband, God rest his soul, and I would think of my Meli and just the thought of his existence somewhere on this planet gave me hope. The fact that people like him existed at all made my lot more bearable for years and years and I wanted to thank him so much for that and for my most wonderful son.'

There are tears in her eyes now and she looks over to Irini who, putting down her bag of pegs, pushes past Frona and Juliet to go behind the counter and put her arm around her mother-in-law.

'I am okay,' Marina sobs, and Irini takes a packet of tissues from the shelf behind her and opens them to hand her one. The shop is silent apart from Marina's snuffling.

'And' – she dries her eyes and sniffs – 'we kissed.'

'Aha!' Frona says with energy.

'Ahhh,' Vasso says with compassion.

'Ah,' Stella says, enlightened.

Juliet remains silent.

'It was the most tender, loving, compassionate kiss I have ever had from a friend.' Marina puts her tissue in the bin.

'Friend? What?' Frona responds.

'Some things you just know, I guess.' Marina leans to Frona and pats her age-spotted hand. 'The years have been too many, our lifestyles too different. The comment on the painting threw this into high relief and allowed us to give each other a kiss that expressed our years of gratitude for that moment in time that we once shared, but we both knew that it was a time that is gone.'

'Umm.' Vasso makes a noise to indicate she understands.

'So after that we had no illusions, just happiness. We had dinner together and I cannot remember laughing as much for years. He has seen

285

so much life, he has so many tales to tell – and how he can tell them. I could not wish for a better baba for Petta, nor a better *petheros* for my Irini here.'

Marina puts her arm around Irini. Then with a sudden grin and a renewal of energy she says, 'And when I told Petta! The joy that boy had! That both men had! You should have seen that reunion. My Petta was the taller, but both big men. It was the Clash of the Titans.'

Her whole body shudders and judders as she laughs, and Vasso joins in, wiping a tear from her eye. Frona looks slightly disappointed but even she cannot help tittering at the image Marina has evoked.

As the laughter naturally declines, Frona says, 'So that's that, then.' The women begin to shuffle, making small movements towards the door without actually having made the decision to leave.

'Well, yes and no,' Marina says. 'He was happy enough to have found his son but I swear the big man just dissolved into tears when I told him he had a grandchild. Sobbed like a baby, he did.' She looks at her daughter-in-law.

Irini nods her confirmation of this event.

Now no one is going anywhere.

'Wasn't he pleased?' Stella asks with a frown and a teasing tone, her intention clearly to fish for more detail, prolong the story.

'Pleased? Pleased? I thought he would just run and suffocate the little man with hugs when Irini brought him from the house all crinkle-faced from his sleep. But he didn't. At first he looked like he was going to burst but then his whole presence softened. He moved slowly towards little Angelos, and as he moved he crouched lower and lower so when they met they were face to face.'

'And all he did was smile,' Irini adds. 'A big grin on his face, and my baby grinned right back.'

'It was like looking at two peas in a pod, only one big and one small. Miltos was so gentle, he picked him up as if he was glass and told him that he loved him right there in front of me and Irini, is that not so?'

Marina turns to her daughter-in-law, who cannot answer for the tears in her eyes, and takes a tissue for herself.

'Does he know the church is booked for the baptism the day after tomorrow?' Stella asks.

'He does. He says he will find a suit to match my dress. I have never seen a man look so proud.'

Chapter 43

Miltos jolts awake, blinking in the half-light, and wonders why it still dark outside.

Slowly he remembers all that life has given him. It is his excitement that has woken him; his eyes open wider and he jumps from his bed in the darkness. The dawn has not yet broken but sleep has gone. As it did yesterday morning too. He may never have a full night's sleep again but he does not care. He is wide awake and he is a father and a grandfather! He wants to shout, to sing, to let the world feel his happiness. Tomorrow he will be in the church when his grandson is baptized: Angelos. And he *is* an Angelos, an angel sent from heaven to make him, Miltos, feel a part of the world, to allow him to belong.

His trousers are on and, pulling his T-shirt over his head, he rushes out of his room and out of the building by the side door, and he strides down towards the beach. The hotel grounds are quiet and still; there is nothing but the rush, the hushed back-and-forth movement of the waves against the tiny pebbles and the sand. The sunbeds are empty, the bar clean and clear of bottles; the bare bulbs hang lifeless. The only light is the grey edge on the horizon out where the sea meets the sky.

The dawn must come. It must come quickly to fill up the huge space that is constantly growing inside of him, the cavern that is being created to contain all his joy. The internal expansion injects energy into his limbs; he wants to jump and shout and tell the world, but the world is asleep. How can it sleep when life is so absolutely amazing?

The land on the far side of the bay is now a flat, pale blue-white, and the sky above it has a cold yellow tinge, which turns slowly to pink as he watches; a sliver of the orange globe peers over the horizon to the east, and as the sky lightens the waves glow orange as if they are on fire. The day is bursting into existence, the land taking shape, the shadows forming, and the sea comes alive with a million reflections of the sun.

'Petta!' He would like to shout the name to the winds but he holds himself back, just hissing it through his teeth, letting just the final 'a' elongate until it becomes an extended outward breath and he runs out of air. He sucks in a lung full of dawn.

'Angelos!' He does the same with his grandson's name, telling the universe that he is staking his claim and that the world had better watch out if anyone or anything tries to come between him and his blood. This action releases some of his excitement. The rest he expends by grabbing a broom and marching to the tennis court, where he sweeps as if he is dancing with the dawn.

He is the first to take breakfast and his cheerful *kalimeras* are returned half-heartedly by the sleepy kitchen staff. After his second coffee he can sit no longer, and even though his day does not officially start till ten he makes his way to the swimming pool to check the pH levels and clear the leaves out of the filter. Tomorrow he will wear a suit. He cannot remember the last time he did that. He will wear a suit and stand next to the woman he once loved and if he doubts that he belongs there she will remind him with a squeeze of his hand. She has promised.

He feels the same peace he experiences when he is underwater. He feels the awe that fills him when he sees a beautiful sunset, or that he once experienced when he observed a butterfly emerging from a chrysalis, its wings, folded and crumpled at first, slowly drying in the sun. He feels the contentment that soaks into his bones when he walks far, far away from civilisation. But he is not far from civilisation now: he is in the hotel, he is in the village, in *his* village, and these people are his home.

The pool is running well, but there is plenty to attend to indoors. There is a dripping tap to fix in number six, a blocked toilet in number fourteen, and Stella has asked him if he can find a lighting system online to rig up over the stage. Oh, and wasn't one of the automatic front doors slow, or sticking, or something? He will do that first, before any guests are around.

'*Kalimera.*' Ellie is already behind reception.

'*Kalimera*, Ellie!' He greets her energetically in return. At least Ellie's youth reflects the energy and excitement he feels about life today. 'How are you?'

'I did not sleep too well,' she says meekly.

'Oh, I am sorry to hear that.'

'Yes, she was kicking.'

This takes Miltos by surprise and he looks at her again. She is pregnant? He has just presumed she enjoys her food, and not once has he thought that she might be pregnant. And besides, she is not married yet. He asked her last week if the wedding had gone well and she related a catalogue of disasters. First the church had been double-booked; then, she said, the priest had become ill, and then, as if that were not enough, her family's flights were first delayed and then cancelled. She said that all of this had given her time to think about what it was that she really wanted and she had decided – how had she put it? Oh yes, "The world and its antiquated expectations can come second for a change." But he had not really understood what she had meant at the time. Now he does. He watches as she smooths her hand over her tiny bump.

'Ah,' is all he can think to say. Having something growing inside him would be unimaginable. But then she is going to have the luxury of a small life in her arms. That he can imagine, because now there is Angelos. 'You will make an amazing mama,' he adds.

She smiles, but a cloud passes over her eyes as if she has some doubt.

'No, really,' he urges. 'You are kind and patient and loving. What more do you need?'

This time her smile has no hesitation.

'So, you are going to have your child first and then get married?' He can hear his own indoctrinated beliefs telling him that this is wrong, that marriage must come first, then children, and then he laughs out loud at his hypocrisy as he thinks of Petta. As he chortles at himself, he wonders, for the first time, how hard the time of the birth must have been for Marina – so young, so alone. He must ask her about it and tell her that if he could turn back time and be there for her he would.

'You think having the child first and then getting married is funny, or is it that you don't approve?' Ellie asks, little worry lines puckering the smooth skin of her forehead.

'No, it is not that!' But inside he questions himself to find what he really thinks, and his answer rings inside him like a clear bell.

'The only way to live is with personal integrity,' he says with confidence – and then he thinks about how being true to his feelings has affected his own life. But he still believes he did what was right for him.

'And sometimes this can mean we make choices that are against the stream of social expectation but ...' He pauses and moves just a little closer and speaks in a deeper but quieter tone. 'No one can truly know what it is you need in your life to keep you physically and mentally strong except yourself.'

Ellie's lines of worry are erased. He steps back and lifts his head as if challenging her.

'If we are not strong in ourselves, what earthly good are we to anyone else?' He points at her small bump.

Now she smiles.

'True, so true.' She seems to be all fun and light again and she picks up her pen and opens the hotel registration book to begin her day's work. 'Oh, and before I forget, Loukas said one of the lights has gone over one of the tables down on the beach. He said to tell you he thinks it has blown the whole circuit.'

Her smile tells him that they are friends and a wave of paternal instinct washes over him. At least that is what he thinks it is, because he suddenly feels all protective towards her but without finding her attractive in the least. This makes him chuckle.

Once the front door is fixed, Miltos collects a screwdriver and some bulbs from his desk drawer and makes his way back through reception to head to the beach. His progress is halted by a couple coming out of the breakfast courtyard arm in arm. They are not young; in fact, the man has a grey streak that dominates his neat haircut. As Miltos walks behind them, slowing his pace to match theirs, he begins to think how, if things had been different, this could have been him and Marina, and a familiar feeling he hadn't expected to return now comes over him.

Chapter 44

It is a feeling he has felt on and off all his life. He has often named it loneliness, and associated it with the notion that he does not belong, having no family, but he has no reason to feel it now. He has a son, a family! He is no longer alone. But the familiar feeling is there anyway. Until now he always thought it meant that something was lacking inside of him, something that needed to be acquired from an external source. Sometimes this feeling has been so strong that it has reduced him to tears – over weddings, for example, or young lovers, or sad films. But right now, walking from the hotel down to the beach, with the sun turning the deep-blue sky almost purple, the sea sparkling and the cicadas blanketing the scene in their own musical mating call, he recognises it for what it really is. It is not the need to take something in, but rather the desperate desire to give something out. And that something is love! But he can give love now, to Petta and to Angelos.

With this thought comes the realisation that he possesses a skill he thought he did not have. He suddenly has the ability to distinguish between different types of love. The love he feels for Petta is a deeper, heavier love than the light, exciting love he feels for Angelos, which is different again from the calm love he feels for Irini and the more personal, but equally calm, love he feels for Marina. Suddenly he is seeing the whole world in terms of love. He hardly knows Ellie, nor is there any reason for them to become closer than the friends they are now, but he feels love for her too – just a tinge, a protective tinge – and he even feels love for Loukas, just because he is Ellie's partner. He also loves Stella, and definitely Mitsos. What a guy! Yes, he loves that man.

The feeling that is upon him now is the love that he has been holding back all his life. The feeling is the love that, until this point, has been extended to only two women in his whole life: his mama and the girl who no longer really exists, whom he called Melissa. But this is the love he most wants to give and is missing – the love for a woman. He feels this need even more acutely now, and his unused love wants to break open his chest and be poured over someone. He wants to give protection and kindness. He wants to release the floodgates of his emotions and give all that he has to offer in terms of that intimate care. He is ready. Probably for the first time in his life, he really feels that he is ready to fall in love.

'A penny for your thoughts.'

The expression shocks him out of his thoughts and he does not look over until he has wiped away the tear that has made its way down to his chin.

'Juliet, *kalimera*,' he replies in Greek. It feels safer somehow, just in this moment.

'*Kalimera*. You were deep in thought? But then I can imagine you have a lot to think over, with all that has happened.' She is sitting on one of the sunbeds marking papers, a large book balanced on her knees for a table, a pen in her hand, and a pair of wire-rimmed glasses on the end of her nose. In the morning light her hair shines gold and orange and pale yellow, and her skin has the deep, even tanned look of someone who does not sunbathe but just lives outdoors.

'It has been quite a … *siezmos*.' He cannot think of the word in English for upheaval so he uses the Greek for earthquake. He feels it has more expression anyway.

'To be honest I cannot imagine what it has been like for you. To find your old love must be one thing, but to discover that you have a son and a grandson too. Wow!' She waves her hand in little circles to express what a storm he must have been through.

'May I?' He points to the sunbed next to her.

'Please.'

He sits on the edge, looking at her.

'It has been amazing, Juliet. May I tell you?'

'Oh, please do.' Juliet puts the book and the papers down on the sand, her pen on top, and rolls onto her hip to face him.

'It is as if I have been born.' He scans her face. 'I know it sounds trite but that is really what it is like.' He looks away, out to sea. The blue is the

296

deepest he has ever seen, the silver wave-tops the most reflective he has ever witnessed. 'I feel as though I have been born and I suddenly have a family and a village and I can feel things I have never felt before. I did not believe such love was possible, nor that love could ever be as strong as the love I now have for Petta, and he is a grown man too! I love a grown man! It is breathtaking. It's as if a casing has been broken away from the outside of my heart and now I can feel things I have never felt before. This morning, for example, I felt love for Ellie and Ellie's unborn child.'

He looks back at Juliet and he can feel his cheeks colour at this display of emotion, but he does not care. He wants to shout his life out to the world; he cannot hold himself back.

'And what I feel for little Angelos, as God is my witness I would die for that little man.' He pauses and looks down at the sand. Juliets papers are ruffling in the slight breeze, and without thought he pulls out the book from underneath them. The cover makes him look twice. It is a book on Berthe Morisot, the impressionist painter. The cover shows a painting he thinks is called *The Cradle*, which he saw in France. He places the book on top of the papers and continues.

'It has also made so much sense of other parts of my life.' He takes a deep breath. 'I understand now why I have held back.' He pauses. 'It was all for the love that I never dared feel for my mama. I closed my heart and I kept moving all my life, Juliet,

297

because I was afraid. Should I be ashamed to tell you that? I feel I should, but I am not. I want to shout it from the hills.'

He lifts his arms and throws his head back. 'But I am not afraid now.' He lowers his hands. 'Last night, I will tell you, Juliet, I cried. I wept and sobbed like a baby. Not from the happiness I should have been feeling at finding my son. No, I cried for the mama I lost when I was five. This is the first time I have done this.'

He looks at her but she says nothing, her face serene. 'And I also cried from relief because I knew these feelings would be sad and that they would hurt, but I knew they could no longer overwhelm me. I knew I would survive because I could no longer drown in these feelings because I have a son, I have a future, hope!'

He stops and breathes deeply. A tear or two escapes him now, but he does not wipe these away. After a moment he gathers himself.

'I hope I have not bored you.' He puts his hands on his knees, ready to stand, giving a little sniff.

'Absolutely not.' Juliet reaches out and touches his forearm, a gesture suggesting that he should stay. 'I lost my father,' she says quietly. 'I was only small. He left me and my mum and wrote letters to me, but my mum, she hid them from me. However, the first letter I did get was to tell me he had died. I know that pain.' Her eyebrows rise in the middle as she speaks.

He can hear the pain behind her words but he can tell that the wounds she is talking about are not fresh, that they have healed, she has dealt with them, and he looks at her again to find the strength that must have taken. All he can see in her countenance is kindness and compassion.

'Here is the weird thing, Juliet.' Her hand is still resting on his forearm and he has an urge to touch her fingernails but he does not give in to it. 'Instead of pulling me under, those tears, painful as they were, they lifted me up. They showed me how great it is to love and how I have not loved all my life because of fear … But I am repeating myself now.'

The need to express himself has subsided a little and he looks away. He is taking up her time, she has her teaching papers to mark. Perhaps he has been selfish to talk to her like this.

'I am so sorry, Juliet. I hardly know you and here I am unloading my world onto you. I am so sorry …' he starts, but she interrupts him.

'You said that this morning you felt love for Ellie and Ellie's unborn child. I understand this. It may be the world's best-kept secret.' Her voice is calm and unhurried.

'Secret?' he asks.

'Yes. Well, it seems to be, because if it is not a secret I cannot understand why more people are not living by it.' Juliet takes away her hand but it does not go far. It hovers in the gap between them.

'What secret is this?' he asks. The urge to touch her fingers has returned.

'That it feels so absolutely amazing, so much more fulfilling, rewarding and powerful to be the giver of love rather than the receiver!'

'Exactly!' He almost shouts the word.

Chapter 45

The collar is too tight and the suit jacket is a little short in the arm, but the colour of the tie matches Marina's dress, and this gives Miltos a measure of confidence.

'Well, don't you brush up handsome.' Stella comes in as Miltos is admiring his reflection in the wardrobe mirror. She brushes his shoulders free of invisible lint with her hand and gives him a more studied appraisal. It was her idea that he borrow one of her husband's suits for the day, and Mitsos insisted that he come over in the morning for coffee and that they all get ready and walk down to the church together.

'But at this rate he is going be going barefoot. I am a size smaller in the shoe than Miltos.' Mitsos pops up from the far side of the bed with a black, dust-covered shoe in his hand.

'I guessed as much,' says Stella. 'So I've borrowed these from Petta. I reckon he is your size.' She takes her shopping bag from her shoulder and fishes out a slightly worn pair of dark brogues. 'I will get the polish.'

Miltos insists he polishes them himself even though Stella offers to do it for him. He takes them into the kitchen so she can get ready in the privacy of her bedroom. True to Stella's prediction, the shoes fit him perfectly. He will be walking in his son's shoes and this makes him smile.

'Right, then we should go. Mitso, come here, your belt has missed a loop at the back of your trousers.' Stella comes into the kitchen looking startlingly glamorous. Mitsos allows her to rearrange his belt, her arms around his waist, and he steals a kiss, making her smile. Miltos slips from the room, out onto the compacted mud of the backyard. The edge of this area is defined by small, brightly painted olive oil drums, from which burst brightly coloured geraniums. Beyond these, in one direction, is a small almond orchard, between the house and the top of the hill, and in the other direction a narrow lane leads past the end of the house and down towards the village.

His village. It gives him such a strange and wonderful feeling to consider that this is his village.

He spots Theo at the *kafenio*, arranging the last of the chairs ready for the celebratory dinner that will be held in the square after the baptism. Eight trestle tables fill the area around the palm tree, between the empty fountain and the kiosk. In front of the *kafenio*, on the road, a small stage has been set up for Sakis, who has offered to play for little Angelos's baptism. It is beyond belief.

A splash of colour catches his eye. Juliet, who is walking with a couple of women he does not know, approaches the square. She was so kind and compassionate yesterday, and he could have talked to her for hours. In fact, they talked for over an hour, and he made her late for her lesson. Her confirmation that he no longer needs to be afraid of anything he feels had been such comfort. It was a clever way to explain it, he thought, hooking into his love of driving.

'Like indicators on a car,' she said, 'feelings just let you know where you are and which way you need to turn. The feeling itself cannot harm you, any more than an indicator can. It is our actions and reactions to the indicators that keep us on the right path.'

'Or cause us to crash,' he added to make her laugh, which she did.

It turned out that the book on Berthe Morisot was not actually hers. It was one she had found at a flea market and it was intended as a present for her son in England. He felt a little disappointment at that.

'But do you like French impressionism?' he asked anyway.

'I think I would if they had not been used so commercially over the years,' she said, and then they went back to talking about languages. However, when she looked at her watch, gasped and hurriedly packed up her work, she added, as she picked her way, shoes in hand, across the hot sand to the hotel's lawns, that he could borrow the book before she sent it off, if he would like that.

'Ah, there you are! Shall we go?' Stella comes out, squinting in the sunshine.

'You look magnificent.' Miltos cannot help himself.

'Here you go.' Mitsos comes out with his jacket on, looking decidedly hot. In his hand he holds three little shot glasses. 'Just to fortify ourselves,' he explains and, with a clink and the call of *yeia mas*, they drink.

By the time they get down to the square the tables are set with clean tablecloths and vases of flowers, and children are running around in their best clothes, chasing each other and being scolded by their mamas.

People are filtering from all the lanes towards the church.

'I am feeling a little on display,' Miltos mutters to Mitsos.

'Ahh, they have nothing to talk about for years and then a stranger walks into the village laying claim to Marina's son, whom she only discovered a while back. They are bound to be curious.'

'Keep walking, man, or you will be late and then all eyes will be on you for sure,' Stella urges, and she links one arm through his and the other through her husband's, and in this fashion Miltos's new friends deliver him to Marina's house.

'Ah, there you are.' Marina has a new blue dress, and the tie she bought him is the perfect match. He wonders if he should have got her something, a pin or a brooch, or just a handful of flowers, as a token of thanks for her generosity. He is not good at thinking about other people, after a lifetime spent making sure that he did not need to. He is going to need to make a more conscious effort until it becomes second nature.

'Right, so where is Petta now?' Marina turns to go back inside. Miltos puts one foot over the threshold.

'I'm here,' a voice booms from above, and with a thunk-thunk-thunk down the stairs Petta almost collides with Miltos, whose heart swells at the sight of him – so much so that he has to fill his lungs with air to make more room, letting it out slowly as they shake each other vigorously by the hand and then pull in for a hug and a backslap.

'Irini, do you have Angelos's clothes?' Marina asks, turning one way and then another but accomplishing nothing.

'They are here.' Stella, having pushed past Miltos, finds them hanging on the back of a chair in the kitchen, on a small coat hanger, protected by a transparent plastic dry-cleaning bag. It is not a big house, and with all of them moving about, looking in mirrors, Irini searching for a comb for Angelos's hair, and Marina losing a shoe, it seems smaller by the minute.

'Come on, let's wait outside.' Petta gives Miltos a nudge and the two of them go out into the street, where people greet them and then stare at Miltos as he and his son make their way to the church behind the shop.

'You see, we would not have this problem if we lived on a boat,' Petta says. 'There would be just the sun, the sea and the sky and no expectations.' He chuckles, a noise that bubbles up from inside his chest.

'You'd better build it big enough for three.' Mitsos joins them. 'But no bigger or the women will want to come.' The men guffaw.

'What are you lot gossiping about?' Stella is the first of the women out of the house, her hair already springing back to its normal frizz.

'Building a boat to get away from you women,' Mitsos teases her as they link arms.

'Irini, come on, the bells have started,' Petta calls, leaning inside.

The scuffling and bumping sounds inside the cottage increase until, finally, Marina joins them on the street; Irini, carrying a sleepy-looking Angelos, follows, and they walk with the others from the village up and across to the church.

Chapter 46

The village swarms out of the church, the men pulling at their ties and the women dabbing at their faces with handkerchiefs. There is a general clicking of lighters, and a hum of conversation. The children break from the confines of the church, running, shouting, chasing one another.

'Kostantino, not too fast, you'll fall. And leave Kristina alone,' a woman calls.

'Ah, leave the children be, let them burn off their energy.' Her husband takes her hand. 'They are excited for the music and food that is to come.'

'They will not last the night.' She leans in towards him.

'Then we can dance under the moonlight, just the two of us.' He inclines his head sideways against hers.

'*Na sas zisi*,' everyone wishes Miltos, 'May he live!'

In the church he stood with Marina on his arm and Petta by his side and he felt a pride he had never experienced before in his life. He expected tears to run down his cheeks, and he had even tucked a handkerchief, which Petta gave him, with black butterflies embroidered on it, up his shirtsleeve just in case he needed it. Surprisingly, though, his eyes remained dry and his chin stayed high and he felt just fantastic.

'He is a fine boy, Petta. A fine boy,' Miltos shakes his own son by his hand, again.

'And tonight we will dance,' Petta says, and he slings an arm around his baba's shoulders and the two of them wander, a head height above everyone else, down to the village square.

'Ah, would you look, Theo has done us proud,' Petta says. On each table there is a carafe of ouzo and a jug of wine, next to a vase of wild flowers.

'I think Juliet and Frona picked the flowers,' Vasso says.

Sakis is on the stage, checking his equipment. When he sees Miltos, he leaves what he is doing and comes over to him.

'Well, who would have thought, eh?' is all he says, but he makes eye contact and Miltos senses that he understands everything that he is feeling about the village and his new life here. Sakis then formally shakes Miltos's hand and wishes his grandchild joy before returning to his soundcheck.

Miltos spots Nicolaos in the crowd with a foreign-looking woman on his arm and a smile on his face, which suggests his toothache is no longer bothering him.

'Eh, look,' Petta says to Miltos. 'I don't think I have ever seen a man look more uncomfortable in his suit than Cosmo does.'

For a moment, Miltos is pleased to see Cosmo deep in conversation with a woman, but then he notes that she looks slightly bored and that makes him sigh and smile at the same time.

Aleko is almost unrecognisable in a pristine white shirt, his oily hands scrubbed and his face clean and free of oil stains. Miltos is not sure why but it surprises him to see that Aleko's wife is very pretty, and, more than that, that they have a set of twins as well as the triplets. No wonder life no longer surprises the mechanic.

'Come and sit here,' Marina suggests, pointing at the central seat of the main trestle table. A dog slides past his legs and slips under the tablecloth. Two women are busy putting baskets of bread on each of the tables and some guests have already found seats and are pouring themselves wine.

Theo hurries over and wishes Petta, Irini, Marina and Miltos all the good wishes in the world. An attractive woman is by Theo's side. Unlike the majority of women at the gathering, she wears no make-up, but somehow it suits her, in a natural, earthy way. Her hair is long and flecked with grey, and she wears it in a knot piled on top of her head. There is an easy manner to her movements, and a hypnotic quality about her. Miltos instantly recognises that this must be the woman who loves Theo but will not marry him. She exudes the strength of someone so completely comfortable and confident within herself that she is slightly unsettling. Miltos can see the boy Theo once was as he tries to please his love. Theo's conversation may be with him, Petta, Marina and Irini but his attention is almost entirely on his reluctant bride. Miltos has not stopped smiling since he left the church but now he smiles even more. Being included in the secret dynamics between Theo and Anastasia makes him feel even more a part of all that is going on, linked by an unbreakable thread.

Anastasia wishes them well and moves off to talk to other villagers. Theo returns to the masculine domain of the *kafenio* and switches the radio on, plugging it into Sakis's amplifier, and suddenly the bustle of people in the square feels exaggerated by the added noise. Most are seated by now. Stella and Mitsos are on the main table and Stella ushers Juliet to sit next to her, opposite Miltos.

Juliet is wearing a caramel-coloured dress that swings as she moves and she has casually pinned up her hair, which falls in curls around her ears.

Something nudges his foot. He looks Juliet in the eye and makes a quick sideways move of his head with an enquiring frown. 'What?' he silently asks. But she does not respond and so he returns his attention to the greetings being given to him, and then a plate of food is put before him. But his foot is nudged again, and so again he looks to Juliet, who smiles.

Is she flirting with him? He studies her as she talks to Stella. Juliet is easy on the eye, of that there can be no denial, and they have a love of language in common. From their conversations so far it seems that she has not travelled as broadly as him, but,

310

since she has lived in both England and Greece long enough to know, to feel, the culture of each and to understand the thinking of each country from the way words are used and the dynamics of syntax, they can talk about the world in similar depth.

It is on the third nudge that he looks down, a little curious to see if she has painted her toenails for the occasion.

The heat burns his cheek in an instant, for there, nudging his foot, is the leg of a dog as it scratches and grooms itself. For the rest of the time they are eating, he finds it hard to talk to Juliet at all.

The food and drink flow endlessly. Theo is loving his role and is running from person to person and back and forth to the *kafenio*, making sure everyone is happy. Miltos catches Anastasia watching him, admiration in her eyes. Glasses chink, and when one person calls *yeia mas*, the salute ripples around the tables and everyone drinks.

Soon the radio is silenced and Sakis begins. This draws everyone's attention, and for a while it is as if Miltos is at a concert at Lycabettus in Athens, but after three songs Sakis calls for attention through the microphone.

'That is enough of the self-indulgence of playing my own music,' he announces. The villagers groan, good-naturedly, in response. 'Instead, I will play all our country's old favourites!' he says, and the villagers cheer, and he only needs to strike a few chords to get the women on their feet. Then tables are pushed back and the dancing begins to the *rebetika* Sakis plays.

'So, when do we start this boat?' Petta leans over and slurs as a full jug of wine is placed on the table.

'As soon as you like,' Miltos replies. Vasso pushes past them to go into the kiosk: someone wants to buy cigarettes, but she waves the money away.

'Tomorrow,' she shouts above the music, 'pay me tomorrow,' and quickly she is back with the other women, dancing, arms flowing, hips swaying. She reaches out her hand into a group of onlookers and her hand is taken and then Juliet is there in the middle, moving to the music, her caramel-coloured dress swaying to the beat.

Chapter 47

The music changes to a faster tempo.

'Opa!' Petta shouts, and his drink is left on the kiosk shelf as he strides to the centre of the cleared area. He begins to dance, reaching out for Marina's hand. She accepts the invitation, her face shining, and Miltos can see the girl he once knew, and a part of him is sad that their lives have made them such different people. Would it be possible for them to fit together, if he tried? His heart tells him that this romantic ending is not a reality, and the sadness that threatened for a moment lifts almost as soon as it started.

Irini is pulled into the dance, leaving Angelos fast asleep in the arms of her neighbour, an old lady dressed in black, who cradles him carefully in her arms. Miltos does not know who the woman is, but he will; maybe not today, or tomorrow, but at some point he will know each and every one of these people. He will know their families and their stories and they in turn will know his. He hopes he has enough to offer them. A little self-doubt reminds him of the feelings that dominated his past. Mentally he clicks off that indicator. He is not going in that direction.

He looks out at the dancers and there, Mitsos, with one sleeve tucked into his waistband, the other arm out to his side, his wrist limp, his fingers clicking, dances as best as his balance will allow, and their eyes meet. With a nod of his head, Mitsos invites Miltos to join him. How long has it been since he danced to Greek music? He cannot even recall. Maybe not since those enforced lessons at school? Has it been that long?

Mitsos nods again, and at the same time Petta dances towards Miltos. When he is close enough he throws an arm around his father's shoulders and shouts *'Opa!'*, leading them back to where Mitsos is dancing. Nicolaos is quick to join them, and Cosmo is reluctantly pulled in, and the line grows further as more of the men of the village join it. Now even Theo forgets his job, and Anastasia, and they all dance to fill their own hearts. Sakis rises to the display and his playing grows stronger and then faster. They dance on and on, growing hot and tired, but elation carries them.

Eventually Mitsos sits down, the empty arm of his shirt swinging free. Then one or two more of the older men sit.

Sakis looks at Petta and Miltos, and Miltos is sure he sees a challenge in Sakis's eye as the music grows in tempo and the dancers are forced to keep up. One by one the men drop out, but Petta seems oblivious, his eyes shut, only his grip on Miltos's shoulder keeping him in this world. They dance on and on, and more and more of the men drop out until there is only Miltos and his son left, their masculinity on display. Miltos cannot imagine being any prouder than this, but in the moment he is only there to support and draw attention to his son, his handsome, strong and good-hearted son. Despite the rapid beating in his veins and his inability to draw in enough oxygen, he wants the moment never to stop ...

And then Sakis begins to slow his rhythm, and Petta returns to the world around him, and finally they stop. The villagers cheer as Petta holds his baba's hand high. They are both winners.

The music does not stop for long – there are other dancers with feelings to express – but Petta and Miltos take a break and drink several glasses of water. The sun is long gone, sunk over the horizon to give way to the stars and the moon, but the air is still warm. Miltos takes out the handkerchief that Petta gave him and Petta takes one out too. They both have black butterflies embroidered on them. Petta shows his to Miltos to emphasise this fact before wiping his brow.

'There is a significance?' Miltos asks.

'Tomorrow, I will tell you such a tale, of black butterflies and Marina's care of her children,' Petta says, and Miltos recognises that his son has inherited his own love of storytelling and so he does not press him – he is happy to wait.

Irini takes Petta away to dance, and for the first time in the whole of this day Miltos finds he is alone. He looks up at the stars. If he is not mistaken, the ink-black sky is turning pale. Surely they cannot have danced till dawn? He does not feel in the least tired. But as he looks over the village square he can see that the tables are half cleared, jugs are empty, glasses abandoned, napkins on the floor and children asleep on chairs and in their mothers' arms.

The older generations, the women in black, have gone home to their beds. Both Marina and Angelos have gone now, as have pregnant Ellie and her beloved Loukas. Nicolaos and his English wife or girlfriend, Sarah, have also gone. Cosmo is asleep across two of the chairs. The village dogs have cleaned the floor of any scraps and they too have now gone.

'Have you had a good time?' Juliet startles him.

'You keep doing that!' he says in English.

'Doing what?' She laughs, and his eyes shine.

'I think you must wait until I am deep in thought before you sneak up behind me,' he teases.

'I do not sneak.' She sounds offended and he is about to apologise when she grins.

'In answer to your question, I have had and I am having the most amazing time. This place is something quite special.'

'Umm. I have pondered this over the last couple of years, and I have come to the conclusion that all the little villages all over Greece must be equally special,' Juliet says seriously. She folds her arms and her stomach growls. 'Pardon me,' she adds.

'You don't think this place is unique then?' To him it is. To him this is the most special place on earth, and he has seen quite a lot of the earth.

'I came to the conclusion a while back that this village may be a little unusual, but then I have not spent enough time living in other villages to be able to compare it properly.' She yawns and her stomach grumbles again.

'Didn't you eat?' Miltos asks.

'Oh, I did, but that was hours and hours ago.' She looks at her watch. 'Gosh, is that the time?'

Sakis is packing away his equipment, and the *kafenio* radio is playing again, but quietly, no longer amplified through the speakers. A cockerel crows once and then again and a dog barks its response, greeting the new day.

'You know what I would like now?' Miltos speaks slowly, checking his emotions and his thoughts as he speaks. He wants to be sure that what he is saying is coming from a good place, a place of which Marina would approve.

'What would that be?' Juliet asks as they stand side by side.

'I would like to look at that book you have bought your son.'

'Now?' It is Juliet's turned to be startled.

'Why not?' Miltos stretches, and the first rays of sun catch the top of the church tower.

317

'Yes, why not!' she says with another grin. 'And I will make you breakfast. Do you like marmalade? I have some great marmalade. I used to buy it online but now I make it myself from a recipe of Frona's.' And she turns to walk in the direction of her house.

They seem to have the same pace of walking, which pleases Miltos, who is in no hurry. And as they make their way out of the square and along the road to her lane, he feels something against his hand, and he looks down to see which of the village dogs it is, ready to shoo the animal away.

He is delighted to find instead that it is Juliet's hand taking his, and he allows her fingers to intertwine with his own.

Good reviews are important to a novel's success and will help others find *A Stranger in the Village*. If you enjoyed it, please be kind and leave a review wherever you purchased the book.

I'm always delighted to receive email from readers, and I welcome new friends on Facebook.

Facebook:
https://www.facebook.com/authorsaraalexi
Email: saraalexi@me.com

Happy reading,

Sara Alexi

Also by Sara Alexi

PUBLISHED BY:

Oneiro Press

Being Enough
Book Seventeen of the Greek Village Collection

Printed in Great Britain
by Amazon